THE OUSIAS

To: Bethany
Congratulations on winning and enjoy
Darryl Spearman

DARRYL SPEARMAN

Copyright © 2011 Darryl Spearman

All rights reserved.

ISBN: 1492722243
ISBN 13: 9781492722243

My gratitude goes out to my family, friends, and coworkers who supported my story.

TABLE OF CONTENTS

Chapter One—The Society	1
Chapter Two—Chosen Ones	7
Chapter Three—The Mysterious Box	15
Chapter Four—Curious for Answers	25
Chapter Five—A Teacher's Secret Is Revealed	39
Chapter Six—Meet My Five-Thousand-Year-Old Friend	51
Chapter Seven—Seth's Pyramid	67
Chapter Eight—Nowhere to Run	77
Chapter Nine—The Aftermath	83
Chapter Ten—The Witmores Escape	89
Chapter Eleven—The Eyes Are upon Them	97
Chapter Twelve—The Unique Map	109
Chapter Thirteen—The Chase Is On	127
Chapter Fourteen—Drake Is One of Us	141
Chapter Fifteen—Great Fiery One	151
Chapter Sixteen—A True Friend in a Time of Need	165
Chapter Seventeen—Go West, Young Teens	173
Chapter Eighteen—The Deceiver	187
Chapter Nineteen—Riddle of the Sphinx	195
Chapter Twenty—The Abyss	203
Chapter Twenty-One—The Great Plagues	209

TABLE OF CONTENTS

Chapter Twenty-Two—Journey through Duat	217
Chapter Twenty-Three—Feather of Ma'at	225
Chapter Twenty-Four—The Eye of Horus	235
Chapter Twenty-Five—Hidden Talents	239
Chapter Twenty-Six—On the Eighth Day	245

1

THE SOCIETY

Throughout history, stories have been told of people and creatures from different mythologies: Egyptian, Greek, Chinese, Norse, and many others. Most people view them as nothing more than just fantasies or legends, but these creatures and people were real. They existed for a period of time; then they eventually passed away. Yet, the essence and magic of some of these beings was too strong to vanish away forever, and many of them returned as a new entity of incorporeal beings. After many long debates over a name to best describe their new existence, they agreed to call themselves Ousia (oo-see-ah). These beings used their combined powers to create a place in the skies, and they called it Utopia, a place of peace and serenity. It is invisible to all humans, but some humans are allowed to visit this wonderful place from time to time.

Utopia contains many levels, like an onion with many layers. The Ousias from all of the different mythologies wished to feel relaxed in their new home. So each part of Utopia was designed to meet every specific personal need and desire, which gave them a great sense of joy in their new home.

In order to maintain this tranquility and order, they formed a group, the Society, but it didn't go over well with every Ousia. Many of them were villains from Egyptian, Greek, and other mythologies who wanted nothing to do with such a society. Their goal was to regain their full powers once again, so they could either enslave or destroy mankind. But the good and heroic Ousias refused to permit this to happen to humanity, so a great war broke out between them and raged for centuries, until the good Ousias finally defeated the evil Ousias in the end. These evil Ousias found themselves in a murky prison for all eternity, and the good Ousias decided to aid mankind.

The Ousias had helped people living in a great city several millennia ago, but their attempt had ended in tragedy for the people. They had promised to never involve themselves in the affairs of mankind, but they couldn't take the chance of any evil Ousias escaping their prison. They resolved this issue by creating three magical items that would go to three chosen humans on Earth. These magical items were placed in a box that would aid them in stopping evil Ousias in the event of their escape. After this, the good Ousias made an important law: noninterference into the lives of mankind.

Our story truly begins on a chilly and windy day in the downtown area of Chicago in February 2011. People are rushing to get home to avoid the oncoming blizzard. A severe snowstorm is approaching the city, and many stores and businesses have closed early to allow their workers to get home. People run to the nearest stores for supplies, or just for an exit out of the area.

But a tall and slender middle-aged man, with long white hair and brown eyes, walks slowly down State Street, and he doesn't have a care in the world. He observes the people taking the opportunity to enjoy watching the local news broadcast through the storefront windows. People who aren't watching the news bump into him as they rush to leave the city. He isn't upset or angry since he understands their desire to get home safely. The snows begins blowing heavily, challenging their vision, and it makes traveling most difficult. People struggle to find their way out of the area, but this middle-aged man stands his ground like a rock.

In fact, he stands in front of Macy's as the clock rings to signal three o'clock. But as the snows blows with incredible force, enough to shake the buildings, everyone hears thunder and observes the brief appearance of lightning in the sky. It's unusual to experience a snowstorm and a thunderstorm at the same time. The strange man seems to be the only person in the downtown area who isn't affected by this storm, but no one notices, since everyone is too busy trying to get home.

The bolts of lightning and the roaring power of the thunder continue to rumble throughout Chicago, forcing people off the streets, with the exception of the stranger. He stands, oddly, in the middle of the sidewalk, until the heavy snowfall starts to cling to him like a magnet. Ultimately, the snow transforms the stranger into a snowman, and the winds lifts him into the air, like he is being shot out of a cannon. The stranger, unnoticed, travels for mere minutes in the sky until he finally lands in a layer of fog. After a few seconds, the fog moves away to reveal a wondrous city. The stranger, dressed in a totally white double linen suit, sees some large golden pyramids in front of him. There are several roads leading to the pyramids that appear to be made of sapphire blue mixed with violet.

A powerful voice speaks out. "Hello, Thoth. It is good to see you after all this time." Thoth recognizes the voice of his best friend, Osiris, a powerful ruler of the underworld to this day and a high ranking figure among the Ousias.

Thoth (also known as Thohth) is one the wisest figures in Egyptian mythology. He had once served as a fellow member of the group referred to as the Society. But Thoth wasn't too happy with being a part of them. He wished to return to Earth. Osiris gave him his permission to watch over mankind, and Thoth had unenthusiastically agreed to become the holder of the vast powers of the Ousias someday. He was able to live a life on Earth for many centuries, since Thoth didn't age there.

Thoth tries seeing Osiris to greet him more properly, but a white fog blocks his vision. Thoth knows Osiris's reasoning for summoning him to Utopia, but he tries to show some surprise on his face at being summoned.

Osiris's deep strong voice rumbles through the fog like a knife cutting butter.

"Don't pretend ignorance about why you were called here, since the blizzard is a signal of an evil Ousia appearing on Earth," says Osiris. "Thoth, destiny calls for your presence to assist mankind again, since they will be in need of your help in the days ahead."

Thoth recalled the days of working side by side with Osiris and how he helped Osiris and the others build this Utopian realm. Thoth had also wanted to watch mankind to grow and develop as a people, but many Ousias refused to share this belief. However, Osiris had spoken up for Thoth and convinced the others that about Thoth was not breaking their law against interfering with mankind. So the other Ousias gave Thoth their permission to watch over mankind, and he had taken different jobs throughout his time on Earth. Thoth's immortality was a problem to his anonymity, so he moved from job to job like a temporary assignments.

Osiris knew that Thoth's pain that still lingered with him. It went back to the very ancient days, when Osiris had ruled over Egypt. Thoth had assisted Osiris out of friendship, but he couldn't handle staying in Utopia. He was glad to take this opportunity to observe mankind, which helped him to ease his own pain from his days in ancient Egypt.

At the time, Osiris had given Thoth an Egyptian box that contained the Ousias' mighty powers. Thoth didn't wish to have any such box in his possession back then, but Osiris had refused to let him walk away from his duty then or now.

Osiris tells Thoth about the escape of the most dangerous evil Ousia in Egyptian mythology history, the evil dark lord, Seth. Thoth's facial expression turns sour, since he has a long history with Seth. Osiris orders him to return to Earth and wait for an Egyptian box to appear in his home. He calmly asks Thoth to fulfill his calling to assist the chosen ones. Osiris doesn't want Thoth to neglect his duty to mentor the chosen ones against Seth. At first, Thoth doesn't wish to help, but in sprite of himself, he becomes curious about their identities. Osiris remains silent.

"If I don't know the identities of these chosen ones, then how am I going to find them?" asks Thoth. "In fact, I don't even know where to go."

Osiris stands quietly in the white foggy atmosphere of Utopia for the next few moments. Then he breaks his silence. "You will go to Chicago and wait for the chosen ones to find you." Osiris watches Thoth's disappearance from Utopia, but he declines to talk to anyone about it. Osiris could have used his magic to track Thoth's movements, but he doesn't want to know the whereabouts of his friend.

Thoth remembers hearing about a pyramid being built in the Chicago River area and quickly discovers this pyramid belongs to Seth. So he magically appears near the pyramid and then moves with the swiftness of a cheetah to remove three pieces from it.

Another Ousia, walking with a veil of fog covering his whole body, approaches Osiris with the Egyptian box, and Osiris transports the box to Thoth's home. The newcomer asks Osiris about Thoth performing his duty as a mentor to the chosen ones.

"Thoth will follow our orders or face our judgment," insists Osiris.

2

CHOSEN ONES

Several months has passed Thoth was able to find a job in Chicago in preparation of meeting the chosen ones. But many Ousias doubt Thoth's desire to obey their wishes in regard to his duty as a mentor to the chosen ones. However, Osiris believes that Thoth will obey the Ousias' orders, but he knows Thoth too well to overlook his tendency to disregard his orders. Osiris didn't wish to think about it the moment, so he calls for the Ousia to reveal the chosen ones of the Ousias to him. The Ousia removes the fog around his body, and the fog changes into images from Earth.

Osiris watches several neighborhoods in Chicago until he sees one neighborhood in particular refer to as Lincoln Park. Osiris views a large detached four-bedroom constructed of brown brick in the city of Chicago. There is a large oak tree in the shape of the letter V out front, and a large pretzel-shaped white-and-black skateboard ramp in the back of the house. Osiris watches as three teens return home from a full day of fun. A middle-aged, bulky man named Malcolm Witmore stands quietly in the living room. Malcolm Witmore is one of the world's most famous archeologists, and a professor who graduated from Cambridge,

England, with honors. He has taught at different schools in the United States and England over the years and has discovered many treasures, relics, and several historical documents over his twenty-five years as a traveling professor.

He retired five years ago, so he could search the globe for ancient relics and spend more time with his family. Malcolm has been a widower for the last two years, since his wife, Rose Witmore, who had worked as a cell phone engineer, passed away. They had both wanted to have children, so they adopted three teens to raise.

Malcolm, dressed in an unusual outfit of alternating stripes of black and silver, waits unhappily for the teens, who are late coming home. He observes the eighteenth-century grandfather clock standing in the right corner of the living room and the large family portrait hanging on the wall near the kitchen to remind him of Rose, who helped design this house. He looks at four five-inch-square mirrors in the living room. Two of the four mirrors hang above the grandfather clock. The other two mirrors are on the sides of the five-blade ceiling fan, reminding him on of how Rose had insisted on putting those mirrors there for fun.

As Malcolm relives the past, he looks at the grandfather clock again. Seeing the hands on five o'clock to revisit his concern, until he hears the sound of the three teens coming home. All three start to push their way inside of the house in order to get inside. A young red-haired-fifteen-year-old girl with chestnut-eyes and cream complexion, Kendra Witmore, uses her wits to shove her two brothers into each other, and she enters the house first.

As her two brothers fall to the ground, Kendra shakes her head at them. "This is what you two so-called gentlemen get for forgetting the basic rule of life: ladies first."

The oldest of the three, Kendra possesses an IQ in the 130s. She does extremely well in most of her subjects, but she excels in computer software and hardware. Kendra doesn't want to be labeled a genius, since she couldn't stand for people to treat her differently because of her intelligence. However, Rose had taught her to embrace her talents and not to deny them for any reason. So she had followed Rose's advice and learned everything connected to a computer, and Kendra's dedication to be the best had finally paid off for her. At fifteen, she is considered the top computer student at her school.

Kendra watches her younger brother. Roland gets to his feet first. Roland is a slightly athletic fourteen-year-old long straight blonde hair and soft pale skin with bright brown eyes. He desires to play in the professional winter X Games someday. Roland knows that he needs to work harder at his grades this year, since he barely passed his classes last year. He doesn't wish to depend on his sister for help, though. Roland wants to make it this year on his own.

Malcolm offers his hand to the remaining Witmore on the floor, but the young teen first declines to accept his helping hand. With an unhappy glance, Juan, a scrawny kid at eleven years old, with short black hair, brown eyes and olive skin, takes his hand. Juan is the most unforgiving of the three, since his rage goes much further than just Malcolm. He struggles not only with his relationship with Malcolm as his adopted father, but he also can't seem to make long-lasting friendships. Juan had spent more time with his mother, than either Kendra or Roland had. But that part of his life had ended in sadness for Juan, when his mother had given him up for adoption at an orphanage on his eighth birthday. Malcolm wishes he could turn the clock back for Juan, since this sorrow keeps Juan from trusting people and from accepting him as his adoptive father.

This goes back to the day that Malcolm and Rose had adopted him. They had already adopted Kendra and Roland, but Rose had wished to adopt another child. Malcolm had decided to follow his wife's suggestion. Malcolm remembers that day about three years ago, a chilly day at Chicago Homebound Orphanage. Juan had gone to several foster homes without opening his heart to any of them. A case worker at the orphanage had heard about Malcolm wishing to adopt another orphan. She gave Malcolm the whole information about Juan, which included the separation from his mother.

Malcolm recalls the worker telling him about Juan watching his mother walking away from him and calling out his mother's name to return. She never did, though, and he was eventually placed in the custody of Malcolm and Rose. Malcolm hopes that Juan will change his mind someday, so he doesn't give up on him, although he does have moments, within himself, when it is hard not to give up the fight. But he won't let doubt creep into his heart like a virus, so Malcolm decides not to rush him. As the teens go upstairs to their rooms, Juan and Roland see Kendra, with a serious look upon her face, looking at Malcolm.

Roland looks at Juan. The scene is familiar. "Fight."

"Definitely fight," says Juan.

"Your rooms await the two of you, so please don't disappoint them," says Kendra, flashing her sword-like eyes.

Roland and Juan know not to argue with Kendra when she looks at them with those eyes. So they both run quickly to their rooms, keeping their doors open slightly to hear the discussion. Malcolm doesn't offer any defense against her rage. He suspects that she wants to talk about the situation at school three weeks ago. He had embarrassed her at summer school, and she had been too upset to talk about it for a long time. Malcolm understands her frustration, so he listens to her with an open mind.

Kendra folds her arms in willful stubbornness. "I needed three weeks to cool off, since your actions made me looks like a fool at school. I'm the oldest one in the family, and I am treated like a little girl. Roland was allowed to go to his former girlfriend's house, but I wasn't allowed to go to my best friend's birthday party with a chaperone there. So why does Roland get treated better than me, since I am the oldest?"

Malcolm had hoped this conversation wouldn't come up. It had reminded him of the worst day in his life this past summer. When he arrived early to pick her up at school, the students were practicing their performance of the story of *Romero and Juliet* at Higher Learning for an upcoming show. Kendra had wanted to surprise Malcolm with her performance, so she hadn't yet told him about it. Malcolm thought Kendra was tutoring at the school. He planned to take her out for pizza to reward her hard work. Malcolm had walked around the school in search of Kendra. The sound of cheering students from within the school auditorium had gotten his attention. Malcolm had strolled into the auditorium to witness Kendra kissing a boy on stage. Malcolm had run on stage like a madman and grabbed the boy by the neck. Everyone had laughed at the situation, but the teen's panic look had made Malcolm feel extremely foolish. Several teachers had run on stage to confront him, and this had forced Kendra to admit Malcolm being her father as well as his terrible lapse of judgment. The teachers came to understand his reaction, but his daughter didn't excuse her father's behavior for a long time.

As both Malcolm and Kendra recover from their embarrassing and painful trip down memory lane, they hear the sound of muffled laughter coming from upstairs.

Malcolm's voice sounds like someone speaking from a bullhorn. "Roland and Juan, I better hear the sound of two closing doors and running to your beds or else I'm going to visit your friends at school next."

They think about it for a millisecond, but Roland and Juan know they can't handle such an embarrassment. So they both close their doors shut and make sure Malcolm hears them getting into their beds for the night. Kendra asks Malcolm to explain why he is more willing to trust Roland than her.

"I don't distrust you, but I'm extremely suspicious of boys seeing my daughter," says Malcolm. "But I do apologize for embarrassing you at school, and I promise to be more trusting of you. It brings back memories of my days at school, when I was a young man dating young ladies."

"Please don't say any more, since it would only freak me out," says Kendra. "There are some things in life that a girl doesn't want to know about her parents. I put your dating days at the top of the list, and I do accept your apology."

Malcolm offers to allow Kendra to go out with a young man to a movie or a chaperoned party, as long as he can meet the young man first. Kendra nods her head in agreement and wonders on what has changed his attitude. But she doesn't want to push her luck, so she thanks Malcolm and walks upstairs to her room. As Kendra approaches her room, Roland and Juan quietly open their doors, as their curiosity has gotten the better of them.

"What did you two talk about, anyway?" asks Roland.

"To quote a famous line from a movie: 'Do you want to see another day?' Or do you want to walk away now?" responds Kendra.

Roland and Juan see Kendra's fist pointing in their direction, so they decide it would be better to enjoy their last two days of freedom rather than finding themselves in the hospital. They have two more days of relaxing before the new school year begins, so Kendra and Juan decide to play some video games in Roland's room. Kendra looks at the posters and pictures of his favorite X Games players and teams which hang proudly over his red-and-black marble desk. Kendra thinks about Juan's room, which is covered with posters of his favorite superheroes that he got from his visit to the last comics convention in Chicago early in April. Kendra marvels at Roland, who is looking for the video game remote in a pile of clothes, and she thinks about Juan's room, which is just as littered with piles of clothes. Roland finds the remote under a pile of clothes near his closet, and Kendra recoils at the boy's lack of cleanliness.

She wonders briefly on how two unrelated people can have the exact same dirty habits, but she comes to the conclusion that it's not worth knowing the answer. Kendra decides to challenge both Roland and Juan to play a knights and dragons video game when she and Roland notice Juan looking nervously around the room. Juan tells them about having the feeling of someone watching them. They laugh at him, since there isn't anyone else room. But Juan doesn't give up. Kendra asks if his feeling may something to do with his feelings toward Malcolm. Juan rejects Kendra's attempt at psychology, and he looks around the room again.

"Are you sensing some other imaginary friend?" asks Kendra.

"Ha Ha," says Juan. "I don't feel anyone else."

"Funny, I can sense something now," says Roland. "It is the overwhelming defeat of Kendra."

"I will be the one who defeats the dragon, and my brothers will the first ones the dragon devour," jokes Kendra.

While the teens play against one another in their video game, Malcolm goes downstairs to the basement, since he didn't want his kids to hear him on the phone. He calls Miss Wallace, a social worker at the Homebound Orphanage who had helped him and Rose with the adoption paperwork. Malcolm thanks Miss Wallace for her advice on helping him out of his blunder. It had been her idea to wait for Kendra to make the first move. Malcolm happily concludes his discussion with her. He walks back upstairs to his office and examines a scroll on his desk about beings called the Ousias.

After many hours of playing video games, everyone decides to go to sleep. In her room, Kendra listens to some music for sometime. She opens up the window for some fresh air and notices a curious event in the sky. A bright comet with two tails like arrows on either end illuminates the skies above like fireworks. It amazes her that she is able to view it without a telescope. Kendra runs into Roland's room first and Juan's room second to find them sleeping like two hibernating bears, so she hits each one with their pillows to get them up. Kendra hurries back into her room to avoid missing the comet, and both Roland and Juan come in with unhappy looks.

"Hey, there better be a good reason for waking us up. It's after midnight." gripes Juan. "I was dreaming about saving the world from the deadly dream aliens from Mars."

"Yeah, I was dreaming about winning my first professional skateboarding X Games. So what's your problem?" asks Roland.

"You two can resume your trip to fantasy land later, but first please look out of my window," insists Kendra.

They all watch in astonishment as the comet with two tails hovers in the skies, and she asks them about this being better than some dream. Kendra recognizes it as the legendary comet Destiny. A scientist named Walter Destiny had discovered this comet with his telescope in 1910, and the unusual two-tailed comet had led to legends being created about people having their destinies fulfilled when it appeared. People added to the myth, saying that a great destiny awaited those toward whom the tails of the comet point to. Kendra points out to her brothers that one of the tails appears to point in the direction of their house, and her brothers concur.

While they observe this sight with wonder, Juan wants to figure out the location where the comet's second tail is pointing. Kendra doesn't know the answer, and they watch the comet moving away from their house. Roland and Juan head back to their rooms, but not before striking Kendra in the head with their pillows. Kendra chases them with her pillow, starting a pillow fight to the finish with them. Before long, they hear Malcolm telling them to go to bed, and they dash to their rooms to turn in for the night.

But it is a different story for Thoth, who is finding it difficult to sleep in his house. He gets a tingling sensation flowing through his body as though something heading toward him. Thoth runs to the window to view the dazzling second tail of the comet Destiny traveling toward his house. The sight gives him no joy. Thoth understands this as another sign of the coming chosen ones' destiny to save the Earth from Seth. The first sign had been the appearance of the Egyptian box in his room.

Thoth changes his mind about involving the chosen ones. He looks outside of his window and notices several garbage cans behind his house. Thoth uses his magic to throw the box several feet to an open garbage can, since he knows the garbage will be picked up tomorrow morning. Thoth stares at the box from within the garbage can and rejects his promise to mentor the chosen ones. Thoth vows to keep the chosen ones safe and returns to his bed to get some rest.

3

THE MYSTERIOUS BOX

The date is Tuesday, September 6, 2011, the beginning of another school term in Chicago. As the sun shines brightly through his windows, Thoth wakes up with a cold sweat. He is still deeply afraid of Seth's return and the potential rise of evil coming to this city but he doesn't regret his action of last night. It is almost time to leave for his new job as a teacher of mythology.

Thoth isn't the only one getting ready the new school year, for three teens at the Witmore house are preparing for the new school term as well. Roland, Kendra, and Juan are getting ready to head to the bus stop. Malcolm gives them some money for lunch. Roland and Juan head for the door, but Malcolm asks for Kendra to wait for a minute. Malcolm whispers to Kendra, so her brothers won't hear any of their conversation. Kendra smiles at Malcolm with some satisfaction. Kendra wants to focus on beginning a new school year and forgetting about this past summer's embarrassment at school. She eventually walks outside to the waiting Roland and Juan, and they see the bus approaching the bus stop. Roland makes it to the bus stop and holds open the door of the bus for the others. They use their time on the bus to discuss everything about school, the comet, and other things.

Roland wants to know the details her earlier conversation with Malcolm, but Kendra doesn't wish to answer him. Juan wonders about going to Higher Learning High School, since this is a place where teens receive the best education. There is a program at Higher Learning to allow a few grade-school students to take some classes there, so they can prepare themselves for life at a high school. Juan is very nervous about attending this school, since he hasn't been very good at making friends at his last school. Juan's attitude makes it hard for people to like him or see him as someone to become friends with. Roland notices Juan's feeling of discomfort, so he places his arm on his shoulder. Roland loves being the big-brother type to Juan, and Juan begins to relax a little about his first semester at Higher Learning.

"I promise to give it my best effort at Higher Learning, but I'm not sure about any of this," says Juan.

"I wasn't the most popular person at one time either, but some people gave me a chance and saw a person worth hanging out with," says Kendra.

Juan doesn't share his siblings' confidence in himself, since they are able to make friends more easily. Kendra joined the debate team with two other girls, and they won the state debate championship. They were rewarded with an all-expenses-paid visit to a movie studio in California. Roland won Higher Learning X Games to gain popularity with other teens. Juan can't see how he can change his unimpressive personality.

Roland reaches over to the unemotional Juan and tells him to let the kind, friendly and good-hearted Juan come out for some fresh air. "Kendra is right for once, but if you need any help, please come to see me, since I'm the master at making friends," says Roland.

Kendra laughs at the idea of Roland being a master at making friends, telling Juan not to let Roland's superiority complex overpower him. Roland uses the opportunity to tell him to give people a chance at school, and Juan agrees to try to make friends. Once again, Juan gets an irresistible feeling of awareness, as if someone is watching him from afar. But he keeps quiet to avoid being laughed at again.

After nearly forty-five minutes of traveling on the bus and train, they find themselves in front of the brown-and-red brick structure of the Higher Learning High School. They hear the eight o'clock bell ringing loudly to signal the beginning of a new semester, so everyone runs to get to their classes in time. They go off to different classes for the first three hours, and then they find themselves in the same Egyptian mythology class. Everyone settles themselves in the traditional seating arrangement of black leather chairs in groups of five enough to accommodate entire thirty students.

Juan's heart begins beating with nerves because this is his first class with high school students. Kendra and Roland are more comfortable. Kendra sees two of her friends sitting two rows behind her. Roland sees his ex-girlfriend, Dawn, a blond medium-built girl with light-brown eyes, but she ignores him to talk to two guys sitting next to her. Roland looks at them with fury in his eyes, and they view him with the same anger. Juan wonders on why was he chosen for this class, and then he remembers the words of Principal Morgan, who had written a letter to Malcolm prior to the beginning of school year.

Dear Mr. Witmore:

I'm happy to inform you that your son, Juan possesses a tremendous knowledge of history and mythology. He meets the requirements for our program that allows grade-school students to take one course with high-school students for one semester. Since both grade-school and high-school students are at the same location, this program lets the grade-school students get a taste of what to expect at the next level.

Juan and five other grade-school students are going to attend several history classes, so Juan won't be the only one there. Please have your son ready to attend our school, since it will be an unforgettable experience for him.
Sincerely,
Pierre Morgan

Juan doesn't feel good about this experience in the least. In the classroom, everyone looks at the clock in their seats. The teacher is a little bit late. Juan observes Kendra happily talking to two people sitting next to her desk, and Roland tells Juan about them winning last year's debate contest.

Roland sees the curiosity on Juan's face, and Juan insists on knowing their names. Roland speaks about the stylish young blonde-haired girl with olive eyes and fair skin named Glitter. Roland remarks about her desire to wear her totally outrageous pink outfits to match her over-the-top personality. Roland tells Juan about her placing colorful sparkles in her blond hair every day. Juan murmurs quietly about how she is allowed to wear this at school, and Roland murmurs quietly about Glitter's father's large yearly donation to the school. Roland mentions about how Principal Morgan looks the other way toward her crazy appearance, so he doesn't upset Glitter's father.

Roland and Juan observe their sister, who is talking nonstop to her other friend next to Glitter. She refers to this strong dazzling young female with long black hair and medium-brown skin as "Eyeshadow" because of her use of makeup. Her eye color, which changes from hazel to a sparkling green like a jade emerald, grabs their attention. Kendra wishes her eyes could change color due to weather, to mood, or to certain clothing like Eyeshadow's.

Roland looks unhappily at a heavyset brown-haired teen who is staring menacingly at Roland. Juan wonders why Roland is so mad at him.

Just then, the door opens up to reveal a slender, fair-skinned middle-aged man, wearing a fancy brown two button suit with black sunglasses. He introduces himself as Mr. Thoth Hermes, which brings some snickers and giggles from the students. Thoth smiles with them and doesn't expresses any anger.

"My name is a bit unusual, so please get it out of your system," says Thoth. "Laughing is supposed to make the body feel good, or something like that. I wouldn't wish to stop this moment of humor, so please refer to me as Thoth instead of Mr. Hermes."

Everyone takes full advantage of this chance, with the laughter going on for several moments. The other teachers wonder what is going in the new teacher's class. Wishing to begin class, Thoth scratches his fingernail on the chalkboard, which makes the students' shudder. Thoth smiles at them with some humor of his own. Thoth surveys the room with the intensity of a bank security guard. Thoth notices a couple of young kids who look no older than eleven. Thoth recalls Principal Morgan's new program that allows students with high grades in grade school to attend high-school-level classes.

Thoth, who possesses the sharp eyes of a hawk, looks at his students with great joy, since he considers teaching his most favorite job. But soon Thoth's happiness turns to pain. He begins to develop an uncomfortable feeling in the pit of his stomach. Thoth starts to feel dizzy, like the room is moving around him, and he crouches down to regain his senses. The students become concerned about him, but the feeling goes away quickly. Thoth rises to his feet with no problem, and he asks the students to give their names along with some basic information about themselves. Soon he gets another feeling, much like eating half-cooked meat, when Kendra, Roland, and Juan raise their hands to introduce themselves. He can't remember ever seeing any of them before.

In spite of his woozy feeling, Thoth shakes off this sudden sensation and has his students finish their introductions. Kendra, Roland, and Juan introduce themselves to the class, while Thoth studies the teens to determine their connection to his dizziness. After everybody gives some information about themselves, Thoth doesn't observe any other bad feeling. Thoth notices the clock is close to recess, and he resumes his lesson on Egyptian mythology.

"So, Osiris loses his life due to his brother, Seth, but Seth didn't get to rule Egypt in the end," says Thoth. "Can anyone tell me why Seth didn't get control and what happened to him?"

Kendra raises her left hand. "It was Osiris's son Horus who fought against his uncle and stopped him from being king. Eventually, Horus killed Seth with the Eye of Horus and saved Egypt from him. Excuse

THE MYSTERIOUS BOX

me, but doesn't the name, Thoth, refer to the wisest person in Egyptian mythology?"

Thoth is very surprised at Kendra's question for a moment, but he gives some standard answer about his mother choosing his name to honor that person. Thoth doesn't want to say anything else about his name, so he quickly changes the subject with a question about Seth's pyramid near the River North area.

"Can anyone give me some details about this pyramid?" asks Thoth.

Some students raised their hands, but then a small hand goes up from the back row. Thoth points over to a shy Juan, who is projecting strong fear and anxiety in answering the question. "In August 2002 an architect, Nicholas O' Reed, wanted to build something different in his career, so he pick this city to build the THES pyramid." answers Juan. "It was designed to be a think tank for people who were working to solve the world's problems, but they couldn't find the right area to put it in Chicago. After many debates over several months, Nicholas O' Reed found an investment group who paid for the THES pyramid construction next to the historic navy pier. Once they finally got the needed improvements and all the legal requirements, then they worked to finish the building over the next couple of years. THES was completed in the summer of 2004 next to the navy pier, and it became the leading think tank in the country."

Thoth marvels at his knowledge of the THES pyramid, and Kendra is completely stunned. Kendra is always the one with the answers, and she wonders how Juan knows so much about the THES pyramid. Juan recalls visiting the place during last year's field trip with his grade-school class. He had enjoyed the architecture boat tour of some of the historic buildings on the Chicago River. Thoth is writing on the blackboard about the many things to see in the River North area, where a stout, unpleasant history teacher with shaggy golden hair and wrinkled clothes enters. He shocks Thoth by presenting him an ancient-looking box. Since Thoth threw this box in the garbage last night, it brings a powerful sense of distress to him.

The teacher tells him a mysterious man in a white linen suit said this box belong to Thoth. Thoth wants to know the identity of this person but the teacher says the person didn't give his name. He leaves Thoth's class to return to his own classroom. Everyone examines the antique-looking box. It is small—nine by five centimeters—and shaped like a hexagon. It is made from light brown, hand-finished wood and inlaid mother of pearl, and it is inscribed with Egyptian hieroglyphics.

Thoth doesn't want to discuss this box with his students, but Kendra wants to know more about it. The rest of the class expresses their desire to examine the box as well, so he allows them to do so with some concern. Each student looks at it for a couple of minutes before passing it along to the next student. Juan doesn't see anything unusual about this box, but his hand begins to feel warm, as if he is touching a radiator. Juan begins to notice that the hieroglyphics on the box are moving slowly. In fear he pulls his hand off the box, and a brilliant white light starts surging out of the box, blanketing the whole room.

Everyone is amazed. Juan tries to let go of the box, but the box is attached to Juan's hands like a magnet. Thoth tries to take the box from Juan but the glow begins increasing enough to fill the entire classroom. Roland and Kendra run over to help Juan, but they find themselves stuck to the box as well. After the intensity of the light show in the classroom, the light decreases to nothing. Thoth finally knocks the box out of their hands to the ground. Thoth places the box in his desk, after which he looks up staring at the teens. Thoth finds it hard to come up with an answer to satisfy their questions.

Kendra shakes her head with disbelief. "That light was nothing more than some cheap magician's trick. Thoth, it was a nice thought, but I've seen better special effects at a movie."

"Kendra is right. I hope my trickery didn't scare anyone here," responds Thoth.

Everyone laughs with Thoth, and one student makes a remarks about not being scared at all. As the eleven o'clock bell rings loudly for recess, everyone runs outside. Roland hopes to get Juan to make a few new friends to help improve his self-esteem, so Roland brings over a few of his skateboarding buddies to meet Juan and his new friends, and everybody enjoys one another's company for a while. But two teens approach them, looking very upset with Roland.

One of the boys is named Chuck. He is the heavyset brown curly hair man with pale skin. Chuck aims his brown eyes at Roland, since Chuck wants express his desire to intimidate Roland. His associate is Drake Gasson, a muscular fair-haired fifteen-year-old with his pale skin, and Drake stares intently at Roland with his strong self-assured hazel eyes. Drake recalled his days of bullying Roland for a time.

That lasted until a couple of years ago. One day on the school playground, Roland refused to be terrorized anymore and stood up to Drake. Drake swung at Roland's face, but Roland was able to evade Drake's fist. They had found themselves battling each others like two boxers. Then Roland delivered the final blow with his fist to Drake's chest to end the fight in his favor. The other students had began to cheer and gather around to give Drake a taste of his own torment. But Roland made them stop and told Drake to never to pick on anyone again.

Since then, Drake can barely look Roland in the face, but he strangely doesn't hold any anger toward Roland. Drake has grudgingly come to respect Roland in his own way. However, Chuck isn't so forgiving of Roland and wishes for nothing more than for Drake to fight him again. Drake focuses his attention on Kendra with fondness and moves toward her. But she looks away from Drake. Chuck observes this nausea-inducing moment between the two of them.

"What is going on with this school when they allow babies, like Roland's little brother, to attend classes with teenagers?" Chuck asks to provoke Roland.

"Probably the same reason the school allows you to attend here, since there isn't a bigger baby than you," responds Kendra.

Chuck stops drinking his pop and tosses it into a pile of leaves. Chuck refers to Kendra as "Daddy's little girl" who needs her father for protection, and he tells her this is the reason no boy is going to ever going date her. But Kendra's friends Glitter and Eyeshadow stand next to Kendra for support. Eyeshadow pretends to see Kendra's father coming toward them, and this causes Chuck to spin around in fear. Chuck still maintains terrible memories of the school play and Kendra's father grabbing him by the neck. Everyone begins to laugh at Chuck, and he looks at Eyeshadow with rage. Chuck wants to repay her, but then a loud, deep voice calls out to Eyeshadow. Chuck looks behind him and sees a burly man, with light grey eyes and dark brown skin, wearing his blue police uniform, is standing just outside of the school's fence. It is Eyeshadow's father, Ray Hightowers, who calls out "Monica," Eyeshadow's real name. She sets off to talk with her father about never using her real name in public.

Chuck, afraid, turns to run back inside of the school. "You are just lucky that I have to get something out of my school bag. But at least, I am not Daddy's little girl."

Drake grabbed hold of Chuck. "You're not leaving until Kendra hears your apology."

"I...am sorry for my bad choice of words. Can I go now?" asks Chuck.

Drake releases his grip of Chuck's arm, and Chuck leaves the area. Kendra smiles at Drake, and Glitter takes notice of them.

"I hadn't realized how Drake is so protective of Kendra. There is a school dance in two weeks, and Kendra hasn't found anyone to attend with," says Glitter.

Eyeshadow sees Kendra's face turning red with rage, and she tells Glitter to leave her at once. Seeing her look, Glitter runs off with Eyeshadow to show off her new dress to other girls. Kendra wants to talk with Drake alone and tells Roland to leave with Juan. As Roland takes Juan to meet other teenagers, Kendra moves over for a one-on-one discussion with Drake. "I wish Glitter would learn to keep her big-mouth shut sometimes, but I do want to thank you for helping me with Chuck," says Kendra. "However, I'm not sure about going to the dance with anyone, since I've got something else to do, Drake."

"I know that you won't give me a chance, since I used to bully Roland," says Drake.

Kendra looks at Drake with uncertainty. Drake hears some of his teammates calling him, so he walks with them to the football field. He looks back at her with some disappointment.

Roland returns with Juan. Juan wants to figure out the secret to Thoth's box and if it is some kind of magic device. "Juan, don't you know a trick, when you see one?" asks Kendra. "It was all done with high-tech microchips or something like that. There was something interesting about the box, though, so maybe I should keep my mouth shut."

Juan and Roland beg Kendra to explain her theory. She says she saw a message written in hieroglyphics on the left side of the box, and Kendra uses her skills at reading hieroglyphics to translate this message for her brothers.

The Dark Lord Seth shall one day return to the world of men to finish that which he began so long ago. The only hope for mankind will be the great power within the box, which only the chosen ones can use against the evil Seth. This incredible power will meet the needs of the chosen ones when they find themselves in danger. They will be able to do implausible things that people will deem unbelievable.

4

CURIOUS FOR ANSWERS

Juan and Roland are curious about Kendra's translation, but she tells them to forget it. The school bell rings loudly, signaling the end of recess. The teens return to finish Thoth's class, and then they complete the rest of their class schedules for the next several hours. As the three o'clock bell rings to announce the end of the day, everyone runs out of the school. Juan tried to reassure everyone that he had used some technology trick with the box, but Juan doesn't believe in his explanation. Juan decides to keep these thoughts to himself, though, until he can prove it to both Kendra and Roland. His stomach starts to growling; it sounds like a bear, bringing laughter from both Kendra and Roland.

Roland notices Juan's hungry expression, and he is tired of hearing the growling noises from his brother, so he suggests making a stop for something to eat. Everyone agrees to this idea, and they take the bus to the downtown area of Chicago, the teens get off. It is an area recognized for good shopping and great food, and Juan is the first one to smell the strong scent of popcorn from several blocks away. Roland bumps into a few people as he tries to keep up with Juan, who is heading to Garrett's for its delicious cheese-caramel popcorn. Roland buys a medium bag of popcorn for them to share and asks the cashier for extra napkins for Juan, whose shirt always get covered with cheese from his hands.

As they head for the train station, Juan asks to stop for something to drink on the ride home. But Kendra looks at the time on her iPhone and tells them about getting on the train. They wait for a moment, and both the brown and red line trains come to a stop. The teens decide to ride the brown line train, and they find some seats to relax for their trip home.

In another part of Chicago, their teacher, Thoth rides the Metra train to his home in the northern suburbs. He is still in shock after discovering his students are the ones chosen to protect mankind from Seth. He can feel the fear growing in his heart. "They can only become the chosen ones when they received the powers within the box," Thoth thinks.

Thoth knows Osiris was the one who came to the school this morning. Thoth thinks about moving the box to another location, but he considers the possibility of either Osiris or another Ousia finding the box to redeliver it to the chosen ones. Thoth decides to keep the box close to him, until he can find a more effective way of getting rid of it. Thoth hates going against the wishes of the Ousias, and he feels a heavy pounding sensation within his heart. He reflects on his agreement with Osiris to train these mysterious chosen ones to face Seth, but Thoth can't allow his students to confront Seth. He shakes his fist in the air, drawing strange looks from the other passengers on the train. Thoth takes the whole thing with a slight smile on his face. He decides to face the consequences of disobeying Osiris and the rest of Ousias for the sake of his students. Feeling peaceful with his decision, Thoth looks outside of his window to observe the sunset.

The teens finally reach the Belmont station, and they walk out of the station for home. Fortunately, it is only a few blocks to their house. Roland uses his key to unlock the door, and they see Malcolm reading over some papers near the fireplace.

"Why are you so late this time?" asks Malcolm. "You should have been home an hour ago."

Kendra is good at giving quick answers to Malcolm. "We were hungry from all our hard work at school, so we stopped for some cheese popcorn. Sorry we caused you to worry about us, but it is nice to hear your concern."

"It is funny that you always use the same sorry speech when you did something wrong," replies Malcolm. "Fine—how was your first day at school today? Did each of you learn something?"

Roland takes a deep breath, relieved about not being in trouble. He smiles over at Malcolm, but Juan's face shows quiet displeasure. Juan's expression doesn't go unnoticed by Malcolm. He knows Juan doesn't totally dislike him, but he refuses to treat Malcolm like a parent. Malcolm becomes a little sad, but he hopes Juan will eventually come to accept him on his own.

"We met a crazy teacher with a weird name, Thoth," says Kendra. "In fact, he said his mom was a big fan of Egyptian mythology, so she chose a name from it."

"Thoth is an unusual name, but that just makes it one of a kind," replies Malcolm. "What is he teaching?"

"He showed us an unusual box with a message written in hieroglyphics on it that talked about the return of Seth," says Kendra.

Malcolm is very intrigued to hear this and wants more information. Kendra says Thoth used some kind of a light trick, and she brings up Juan's believing in the probability of this box being real. He doesn't want to upset Juan by agreeing with Kendra, so he refuses to respond to their story. Malcolm tells them to get ready for dinner.

Malcolm begins to take the food out of the kitchen and place different dishes on the table. But then he gets curious and goes upstairs to the attic for further study. Over the years, Malcolm enjoyed keeping much of his discovery in his attic for his study, and this mystery box has filled his head with too much interest for him not to investigate. He slowly opens the door and looks at his unique attic full of ancient Egyptians artifacts: pictures, jewelry, maps, medium-size canopic jars filled with several scrolls wrapped in plastic to protect them from fading. He moves toward a square steel table where he keeps the scrolls to scrutinize. These scrolls contain an outline of the chamber that Malcolm has studied off and on for the past five years with his archeological team in Egypt.

There was a reference on one of the scrolls about a time in ancient Egypt when Osiris had ruled Egypt with his brother, Seth, for many years. Sadly, Seth's jealousy of his brother had caused him to murder him. But Osiris's son Horus, killed Seth to avenge his father's death and brought peace back to the land as ruler of Egypt. A wise man had recorded every historical event that happened in ancient Egypt on many tablets and scrolls. He was named Thoth. The scrolls made reference to a box with hieroglyphics writing on it. It was said to contain the great power of the Ousias. Malcolm scratches his head in confusion, since he was never heard of the Ousias. Malcolm figures this mystery box could answer his questions. However, this box had disappeared from the pyramid, and it was believed to be either lost or stolen. Malcolm had became obsessed about the location of this mysterious box.

"Could this be the missing box from the pyramid—no archeologists were ever able to find it with the other artifacts inside of the pyramid," muses Malcolm. "Not to mention, the message on the box talked about the Ousias."

The teens walk into the dining room and see the tasty-looking collection of appetizing dishes on the dining room table. Everybody calls out for Malcolm. So Malcolm puts down his scrolls and runs downstairs. Just as the teens are starting to lose patience, Malcolm finally makes his way to the table. Malcolm wants to hear their feedback to the meal, since his busy schedule, at researching relics and artifacts, doesn't give him a lot of time to cook. Malcolm had spent the last few hours cooking the different dishes, and he moves with great speed to his chair, eager to observe their reaction to the meal. Everybody begins to eat from plates filled with pot roast, mashed potatoes with gravy, and green bean casserole. Kendra and Roland nod their heads and express approval of Malcolm's cooking skills.

As Juan wolfs down the food on his plate, Kendra whispers to him to acknowledge Malcolm's efforts in preparing the perfect meal. A part of Juan wants to give credit to Malcolm, but then he recalls an old memory of his mother. Juan starts getting upset, and Malcolm notices the awkward look on his face.

Kendra is very sympathetic toward her brother, though; she is tired of his attitude.

"Juan can't see beyond the past to appreciate the present, but what do you expect from someone who believes in a fantasy box being real?" says Kendra.

"At least I'm not going to date some bully at a cheesy dance," replies Juan.

Kendra kicks Juan with extreme force under the table again, and he calls out to her to stop it. Roland pretends not to notice any of this, but he waits to see how Kendra will get herself out of this one. Kendra's face turns as red as an apple at a grocery store, and she reaches over to attack Juan. Kendra desires to wring Juan's neck, but Malcolm asks her to use some self-control toward her brother. Malcolm wants to have a discussion about this so-called date.

But Kendra doesn't even see Drake as worthy of going to a dating and wishes not to continue the conversation. "I'm not interested in dating anyone, but if I am, I promise I'll talk it over with you first, Dad," Kendra says to Malcolm.

Kendra would have rather avoid the subject, but she knows Malcolm will ask her about it. Kendra thinks again about being the oldest one and the lack of respect. Malcolm breathes a sigh of relief to hear this, but Malcolm also realizes Juan's attitude is hiding a deeper issue within him.

"Is everything all right with you? This attitude seems to go against your personality?" says Malcolm.

"How can you truly know someone who you have raised for only three years!" shouted Juan.

Malcolm stops in midsentence, chills running down his spine. "Juan, I'm sorry for not realizing this."

Malcolm realizes, too late, that Juan is still angry about his mother, and he is unable to completely let go of the past. Malcolm tries to make peace with him now, since he understands Juan's lack of trust.

But Kendra refuses to make peace with Juan, since he got Kendra into trouble. She demands that Juan start living in the here and now. Juan, in a fit of anger, knocks his chair to the ground and runs back to his room. He slams the door shut hard enough to shake the entire house.

"Let me go upstairs to talk with him," says Roland.

"No, Juan needs to be alone for a while, so he can hopefully come to terms with his angry," replies Malcolm. "Even though I'm wondering if Juan will ever trust me, or even let me be a part of his life."

"Dad, don't give up on Juan; after all, we were not easy to deal with either," says Roland. "Even though I'm the easiest one of the bunch to handle since Kendra can so be overbearing at times."

Kendra pinches Roland on his left arm. "Hey, I'm the easiest one and the smartest one, right?"

Malcolm smiles at them, and he speaks like a diplomat about both of them being great to have as his own children. Malcolm changes the subject back to their new teacher, and he listens with interest to their answers. He asks Kendra if she knows how their teacher had come to possess this unique box. She puts down her food and tells him everything she can remember about the box. Roland goes into the kitchen and places some Neapolitan ice cream and slices of a double-layer German chocolate cake on two plates. As Kendra and Malcolm continue to eat their food and talk, Roland sneaks around them to carry both plates upstairs to Juan's room. He patiently knocks on the door and waits for him to respond, but Juan is too upset with Malcolm and everything else to answer the door.

After a while, Roland starts eating, expressing some shame out loud about his eating all the ice cream and cake. Juan listens to Roland making slurping sounds through the door for several minutes until it is too much for Juan to bear any longer. Juan finally opens the door to Roland holding his two favorite desserts in both hands. He reaches out to grab the plates, but Roland uses his arm as a barrier to block him. Roland tosses some of the ice cream high in the air, and Juan watches some of it fall on Roland's face. This fills Juan with uncontrolled laughter, and Roland walks into the room and puts the plates on his desk.

The teens finish off their dessert. Roland waits for the right moment to inquire about Juan's attitude toward Malcolm. However, Juan gets curious about Malcolm and Kendra's conversation, so they tiptoe downstairs to eavesdrop on them. Kendra is taking this moment without Juan and Roland around to express her own curiosity about the mysterious box. Unfortunately, she has underestimated her brothers' need-to-know natures as they step quietly down the stairs.

"I believe the box in your teacher's possession could be from a pyramid in Egypt," says Malcolm. "There was a message written on a stone that referred to a 'great power' contained within a box. It is said that the Ousias were of great power, but we couldn't find any such box in the pyramid. The box was to remain in this pyramid until the day the chosen ones opened the box to claim this great power from within. There was very little information about the location of the box, so we couldn't figure out the meaning behind the message about the chosen ones or the 'great power' reference, either."

Malcolm tells Kendra that he found this pyramid during one of his archeological dig in Egypt. Malcolm discovered a secret chamber with many artifacts and scrolls referring to a mysterious box of the Ousias. The Egypt government allowed Malcolm to keep some of the artifacts and scrolls, but they kept the varieties of gold, silver, and other jewelry discovered in the pyramid. Malcolm didn't have a problem, since he was interested in the historic values of the artifacts. But Malcolm wonders if the teens' teacher could have the actual box in his possession. Kendra talks about a message on the box that mentioned the coming of Seth. Kendra hears the ringtone from her iPhone, and she knows her friends are trying to reach her. So she fakes being exhausted from the first school day, and Malcolm decides they can continue with this discussion tomorrow. Both Roland and Juan practically knock each other down in their return to Juan's room so Kendra doesn't catch them in the act.

Before she leaves, Kendra tells Malcolm not to give up on Juan, since she believes he is coming around. She offers to help clean up the kitchen and dining room, but Malcolm motions for her to go to bed. Malcolm cleans up both rooms promptly. He is eager to do some more research into the mystery of this box and these Ousias.

Kendra strolls past Juan's room with some anger. She continues on to her room to talk with her friends, but Roland stays in Juan's room.

"Hey, bro," he says "Dad is trying to reach out to you, so why is it so hard to reach back a little?"

Juan doesn't like talking to Kendra, since she always wants to judge or lecture him. But Roland is more understanding about stuff. Juan decides to listen to him. Roland moves a chair near the door, close to the bed.

"Roland, I have nothing against Malcolm, but it's just too hard for me to accept him," says Juan. "Besides, I'm getting tired now, so can we talk about this another time?"

"OK, but you're going to tell me the real reason that you can't accept or even refer to Malcolm as Dad," replies Roland.

"You want the real reason? Then this how it is, Roland," he says. "When my mom dumped me off at the orphanage, she promised to return for me soon. She never came back to get me or even check up on me, so she lied to her own son. This is why I can't allow myself to trust anyone, including Malcolm, so please stop telling me how wrong I am to feel this way."

Roland doesn't judge Juan. He simply places his arm on his shoulder, like a big brother would. "Malcolm isn't your mother. You can't continue to judge him so harshly. Why don't you focus on the fact that Malcolm loves all of us equally?"

Juan listens with an open mind, since he knows Malcolm desires nothing more than to become a part of his life. Roland walks over to Juan's desk, and he brings out a picture with everyone in it. "Kendra and I used to get upset about our parents leaving us behind. Then we came to live with Malcolm, and he treated us like his own children," says Roland.

"I...guess I can't argument with that," replies Juan. "I won't make any promises, but I'll try to trust him."

Juan wants to think about this some more in the morning, since it is almost eleven o'clock. But Roland tells Juan to get dressed, since he wants to go outside for a reason of his own. Juan thinks Roland is crazy, and that they are going to get into trouble again for being out so late. But Roland loves to go skateboarding; it relaxes him, and it always helps

Juan to feel better about things as well. So Juan doesn't argue with his brother; he puts on his light-blue shorts and a maroon shirt. Before long, they quietly open the door to sneak outside. They move with complete stealth to keep their father and Kendra from hearing them.

Kendra is on her new universal multiphone, which allows one person to not only talk to but to view two people from different location. Kendra is able to watch both Glitter and Eyeshadow on a split screen. Glitter is still wearing her bright pink dress, which leaves Eyeshadow and Kendra pondering her self-absorbed attitude. Glitter is busy telling them about how they can look fabulous.

Eyeshadow and Kendra shake their heads. What was the use in trying to change Glitter in the middle of the night? Glitter offers to make amend to Kendra for telling her private business in front of her brothers and Drake, and Kendra accepts her words with the agreement to not do it again. Through the iPhone, Glitter smiles at them, which made her appear sincere, but she then spoils the moment with a discussion about them going to mall this weekend.

Eyeshadow rolls her eyes and says, "Glitter, you are making progress at being a less self-absorbed person, but your personality needs a total makeover."

Kendra changes the subject, telling the girls that her little brother told her father she was dating some boy at school. Kendra refuses to discuss this any further with her friends. But Eyeshadow and Glitter know she must be talking about Drake, since they know her too well for it to be anyone else. Nevertheless, they allow Kendra to keep her feeling about him to herself. They also figure on her hoping to attend the school dance with him, so they don't want to freak her out again with more questions about Drake.

Kendra hears a minor creaking of the wooden floor in the hallway. She slightly opens her bedroom door to watch Roland and Juan leaving with their skateboards. Kendra shakes her head at their craziness and closes the door to resume her discussion with her friends.

"How come the oldest female teen can't go out on a date, but her little brother can go out with whomever he wants to?" says Kendra, aggravated.

Eyeshadow and Glitter talk about their parents treating them the same way, and they agree not to mention this subject in front of Kendra's little brothers next time. Glitter talks about her father, Roger Bergon, and her mother Martha Bergon, who are co-owners of the Fragrance Enterprise, a company that sells premium perfume and cologne. "Fragrance Enterprises products guarantee give men or women the finest aroma of a lifetime. But they needed something more to catch the interest of the younger market, so my mom had come up with an idea that delighted my father," Glitter says.

Glitter's parents had told their daughter, Suzanne, to refer to herself as Glitter, so they could use her as part of their marketing plan. It worked out perfectly for them, since everyone would immediately recognize their daughter on television in her pink outfits. She used the perfume to demonstrate its quality, and her beauty and youth completely sold it to the people. The success of the campaign went to straight to her head, but neither parents saw this as a problem. Instead, Mr. Bergon gave her gifts and money for her help. Her parents were always traveling on business trips, and they didn't offer any apology for their absence except with jewelry, fancy clothes, and money. This had given her immense satisfaction, and Glitter began to use her good fortune to look down on people who didn't have her wealth and status.

In fact, it turned her heart as cold as ice inside of her for a long time, until she met Kendra and Eyeshadow at school. At first, they didn't want anything to do with her, since she was too absorbed in herself. One day, Glitter found herself lost in the far northwest part of the city, and she recognized Kendra and Eyeshadow walking down the street. She asked them for their assistance, and they decided to help her in spite of her selfish behavior. Glitter agreed to change her ways, and they formed a strong friendship. But they kept her accountable for her actions, and she worked hard to be a better person, at least to them.

Kendra and Eyeshadow are the closest things to real friends for her, and it feels like her old heart has been exchanged for a new heart with a faster beat. They talked about everything to each other, but she never mentions anything about how her parents chose her nickname. Too embarrassing for words.

Eyeshadow's father, Ray Hightowers, wants to provide with the best for his daughter, so he works lots of overtime patrolling the street of Chicago. He hopes to one day become a detective for a little more money. Eyeshadow wishes her parents would trust her more as well. Once, when she stayed too long at a friend's house, Ray had the whole police department driving through the neighborhood with the sirens on their cruisers blasting superloud. After that situation, none of the neighbors would let Eyeshadow visit their homes or to even let their kids go to her house.

The girls say they hope that their parents will become more mature someday, and then they begin laughing their heads in disbelief about such an idea.

Roland and Juan walk around the back of the house, where Malcolm had built a small black-and-silver skateboarding rink.

This pretzel-like rink allows them to practice skateboarding for their upcoming competitions, but Juan knows Roland prefers to go to the park to show off some of his moves for the girls. However, Juan doesn't want to upset Roland with his observations as he did with Kendra, so he focuses on doing some trick maneuvers like his brother. Roland tries to ride the top of the rink, so he can land safely on the ground, but he can't get too high in the air so he falls hard to the ground. Juan isn't any better at achieving a high level into the night sky. Then they try leaping over the front gate, but neither is successful enough to keep them from falling on their rear ends. Roland and Juan continue to perform other tricks.

Juan asks about Thoth's box. "Hey I got a thought here," says Juan. "Don't you think it is strange that Thoth's box is similar to the one box missing from the pyramid? What if the box is the same one—how did it get out of the pyramid?"

"We don't know if it's the same box or not, so why don't we get some rest for the night?" says Roland. "I'm getting tired from riding this skateboard. Why don't we focus on it tomorrow."

"Thanks," answers Juan. "I'll try to give Malcolm a chance, too. We'd better get back inside."

Roland grins at Juan, and they both sneak back inside of the house.

In his room, Malcolm doesn't hear a thing. He keeps drifting back to the box in Thoth's class, thinking it might be the link to a great Egyptian mystery. Malcolm looks at one of the scrolls that was found inside of an ancient canopic jar near the pyramid's entrance, and he reads something extremely interesting about the evil Seth. But Malcolm is too tired to try to solve the riddle tonight, so he goes to sleep, hoping to find the answers tomorrow.

It is 11:35 p.m., and Thoth can't sleep at all. It is a good thing he doesn't need a lot of sleep like regular people, and he is able to stay awake for long periods. Thoth looks around his house and sees nothing out of the ordinary. But his main concern is still on his students being the chosen ones. He doesn't want three teenagers to have to face Seth. Thoth goes into his closet and pulls out a sledgehammer to smash the box. He strikes the box with all his might, but the box isn't even scratched. Thoth realizes Osiris has protected this box with powerful magic, ensuring that nothing can either damage or destroy it. In frustration, he screams out loud for Osiris to give him an explanation. But there is only silence, and Thoth stares at an empty room. He ponders on his three students who were chosen. The skies over Chicago fill with a sudden thunderstorm, even though no such storm had been forecasted by the weather experts. Thoth tries to find a way to get rid of the box. But he knew Osiris would immediately take the box to the chosen ones. Thoth decides to keep the box close to him and hopes Osiris won't interfere. Thoth gets some rest for the night. He will deal with the consequences of his choices in the morning.

As the clock ticks closer to midnight, several lightning bolts strike the John Hancock building and the rooftops of other nearby downtown buildings with a dazzling forces. Those who see this marvelous event with their own eyes use their phones and other devices to take photos of the phenomenon, but the intensity of the storm causes most people to run for safety. News people will later air their photos.

The lightning bolts strike multiple buildings until they focuses on one building in particular, the Willis Tower, once called the Sears Tower. One of the lightning bolts hits the tower and continues to the ground in front of the tower at the stroke of midnight. The storm comes to an immediate halt, and a man appears on the spot of the lighting strike. He wears leopard skins over his shoulders and a black headdress with gold accents on his head. A black limousine pulls up to the front of the building, and several men in two or three button suits approach him with caution.

One of the men speaks with fear. "My lord Seth, we celebrate your return to the world of men."

"If you are one of my followers, then show me your proof of this now," says Seth.

The man moves the sleeve on his left arm, and he shows Seth a tattoo of Seth in hieroglyphics. Lord Seth nods his head to acknowledge, and he asks for his name along with the name of this place.

"My name is Tek, and you are in the windy city known as Chicago," replies the man.

"What is today's date?" asks Seth.

"It is Wednesday, September, 7," says Tek.

Seth thinks he has only a week to possess the power of the Ousias from the chosen ones. Tek wants to send a group of Seth's followers to capture the chosen ones. But Seth tells Tek to keep his followers away from the chosen ones and Thoth, since he desires to deal with them personally. Tek agrees, and Seth laughs with an evil-looking gleam in his eyes. Seth looks around at the Willis tower, marveling at its height, and he observes the other buildings with similar appearances. Seth views the limousine with delight and thinks how this horseless chariot would put the pharaoh's chariot to shame. Seth wishes to know more about the people of this time, so he can better prepare to take over the city and the entire modern world. The limousine drives away with great speed, and Seth expresses amusement at his newfound freedom from his dark prison.

"I have returned to the land of man and woe unto all who inhabit this world," says a ruthless Seth. "For all will come to follow me as their ruler or die in their rejection of me."

5

A TEACHER'S SECRET IS REVEALED

The next day, after everyone finish eating their breakfast, they go upstairs to get their backpacks. Malcolm tells them to get ready to leave for school. Juan shows off his speed running down the stairs like a racecar, but Kendra pulls hard on his shirt to stop his movement. Kendra is still upset with Juan for his comment last night. She stands patiently in front of him. Juan knows he has made a mistake with Kendra, so he offers his apology to her swiftly. Kendra nods her head and warns him not repeat such a mistake again, or else. She shoots daggers at him with her eyes to prove her point, and Juan, fearful of his sister's wrath, gives her word.

Roland slowly makes it down the stairs, resting himself next to Juan and Kendra. Roland was injured in his wild skateboarding stunts last night. Juan looks to his right and observes Roland motioning his head toward Malcolm. Juan suddenly rubs his ankle as well and nods a hello to Malcolm. They all turn toward the TV in the living room as the newscaster announces a series of bizarre lightning strike over the downtown area last night.

A TEACHER'S SECRET IS REVEALED

"Do you think the lightning strikes, the comet flying over the neighborhood the other night, and the mysterious box at school are all part of a conspiracy to fulfill some destiny?" asks Juan.

"There isn't any evidence to support your crazy theory, so please rejoin us in the real world," answers Kendra.

Malcolm tells Juan to document everything, and see if he can find a connection.

"Thanks for supporting me, and I'm going to prove my theory," says a determined Juan.

Roland speaks out in support of his brother as well, but he is doing this more out of anger at Kendra than with any thought of agreeing with Juan's destiny theory.

"I'm going to lecture at the John Hancock Building on my archeological career and discoveries," says Malcolm. "I might be a little late getting home, so I'm going to get our babysitter, Ms. Hawkinson, to care of you."

Malcolm sees the concerned expressions on their faces, since he doesn't always spend a lot of time with them. Roland wants to spend some time with Malcolm. And none of them want to have babysitters or nannies taking care of them. Roland expresses his displeasure at having a babysitter, since this causes Juan to regain his doubts with Malcolm. But Kendra understands more than her brothers that Malcolm is still regarded as an excellent professor, who doesn't want to miss too many of these speaking engagement.

"I understand your desire to spend time with me, Roland. This will be my last speaking engagement, so I can spend more time with all of you," says Malcolm.

Before they leave for school, Malcolm wants to talk with Kendra about finding the name Ousia in the scrolls. Roland looks at his iPhone and observes that it is almost time to catch the train to school. He and Juan head outside.

Kendra lingers, wanting to hear more. Malcolm says that there were many different meanings to this word, but there is a Greek reference that *Ousia* means substance, essence, or entity. Malcolm promises to continue to search for answers about the Ousias. Malcolm asks to talk with Kendra about their teacher.

Roland and Juan wait for Kendra at the front gate and hope her conversation won't be too long. Juan and Roland watch the bright blue sky, but soon their focus changes to something else. They witness an incredible upside-down rainbow in the sky, but it begins to disappear, little by little, from the sky. Juan quickly uses his iPhone to get pictures. He gets a very good snapshot of the rainbow before it completely vanishes from sight.

As they continue to wait for Kendra, they notice their neighbor, Ted Hardgrove, an elderly, lanky man with black eyes to match his bushy silver hair, comes slowly out of his house, walking with a limp. He picks up his daily newspaper at the same time every day, using a twisted cane with the head of a falcon on top to help him get around. He waves hello to them and both teens return the greeting to him. Juan recalls how he used to be nervous around Hardgrove, but he has been a good friend to Malcolm and the teens for many years. Kendra finally emerges from the house, they all run off to catch the bus for school.

They travel for sometime on the train, but Juan doesn't care about the train ride. His attention is on Thoth's mysterious box and its potential relationship to the missing box from Malcolm's archeology dig in Egypt. They arrive at Higher Learning with only a few minutes to spare before eight o'clock, and they head off to their different classes.

After several hours of attending classes, they arrive at Thoth's Egyptian mythology class, Juan, who wants some answers about his teacher's box is excited. The students gather outside of the classroom, waiting for Thoth to finish with the previous class. Kendra takes this opportunity to start her usual conversation with Glitter and Eyeshadow. Drake moves behind Kendra with the intention of asking her to go on a date. Drake hopes that Kendra will change her mind. Roland sees Drake standing near Kendra and runs over to give his support to her.

"I'm telling you to stay away from my sister," states Roland.

"Kendra is a big girl, and she doesn't need your protection," replies Drake.

A TEACHER'S SECRET IS REVEALED

"Roland, I can handle this on my own. I want Drake to hear this from me," says Kendra. To Drake, she says, "I don't go out with people who need to belittle others to feel big."

"Why can't you look beyond my past and give me a second chance to prove myself, Kendra?" Drake asks.

"It's very simple. A leopard doesn't change his spots," says Roland.

Kendra shakes her head with sadness. "Roland is right. I can't believe you. I'm actually starting to feel sorry for you, since you'll never see anything or anyone beyond your ego. Maybe if you could see people as people, then I might want to..."

Kendra just can't forget Drake's mistakes in grade school, when he had taken pleasure in bullying others. The many battles between Drake and Roland continue to haunt her mind like a nightmare. During those days, Drake was treated like a king there. He resumed his treatment of others as less than human at Higher Learning until Roland had stood up to him. As much as Kendra wants to believe Drake, she can't allow herself to. Kendra places her hand on Roland's chest to move him away from Drake, but Chuck walks in front of Drake to defend him.

"This is what happens when someone thinks too highly of herself," says Chuck.

Roland throws down his backpack in a fit of anger and moves toward Chuck. But Eyeshadow and Glitter move in front of him so Roland won't get into trouble for fighting. Glitter, who is wearing her pink pants with her pink high heel shoes, stands next to Kendra with her ever-loving devotion. Eyeshadow is equally full of strong devotion to Kendra like Glitter but she is more forceful than Glitter in defending Kendra. Eyeshadow asks Chuck to recall how Malcolm had held him in the air; he had looked like a scared rabbit in the school auditorium this summer. Glitter finishes Eyeshadow's thought by saying, "That was an insult to rabbits everywhere." Everybody begins laughing at Chuck, but it only adds to his hatred of them.

Chuck's face turns red with embarrassment and rage, "All of you are going to regret making fun of me, so you better enjoy yourself now. I promise a swift revenge to everyone here, so watch your backs."

"Hey, Chuck," replies Eyeshadow. "You need to come up with some new threats, since those are as old as your clothes there."

Chuck runs off with anger in his heart, and Drake looks disappointed with the whole thing. Drake walks toward his class, but he looks back at Kendra with sadness about her mistrusting him. Roland thanks Eyeshadow for saving him from punching Chuck's lights out and getting suspended for fighting. Eyeshadow regrets her decision to interfere, since she would have enjoyed watching that, but Kendra tells her not to encourage Roland. Thoth finally opens the classroom door, and everybody moves to their seats. Thoth apologizes to the class, saying he was in a teacher's meeting.

As the bell rings for the start of the class, Thoth tells his classroom that vice principal, Mr. J. D. Aster, will be in charge for the rest of the week. It brings some discomfort to the other students, since they know Mr. Aster likes to run the school like a boot camp in Mr. Morgan's absence. Roland listens to the kids' discussion about Mr. Aster and how he desires to become the principal of Higher Learning school. Soon after, a student walks into class, and he tells Thoth that Mr. Aster wishes for every student at Higher Learning to take a short test to evaluate their reading and math skills.

"Why would they need to take this evaluation test, since every student already took this test prior to the beginning of the semester?" asks Thoth.

The student could only respond with just following the orders of the vice principal. Thoth gives his permission and the student pass out the test to everyone. However, the student didn't have enough test sheets for Roland, Kendra, and Juan, but he promises to get them more. The student tells Thoth that Mr. Aster is going to allow every student who complete the test to go outside for an early recess. As time goes by, each student finds it takes no time to finish the test, and they head outside for some fun. But the teens are waiting for their copy of this test. Thoth doesn't like this delay and leaves to confront Mr. Aster.

After several minutes, Mr. Aster tells Thoth that the non-profit organization, Improving of Students Skills, didn't sent enough of the evaluation test. Mr. Aster promises Thoth that the organization will deliver more copies as soon as possible. Thoth refuses to accept this delay and argue to use the school's copier to make more. But Mr. Aster refuses to allow it for any reason. "There are other students that don't have the test either. I don't see their teachers complaining about it," Aster says.

"I don't want my students to just sit around, while their classmates are enjoying themselves outside," says Thoth.

Mr. Aster doesn't wish to hear this discussion anymore, and he tells Thoth to leave. Thoth heads for his class with a worried look on his face. Thoth opens the door and notices the Witmores are the only ones left in his class. Thoth tells the teens that Aster doesn't have enough copies. But Mr. Aster expects to receive some more copies.

Kendra expresses her displeasure and Thoth shares her feeling. "This test isn't even a long one and it took no time for them to finish it. I don't want to sound disrespectful, but Mr. Aster is always trying to pull something crazy like this."

Roland and Juan agree with Kendra. Thoth asks them to wait a little while longer and offers to let them go outside. He promises to bear the blame. In the meantime, Juan takes this opportunity to ask Thoth something important. "Thoth, is the message on the box part of some destiny, since the comet Destiny flew over our house a few days ago? And then a bright light appeared out of the box. Please tell my doubting sister that this all part of some grand plan."

Kendra knocks her books to the ground with frustration. "Please, Thoth, don't give any credit to my brother's crazy idea. He is living in his own dream world."

Roland sits quietly in his seat, since he'd rather avoid getting in the middle of his siblings' argument. But Thoth doesn't dismiss Juan's theory. Instead, he tells Kendra that every theory has a right to be proved right or wrong. Kendra stands on her feet, craving to put this nonsensical idea to rest. Thoth refuses to wait another minute for Mr. Aster and tells his students to leave. When the fire alarm rings to alert them to a possible fire, Thoth tells them to follow him.

Thoth heads for the door, but thick, dark smoke is flowing under the door, and Thoth orders them swiftly to the front window, since their classroom is on the first floor Thoth tries to open the window; however, they observe a thick layer of smokes covering the window as well, so he moves the teens away from the window to figure out another way out. Thoth feels the classroom door, discovering the door isn't hot. Kendra and the others are nervous about getting to safety, but Thoth confidently tells them to prepare to crawl on the ground. Thoth is just about to open the door slightly to check for anything out of ordinary, but at that moment the doorknob turns ever so gently. A stocky man with a black ponytail opens the door.

Everyone relaxes to discover it is Mr. Aster, since they think he's there to rescue them from danger. However, Thoth tells the teens to stand behind him, and they soon see Thoth's reason for concern firsthand. Aster's facial expression is as silent as a corpse's, and he moves in front of them to hinder their attempt to escape. Thoth begs him to allow his students to getaway, but he refuses to step aside.

"I can't believe how easy it was to fool you," says Aster. "You must really care about these teens, so why don't you just give the chosen ones their powers. Then they can surrender their powers to me, and I can hand it over to my master, Seth."

"Never," says a defiant Thoth.

A courageous Juan challenges Aster to a fight, but Roland yanks Juan behind him for safety. Aster sneers at him to create fear in the teen and Thoth waves his hand in the air, tossing Aster against the far wall near the window. As the teens gasp with amazement, Thoth lead the teens to the door. Aster struggles with some discomfort to get back on his feet. He opens his hand to release thick shadowy gray smoke out of it in front of everyone. The smoke goes underneath the crack of the door. Everyone shakes their heads in confusion. They hears the hooves of horses coming closer and closer to the door. Thoth pushes the teens several feet to the left side of the door.

"You should be honor here, since I went to all the trouble of creating a fake test and false alarm," says Aster. "This was all for the benefit of the chosen ones but wait the best is yet to come."

Within moments, the door splits into pieces like tissue paper. Thoth wasn't able to move out of the way in time to avoid the creatures' forceful hit on his body. Thoth goes sailing in the air toward nearby chairs, smashing into them. The teens run to examine Thoth for any physical damage. Roland and Juan move away some of the chairs from Thoth's body, and they can see blood dripping from his forehead. They look fearfully at the newcomers, two powerful charcoal-colored bulls with a pale, eel-shaped stripe on their bodies. Kendra calls out to Thoth that she recognizes these bulls. She remembers reading about them in Egyptian mythology as the extinct aurochs of ancient times.

The bulls aren't the same creatures from the legends, since they are huge, standing almost six feet tall and weighing each. Their dark-red savage eyes and their lyre-shaped horns are fixed on Thoth. Thoth knows all too well about Seth's fondness for changing simple creatures into deadly meat-eaters that turn ferocious at the sight of blood. The aurochs start to use their horns to knock chairs away from Thoth, since they like to charge a potential prey at full speed. Thoth orders the teens to stay behind him, so he can use his power to move them away. But the bulls aren't affected in the least, since Thoth is too weak from the bulls' first attack to focus his power. The aurochs knock away enough of the chairs, and they begin growling at Thoth with slobber dripping out of their mouths. Aster happily raises his hand in one last attempt to get Thoth to change his mind.

"Thoth, you can't win against these powerful creatures, so why prolong this useless struggle?" asks Aster. "These bulls can't be stopped in their obedience to my will. Give the chosen ones their powers, so they can hand them over to me as I gift to Seth. I will let them go home free once they release the power to me. Or they can watch helplessly as these aurochs rip your flesh and bones to pieces like ribs at an all-you-can-eat buffet."

Roland, Juan, and Kendra want to help him, but Thoth doesn't trust Aster to keep his word. Thoth can see the fear upon them. He motions calmly for them to come toward him, and he whispers to them to run for the door, telling them not to stop for any reason, but they don't like this plan. However, Thoth insists they obey his wishes in this matter, so Kendra nods her head to sort of agree for all of them. Aster is getting impatient for an answer from Thoth, so he yells out for the bulls to proceed toward them. The aurochs approach Thoth, hungry for his flesh, but he lifts his hands in the air to surrender. Thoth and the teens head for Thoth's desk, which the bulls had damaged a little in their earlier entrance. Thoth uses his remaining power to physically move the desk with great speed and strength at the bulls. His last ounce of power knocks both the bulls and Aster to the other side of the classroom with such might that they are temporarily stunned. But Thoth is too weak to leave with the teens, and he orders them to run home without thinking about him.

With deep regret, the teens dash out of the room, gasping at thick, blinding smoke in the hallway. Roland had once been on a fire patrol person at the school and assisted his fellow students in several fire drills, so he tells his siblings to crawl onto the ground to locate the nearest exit. They are able to maneuver on the ground and avoid breathing in the smoke for a few minutes. Roland finds one of the exits straight ahead and tells them to follow him. But Juan refuses to leave the building.

A terrified Kendra confronts him. "We can't just stay here and wait for those monsters to find us."

"No, I won't leave Thoth behind while we run off to save our butts," says Juan.

Roland moves next to Juan and says he agrees with Kendra that they must leave the building. They don't have the power to help Thoth, and Thoth told them to get away. As they deliberate over wanting to help him, a voice yelling out in pain rings throughout the hallway.

Thoth finds himself bruised and throbbing in pain from being tossed around in the air and landing on top of his desk. Aster delights in observing Thoth's broken body.

One of the aurochs rushes at Thoth like a bull in a china shop and rips the desk to pieces. The force of the horns open a lock drawer on the desk and the mysterious box falls to the ground. The box opens to release three lights of energy, which speed like lightning out of the classroom.

A TEACHER'S SECRET IS REVEALED

Roland has just convinced Juan to leave with them when they spot this surge of energy approaching them at tremendous speed. They try running away to avoid the light, but the wave of energy strikes each one to form a glow on the three. It leaves a platinum and white gold bracelet that reside on the teens' left or right arm. When the glow disappears, they see ancient hieroglyphic writing on them. Kendra is able to interpret the glyphs as being similar to the ones that are on the box.

Kendra doesn't even want to think about some "chosen one" destiny, and she decides to remove the bracelet. But Juan refuses to consider taking off his bracelet. Immediate after, he gets a terrible headache. Roland and Kendra run over to check on him, and he comes to his senses. Juan, without ever being in Aster's office, crawls his way there, as a worried Roland and Kendra pursue him. Juan struggles to catch his breath. The overwhelming smell of the smoke causes great discomfort to him. They look around to see textbooks, homework papers, and an antique lavender desk in the room. Roland listens to his brother gasp for fresh air.

"There is nothing in here to justify this foolish stunt of yours. We're having a hard time breathing in here," Roland reminds him. "I want to help Thoth, too, but we don't know how to use these bracelets to help anyone."

Roland turns to Kendra for help, but she heads toward the desk nearest the window. Kendra observes a combination padlock on a drawer, and she tries to figure out the combination to unlock the drawer. After several moments of intense guessing, Kendra is worried about not finding the solution in time to save Thoth, until she starts to experience a strong jolt of static friction all over her body. Both brothers fear for her, but Kendra successfully unlocks the padlock. She moves her hand inside of the drawer and brings out two glasses two inches long, with smoke inside of them.

"How did you know the combination to the padlock so fast?" questions Juan.

"Yeah, how did you know the glass pyramids were in the desk to begin with?" asks Roland.

"It's hard to put into words, but I could hear the thoughts of Aster shouting in my head," answers Kendra. "He was so furious with Thoth from helping us to escape that Aster gave away the hiding place of these glass pyramids. I can't explain it but his emotional state was like a roadmap to his hidden thoughts. Aster was thinking about using them to summon more aurochs to catch us when the aurochs finish off Thoth."

Juan goes over to smash the pyramids, but she stops him. She tells them to take the pyramids back to Thoth's classroom, so they go quickly.

In the classroom, Aster gives him one last chance to save his life, but Thoth tells Aster to shove his offer. In a fix of rage, Aster gives the bulls permission to completely destroy Thoth. The aurochs rushes over to Thoth like piranhas, and they start biting away at him like a four-course meal. With no concern for their safety, the teens enter the room like warriors and order Aster to release Thoth.

Aster laughs at them, since he knows they don't have any power. However, they stand their ground together like soldiers, and Aster orders the bulls to attack the teens instead. Thoth tells the teens to leave him, but this time they disregard his order. Aster prepares to enjoy the moment, but then he sees his glass pyramids in their hands and the bracelets on their arms.

The aurochs run at the teens at full force. Roland smashes the glass pyramids on the ground into pieces. The bulls disperse quietly in the air, and the teens run over to check on Thoth.

"Why couldn't I have just smashed the pyramids earlier, Kendra?" asks Juan.

"The power of the glass pyramid needed to be near the aurochs, so the magic would destroy them." answers Kendra. "I could read the intense desire in Aster's mind, calculating the possible distance of those pyramids to use against us."

Aster fears the power of the bracelets on the teens' arms, so he dashes for the door to escape them. Roland goes after Aster, but Thoth pulls on his shirt to stop him as he endeavors to catch his breath. They hear the sounds of the fire engine coming to the scene, and Thoth tells them to follow him to another exit out of the building.

Thoth doesn't want to clarify his reason to be inside of a building consumed by smoke, and they go downstairs to the basement. Thoth opens a back door to the outside, so no one would see them leaving the school. They find themselves near the playground, and Thoth doesn't see anybody in the area. The teens take this opportunity to breathe in fresh air, but Thoth doesn't want to waste time standing around. Since people are waiting outside of the building for the firemen and police, he seizes this opportunity to lead the teens to his blue car parked near the playground. He drives around to the main entrance, where parents are picking up their kids, and firemen are going through the building to check for other people inside. One fireman talks about finding no cause for the thick smoke in the building, and Thoth casually walks over to an officer. He tells the officer that he's their teacher, and he's taking these students home to their father. The officer gives his OK and watches Thoth and the kids get into the car.

"I know you have a lot of questions about this whole situation, and I promise to answer them somewhere else," says Thoth.

"OK, but we want to know the whole thing from the beginning," replies Kendra.

Roland and Juan agree with Kendra. As they drive away, they witness Aster telling the police and fire department about the smoke, mostly lying to them. Thoth drives past the school, but it isn't easy for him to drive. The force of the bull's attack has left him a little weak, but he is able to drive without having to explain this to his nervous students. Thoth wonders about the teens being able to handle the truth of him or their role as the chosen ones. Thoth reflects on the saying "It's going to be a long story." Thoth drives far away from the school, and he looks at those bracelets on the teens' arms as a sign of the beginning of things to come.

6

MEET MY FIVE-THOUSAND-YEAR-OLD FRIEND

As the fire fighters and the police finish their investigation, two of the officers, Tek Argo and Ray Hightowers talk for a long time with Aster, finding no answers for the smoke. Aster tells them that he views this as a prank by one of his students. Officer Tek, a husky man with blond curly-haired and grey eyes, tells Mr. Aster to leave the investigation to the professionals. Ray goes off to check on his daughter, Eyeshadow, and Tek uses this time to get in some private words with Aster.

"Thoth and the chosen ones escaped from school on your watch with the bracelets, and I get to clean up your mess," says Tek. "Seth told us to leave Thoth and the chosen ones for him to deal with, and he won't understand your failure here. But I'll let you explain this to him, since he wishes to talk with you as soon as possible."

Aster turns pale at the idea of facing Seth and explaining why he had ignored Seth's request about taking on Thoth and the chosen ones.

Aster grabs hold of Tek's arm with Seth's tattoo on it, and Tek promptly removes his arm from Aster's grip. Ray is walking back toward Tek, so he orders Aster to leave his sight immediately. Tek reiterates to him about not missing tonight's meeting with Seth, or he will face his wrath. Aster gives his word to attend the meeting with Seth, but he is as frighten as a fish out of water. Ray returns to tell Tek that he is taking his daughter home from school, since his wife is working late. Tek offers to finish up the paperwork about the incident, and Ray taps him on the shoulder as a gesture of thanks.

Tek uses his iPhone to makes a desperate call. "Aster is about to runaway like a coward, so please be ready to stop him and return him to Seth."

Thoth uses his magic to heal his injuries and make them disappear, and they watch him being made whole again with bewilderment. Thoth knows the teens' desire to learn the truth. He takes this chance to explain the whole situation. Thoth tells the teens with caution that they must be trained to protect their world from an evil Ousia, but he expresses little interest in being their mentor. Roland and Juan look very confused, but Kendra recognizes the term "Ousia."

Thoth explains that every mythological being in history existed on Earth at one time, but they passed away in some fashion in their lives. Thoth speaks about how their magic was too strong to stay gone, and many of these beings inexplicably returned to Earth in an incorporeal form two millennia ago. Thoth tells the teens that some of the mythological beings didn't get a second chance at life. Kendra wants to understand the reason for this, but Thoth couldn't give her an answer. Thoth admits that many of these beings was able to become corporeal beings for a limited amount of time. However, most of them couldn't achieve this without certain conditions. Thoth reveals how they renamed themselves the Ousias and formed a group referred to as the Society to help make life better for all mankind.

However, many of the evil figures from different mythologies weren't in favor of this society, since they'd rather to conquer or annihilate mankind. A great war ensued between the good and evil Ousias, and eventually the good Ousias won the war against them and imprisoned the evil ones for all eternity. Roland, Juan, and Kendra become very interested in hearing more of Thoth's tale.

Thoth finds it complicated to finish his thoughts, so he takes a deep breath for two seconds. He then informs them that an evil Ousia from Egyptian mythology had escaped from his prison, and he was here in Chicago.

"If Loki and Hades are examples of these evil Ousias, and then this must mean Zeus, Odin, Thor, and Hercules are examples of the good Ousias?" says Juan.

"Yes, those names represent both good and evil Ousias, since they and many others became entities," answers Thoth.

A jumpy Kendra keeps calm with lots of difficulty. "So this evil Ousia couldn't be the horrific Seth from Egyptian mythology who killed Osiris in his attempt to conquer Egypt, since he was slain by Horus, right. So does this mean that Seth and Osiris are alive and well?"

Thoth admits that Kendra is right about Seth and Osiris being alive. Thoth tells the teens that Seth has returned to try again to conquer not just Egypt, but the whole world. Seth had been one of many evil Ousias imprisoned forever. There wasn't enough time for Thoth to explain the whole story, but he explains that Osiris ordered him to train the chosen ones to use the bracelets, so they could help to defeat Seth. But Thoth cannot allow this to happen, since it is dangerous for any of them to confront Seth.

"I don't care about the dangers, if the bracelets will give us the powers to stop Seth," says Juan.

Kendra looks at Juan. "This isn't some video game. This is real life here. We were lucky those aurochs didn't hurt us or kill Thoth."

"This is what I wanted to protect you from, so I tried to prevent your being dragged into this mythological fight," says Thoth. "Unfortunately, my power was reduced due to my unwillingness to become your mentor, and I was too weak to fight those aurochs."

Roland supports for his brother, since he saw enough to convince him that they need to learn how to defend themselves from Seth and his followers. Roland reminds Thoth that he is responsible for their safety. They have to be able to use the bracelets. Thoth listens to their arguments for several moments before he finally gives in to Roland and Juan. Even Kendra finally comes around, saying they need to know to use those bracelets to protect themselves and Malcolm. The teens explain how they were able to do certain things at the school to help Thoth and stop the bulls. Thoth turns off the Kennedy expressway and parks near a vacant lot. He asks them to bring their bracelets closer to him, and he examines each one to figure out the power within. Thoth finds some hidden hieroglyphics on each bracelet, which he realizes only an Ousia can see.

Thoth asks them to get out of the car, and he explains their powers to them. He informs Roland that he will be able to move some objects with his bracelet and sees the look of excitement on Roland's face. Thoth asks him to calm down, so he can tell him about this ability. Roland stands at an attention like a soldier, and Thoth mentions that he will be able to bring certain inanimate objects to life for a limited time.

"I want to test these magical powers immediately," says Roland.

"No, these powers should only be used in a time of trouble," answers Thoth. "If you use these abilities too often, it will drain your energy to the point of exhaustion."

"What abilities do I have?" asks Kendra.

"You have the ability to know the inner feelings of most individuals," says Thoth. "This gives you the ability to know the details of a person's secret. But this ability won't tell everything there is to know about the person."

"OK, you have saved the best for last for me," shouts Juan.

"Your ability is seeing future and past events," answers Thoth.

Unexpectedly, Roland sees a chance to test his powers. A car speeding out of control is about to strike a pedestrian, but Roland uses his bracelet to force the car out of the pedestrian's way. The person appears to be OK, and the driver stops his car to check on him and offer an apology for his lapse of judgment. Thoth smiles at Roland's quick reaction. But he cautions them to limit using these powers.

Kendra looks at Thoth with her new ability, and she senses his desire to protect them. He has come to care about them. She tells her brothers that he is on their side, but Thoth isn't feeling so easy inside.

In fact, she gets a slight feeling that his interest in being a mentor goes deeper than a concern for their safety. Unfortunately, Kendra doesn't have the power to dig too deep inside of him, which brings strong relief to Thoth. But her brothers aren't believers in Kendra's ability, even though she sensed Aster's thoughts at the school. Kendra is determined to prove them wrong, so she takes a hard look at Juan and Roland. She notifies them that she knows that they sold some coins from their collection so they could attend the comic convention event last April at McCormick Place. Their faces turn pale at the thought of their sister reading their secrets and feelings. Juan isn't satisfied with his ability, hoping to have a cooler ability than Kendra. Thoth tells him to clear his mind of everything.

"That shouldn't be hard for Juan, since his mind is a blank slate to begin with," answers Kendra.

Juan ignores her to clear his head, and a vision of water flooding a room appears to him. Thoth asks Juan about noticing anything else in the room, so he could figure out the whole picture behind the vision. Juan couldn't see anything else. Thoth tells him to relax, since the vision will reveal itself in time. He makes it clear to them that the bracelets' power will aid them in times of great need, and Thoth mentions the limitations of each bracelet.

"I don't understand why would the Ousias would put limits on these bracelets, since we're called to help protect mankind," says Roland.

"Yeah, and why does Roland have all the cool physical powers to move things and bring objects to life, but I have some weak mental power?" asks Juan.

"The Ousias require the chosen ones to display your level of maturity, before they will remove the limitation on those magical bracelets," answered Thoth. "Besides, mental abilities of yours and Kendra's will come in handy when physical abilities aren't enough to save the day."

Thoth tell the teens about managing their emotions, since their abilities may spiral out of control from their feelings. He tells the teens that they can't use their powers against an innocent. But Juan still wants the cooler powers. He wants the pressure of being able to handle real power. Juan starts feeling dizzy. They others notice blood dripping out of his nose. Thoth tells him to stop focusing on it. As Juan's nose continues to bleed a little faster, Roland and Kendra want to help their brother. Thoth tells them to stay there and orders Juan to concentrate on him. He follows Thoth's suggestion, and Juan's headache disappears and his nosebleed stops. Juan tells the others about his vision of being inside a forest of spike-like trees. Juan says he could feel the pain of being struck in the back by these long, needle-like thorns. Juan says that he now has no feeling of any kind—kind of like frostbite. Thoth doesn't want to alarm him about these visions, but he speculates that this vision could be of some future danger yet to come.

Thoth suggests to Juan that he shouldn't try to force the vision to appear. He says the vision will appear in a simple flow, like a river moving downstream. Juan nods his head in agreement to the advice to let the visions come naturally. Thoth knows the danger of trying to look too far into the future, and Thoth recalls his experience of possessing a similar talent.

Two millennia ago, when Thoth had been working with Osiris at Utopia he had the ability to see the future, which he used to assist Osiris to improve the lives of mankind. Thoth helped Osiris successfully foresee the great battle against the evil Ousias. But the abilities were giving Thoth's horrible headaches, worsening to the point of death. Osiris had no choice but to take these abilities away. However, it came at a cost—Thoth wasn't able to foresee an event later, which changed his life forever.

Thoth offers an important lesson to them. He tells them to stand together. The teens move closer together with some discomfort for each of them until they understand his reasoning for this exercise. Thoth suggests that they concentrate on their bracelets, and he asks them to think of an invisible field surrounding them. They don't feel any different, so they try walking away from one another. But their movement was stopped with a hard bump, like hitting a brick wall. They realize Thoth wasn't kidding about this invisible force field. Thoth laughs at them and tells them to think about the invisible field being gone. Everyone smiles back at Thoth as they follow his command with no doubts. They are able to walk forward without no problem. Kendra wants to know about any limitations on this force field.

Thoth orders them to listen carefully. "This force field will protect you from most attacks, but any out-of-control emotions will decrease the power of field. And Seth will endeavor to use his power against you, but Seth can't take the bracelets. The chosen ones must give him the bracelets of their own free will. Don't forget these words, no matter what is coming at you."

Kendra's phone starts to ring, and she sees Malcolm's ID on it. He saw the news story about the school on television, and he was driving to the school. Kendra answers it to inform him of their safety. She tells Malcolm that they are in the company of their teacher. Thoth takes the phone from Kendra and tells him that his kids are safe from the smoke at school. Thoth reassures him that he will bring them home immediately. They each talk briefly to Malcolm, who sounds relieved to hear their voices. Malcolm agrees to return to the house and waits for them. But Juan can't stop thinking about his vision, and he asks Thoth about the meaning behind the vision.

Thoth contemplates his question. "It would be nice to learn about this mysterious vision of yours, but there are more important things right now. Mr. Witmore is probably still worried, so I think it's best to get everybody home at once. Especially since these followers of Seth now know of us, so they may try to set a trap at your house. We need to explain to him about everything."

"That is assuming Dad will even believe us," says Kendra.

"Yeah, I can't even get myself to accept this whole craziness," replies Juan.

Thoth agrees to help them convince Malcolm, and they all get into his car. Everyone thinks about Thoth and his and her new powers. But each one is worried for Malcolm, since they have gotten a taste of what Seth's followers can do. They also fear for their adoptive father's safety. They drive for several minutes, and Thoth reassures them that he will do everything in his power to protect them all. This brings some relief to their fearful hearts, until they think about explaining this to Malcolm.

Eventually, Thoth arrives and parks the car in front of their home. Thoth follows Roland and the others to their house, nervousness engulfing them. Juan and Roland reach out to knock on the door, but Kendra regains her senses, grabbing their arms. She motions for them to catch their breathe and relax, sensing their concern. Kendra uses her own key to open the door, and Thoth tells them to remain calm as well.

Upon hearing the kids' arrival, Malcolm immediately runs over to the door. He moves with the quickness of a jackrabbit, and his smile lights up the room. Roland and Kendra show equal excitement and relief upon seeing Malcolm, and it includes their little brother, too, for the most part. Malcolm starts to inquire to about the smoke at school when he spots someone waiting outside to come in. Malcolm was so filled with concern for his kids that he completely ignored him. Kendra introduces Thoth as their teacher from school, and Malcolm invites Thoth to come into his house.

As everyone walks into the house, Malcolm notices the bracelets on each of their arms. He notes the excellent craftsmanship. Kendra casually mentions that Thoth gave them the bracelets, and Malcolm invites Thoth to sit on the mahogany couch in the middle of the living room. Roland and the others are too nervous to move, and Malcolm tells them to sit down. So they each sit on one of the four wood chairs that are arranged on either side of the couch.

"Thoth, your name is the same as the one of the great Egyptian legends in mythology," says Malcolm. "I'm really intrigued with those bracelets. They seem too valuable to just give away. Where in the world did you find such unique objects?"

Malcolm walks to Roland to get a closer look at his bracelet and observes that the other bracelets are indeed very valuable, made of platinum and gold, and they appear ancient. Malcolm remembers the missing box at the pyramid in Egypt, which had similar markings similar to those on the bracelets, and he wonders about how Thoth has come to possess them. He turns to Thoth for an answer, but Thoth doesn't have one to give him.

"How did you get a hold of these bracelets? These markings relate to an ancient box that has been missing for thousands of years," says Malcolm. "I want the truth here."

"Dad, there is a connection between the box and our bracelets," said Kendra.

"Yes, and you may not be able to handle the whole truth," adds Roland.

"That depends on how you define 'whole truth,' since I'm still feeling a little...shocked on the subject," says Juan.

Thoth looks Malcolm in the eye. "I feel that you need to know the truth about me. You are curious about those bracelets and the missing box, and the truth is I took the box out of Egypt some millennia ago. I'm the actual Thoth from Egyptian mythology, and those bracelets came out of that same ancient box. Now these bracelets belong to your children, the chosen ones."

Malcolm become extremely angry at Thoth. "I don't know what kind of sick game you are playing with my children, but I want you to leave my house at once. Kendra, Roland, and Juan—I want all of you to go upstairs now."

"No, Thoth is telling the truth. Please listen to him," replies Juan.

"I'm telling you to do as I've told you," Malcolm demands.

"No! You aren't my real father, so don't start acting like one," yells Juan.

This was the last straw for Malcolm, who had tried very hard to be patient with Juan. He yells for Juan to obey his wishes at once. Thoth observes the anger building on Malcolm's face like a volcano getting ready to blow its top, so he offers Malcolm proof about his identity. Malcolm doesn't want to hear from someone who has apparently lost his mind, so he put his fists forward, sending a clear message for Thoth to leave his house.

Thoth pulls at the back of his head until his face comes off like a mask. Everyone is shocked to see Thoth's face isn't human, but it is actually the face of an ibis with a downward-curving beak. Everyone else stands stunned unable to speak. Thoth moves a few steps back, holding out his left hand to indicate friendship. Roland approaches Thoth calmly to shake hands with him. After their initial shock, Kendra and Juan convince Malcolm that there is nothing to fear. Even after viewing Thoth's true face, Malcolm is still nervous about trusting this person, but he decides to trust his children. Malcolm asks Thoth to explain this. Thoth holds out his hand toward Malcolm to demonstrate his good intention to Malcolm who returns the favor. Thoth sits back down on the couch, and the teens settle again on the chairs.

"Thoth, what are you, if I may be so bold to ask?" asks Malcolm.

"I'm a being known as an Ousia, and your kids are the ones chosen by the Ousias to save the world," says Thoth. "I would like to apologize for looking so scary, so please let explain this to you." Thoth gave Malcolm the story how they came to call themselves Ousias.

After nearly a half an hour of explaining this to Malcolm, Malcolm starts to develop strong feeling of anxiety. At the thoughts of Seth being an evil Ousia, escaping from prison. Not to mention, his kids being chosen to stop him that Malcolm can't bring himself to accept any of this. He asks Thoth, "Why were they picked to protect mankind from these evil Ousias? If these good Ousias have such great power, then why can't they just recapture Seth?"

"The other good Ousias try to help mankind, but their attempts have caused great disaster for the people of this world in the past," answered Thoth. "They decided not to interfere with the affairs of mankind, so they made these bracelets of power that are meant to attach themselves to the best chosen ones of this world. These bracelets will glow only in the presence of the chosen ones, but I never thought any of my students would be the chosen ones. For this reason, I refused to train your children as the chosen ones, and that caused my power to be cut in half for my disobedience to Osiris and the other good Ousias. It made me unable to defeat one of Seth's followers at the school."

"Are you saying that someone at the school was trying to hurt my kids?" asks Malcolm.

"Yes, it was the vice principal, Mr. Aster, who tried to kill Thoth and forced us to give him our powers," says Juan.

"My word," replies Malcolm. "This would be too dangerous for adult to deal with, let alone for teenagers. These Ousias must find some other chosen ones to save the world."

"Osiris and the others Ousias believe it is the destiny of your children to save mankind from the evil Ousias like Seth, but I don't desire for any of your teens to fight in our battle against Seth," answers Thoth.

Malcolm is trying to understand this whole thing, but it's becoming more difficult to accept Thoth's answers. He sits down very hard on his couch, as if he is going to faint, but the teens are calm for the most part. Kendra runs into the kitchen and pours some water into a cup, which she quickly gives it to Malcolm. He begins drinking the water too fast, feeling like his nerves are about to explode out of his body. Malcolm begs Thoth to find another solution to this, but Thoth explains how Osiris is the most inflexible person who ever lived, and he has never changed his mind on anything.

"I say that we should decide for ourselves on this," Juan says. "After all, it is *our* destiny. What other choice do we have here?"

Malcolm knows Juan has strong issues with him, but he's still red with anger. "I know that you don't want to accept me as your guardian, parent, or anything else. However, I care about what happens to all of you, so don't expect me not to care about your safety here. Thoth, I know that Osiris decreased your powers, but isn't there some way to stop Seth on your own without involving them? Because there is no telling how many other followers like the vice principal, are waiting for their chance to attack my children."

Thoth moves back and forth on the floor, leaving an impression on the brown carpet. He appears not to hear Malcolm or any of his kids talking in the room. Thoth's thoughts are about Seth and when he will find them here. Malcolm can see Thoth is distraught about something, so he repeats his question to Thoth in a louder tone.

"Please forgive me for not listening earlier, but I don't have the power to stop Seth," answers Thoth. "However, evil Ousias have weaknesses of their own, but I don't know what they could be."

Thoth tells them that Seth has seven days from his escape from prison to capture their bracelets, and this news brings a collective feeling of dread. It is a whole new spin on a scary situation. It is down to the six days.

As the grandfather clock ticks, Thoth says that every Ousias, either good or evil, has a weakness of his or her own, so that neither group can take advantage of mankind for its own purposes. Thoth mentions that he took three pyramid pieces from Seth's pyramid, so he wouldn't be able to complete his evil plan of conquest.

Thoth offers some good news for them. "Seth can't take your bracelets with any kind of force. The chosen ones must give him their bracelets of their own freewill, and Seth must also get possession of his three missing pyramid pieces."

Kendra asks Thoth why Seth might need these pieces, since the pyramid is already put together. Thoth informs them that's just the outside of the pyramid—the inner, magical part of the pyramid needs to be whole prior to the seventh day since Seth's escape from prison.

This gives them some hope since Seth can't take their bracelets with force. Everyone thinks about ways to avoid Seth for the next several days, so he won't succeed in his plan. Malcolm begins to question Thoth about Seth falling to gain these items in time, and Thoth says that Seth will die if he is unable to gather these items, which provides some relief.

Thoth offers to take them out of the city. Juan wants to face Seth like a hero, but Kendra wants to go away. Roland doesn't like to run away from a fight; however, he doesn't want anyone to get hurt. Malcolm agrees about getting his family out of town. Juan would rather figure out Seth's weakness, so they can use it against him.

Juan wonders to himself about his attitude toward Malcolm. Then, his bracelet starts to glow with an intense brightness, like a small sun illuminating the whole house. Kendra and everyone else shut their eyes to avoid the strong light, but Juan is strangely able to see a vision in the light. He sees a dark figure with a face too strange for him to recognize standing in the middle of a room. The figure is bending over in pain, as he tries not to look at the walls. The light of the bracelet begins to decrease, and gradually everybody is able to see again.

"Quickly—what did the bracelet show you?" asks Thoth.

"The bracelet showed me a figure of someone standing with four walls around him, and this person was in great pain as he tried to shield himself from looking at the wall," replies Juan. "I could feel his hatred for the living, so it's got to be Seth, right?"

"Do you think Juan is right about seeing Seth? What does the vision mean?" asks Roland.

"Yes, but we better keep focusing on the vision for a solution, since it may be helpful later," answers Thoth. "For the moment, we have to get out of here, since Seth may know your location. Seth can't be trusted not to try to hurt your children, since he desires those bracelets."

"Why would Seth want to hurt them? They're too young to be a threat to him," asks Malcolm.

"Because the power of those bracelets gives them the ability to stop him, when they are used in the right way," says Thoth. "Seth doesn't want to leave anything to chance, since he has failed before in his attempt to rule Egypt. Also, Seth hopes to open a doorway into the underworld and release his army upon the world."

Malcolm interrupts Thoth. He has just recalled something from his research. He recounts finding a piece of a lost pyramid in a jar near the entrance of the pyramid he had excavated near Cairo, Egypt. His research assistants had felt the jar was an original canopic jar, in which parts of the human body were placed for the afterlife. Malcolm had looked inside to find no body parts, but he had found something just as interesting. He discovered an inscription written on a scroll that warned about the evil lord Seth trying to rebuild the pyramid as a gateway to the underworld.

Thoth confirms Malcolm's thoughts. He says that Seth will unleash the plagues of ancient Egypt as well, but while everyone is trying to absorb this terrible possibility. Thoth reveals something much worse that only adds to their fears. Thoth concludes that Seth can keep this gateway open till the beginning of the eighth day, he will become fully corporeal with all of his power. The armies of the underworld will enslave the human race, with Seth as their pharaoh.

However, Thoth maintains that Seth will be gone forever in the event, that he fails to keep the gateway to the underworld prior to the start of the next day. Everyone gasps for breath on hearing this information, and Malcolm looks concerned for the teens. Thoth sees the fear on Malcolm, so he once again explains their advantages over Seth. Seth can't force any of the teens to give him those bracelets, and Seth will die without the bracelets in his hand on the seventh day.

"Thoth, why would his failure lead to his destruction in seven days?" asks Roland.

"When I chose to return back to Earth, I was able to survive in a temporary corporeal form," responds Thoth. "But it came at a paid, and the price was to train and protect the chosen ones who would use their power to protect the earth from the evil Ousias. All evil Ousias have some kind of limitation of their powers that prevent them from dominating mankind. Even good Ousias have limits, so they won't be tempted to misuse their powers. Many of us didn't like having restrictions on our magic, but we didn't argue with those who were tasked with managing the balance between order and chaos. Unfortunately, evil Ousias like Seth, have found a way around this limitation, leading to his escape and a potential threat to humanity."

"I get it now," says Kendra. "Do you have a limitation of your own, Thoth?"

Thoth knows Kendra is only trying to be helpful, but he can't tell this secret to anyone. Thoth can't risk Seth finding out about it. He refuses to answer, and Kendra can see the fear on his face. She doesn't question him any more about this.

To demonstrate a trick that might help them out in an emergency, he tells the teens to think about hiding their bracelets, and they do as Thoth tells them. The bracelets are transformed into tattoos of hieroglyphics, each with a different design, amazing everyone.

As the teens marvel at their bracelets, Thoth tells them that the bracelets will form a shield to surround each teen separately, or they can form a group barrier around the three in times of great need. Kendra inquires if they can protect friends as well, Thoth nods, adding that the individual or individuals must be within range of their bracelets to protect them from Seth. Everyone begins to relax, but Malcolm is still on edge, thinking about the evil creature looking for his children. Thoth suggests one last idea to them; he asks the teens to think about their bracelets. The tattoos turn magically back into the bracelets again.

Malcolm expresses his desire to leave without any more delay. Thoth's main goal is to leave the city with everybody, and Malcolm agrees with him. Malcolm tells them to grab some clothes since they won't be returning here for a while. Thoth takes back his mask and places it back on his face. To the delight of Malcolm, Thoth appears human again. Everyone goes upstairs to pack their things to leave before Seth finds them there. Malcolm is the first one to make it downstairs, noticing Thoth attempting to hide his fear and worry. But Malcolm doesn't need any powers to notice his anxiety, since he shares the same concern.

7

SETH'S PYRAMID

The teens finish packing their stuff, and they place each bag into the trunk of Malcolm's car. The kids feel excited, as if they were going on a trip. Malcolm thinks about the craziness of the situation, but he knows this is the only way to protect his kids. Thoth asks Malcolm if he can drive his car. Malcolm doesn't trust his car to just anyone, but this isn't a normal situation. Thoth starts the engine and drives toward the expressway.

Thoth asks Kendra, Roland, and Juan to sit in the backseat so he and Malcolm can talk privately about Seth. Malcolm's car has a backseat radio with headphones, so passengers can enjoy listening to music during long road trips in private. Both Kendra and Roland enjoy listening to music on their headphones, but Juan, who is beginning to feel guilty about his argument with Malcolm, stares silently outside of the window.

Roland takes off his headphone and taps Kendra on the shoulder. "Hey, Kendra."

"What is it, Roland?"

Roland places his hand over Kendra's mouth and speaks softly to her. "Please don't yell. I wish we could go to the pyramid and put an end to Seth ourselves."

"Yeah, it would be great to get back to a normal life again, but what are the chances of that?" inquires a skeptical Kendra.

Juan notices Kendra and Roland talking quietly to each other, and he wants to be a part of their discussion. Juan is about to loudly speak his mind when Roland places his finger in front of Juan's mouth. Roland explains to Juan in quiet tones about going after Seth. Roland remembers taking a boat tour of the Chicago River. A tour guide talked about the buildings along the river. He recalls a large sapphire-colored building shaped like a pyramid near the north bank of the Chicago River. The pyramid is one-third smaller than the size of the great pyramid in Giza and realizes this place is Seth's pyramid.

Kendra adds this pyramid was created as a think tank for highly educated individuals, a group referred to as THES, to help improve the lives of mankind. Kendra mentions that "THES" group took the initials words, Triumph, Happiness, Equality, and Success. The THES group promises positive change and great knowledge will come to mankind when humanity opens its mind to it. The teens realize this so-called think tank group is in reality followers of Seth, wanting to share in Seth's conquest of mankind.

"It would be very easy to find him there," says Kendra. "But I don't get any pleasure from being inside of a blue glass structure, trying not to die at the hand of Seth. However, I did a little checking on my iPhone and found something very interesting."

"Be careful, Juan," whispers Roland. "Kendra is going to show off her super brain again, so we need to stand back in order to avoid being blinded by her brilliance."

Kendra takes out her iPhone from her left pocket and uses the universal app that rearranges anagrams and translates different languages. But she reads her brother's feelings and knows they've already figured out that THES is an anagram for Seth. But she points out to them that there are words after THES: 'THES—THE BRINGERS OF KNOWLEDGE AND CHANGE.' They watch Kendra take out several letters of the sentence, spelling its true meaning. 'SETH—BRINGER OF DEATH AND CHAOS.' The brothers look at Kendra and a wave of panic takes hold of their hearts.

"This is why we have to stop Seth ourselves," says Juan.

"I have to agree with Juan," replies Roland.

"Listen—we can't confront Seth without Thoth's help," answers Kendra. "Don't make me regret my decision to show you that message."

Juan and Roland ask Kendra if she can use her ability to know the details of Malcolm and Thoth's conversation. After several minutes, Kendra can't get anything about their discussion, wondering if she is doing something wrong with her ability. But Kendra does get something about Thoth, hiding a tragic mistake from his past. Kendra can't seem to get any more details about this mistake. As Thoth senses Kendra's attempt to read his feeling for information, he uses his own powers, concealing his secrets and the conversation with Malcolm.

Juan tries to recreate the vision he had at the house with no success. Thoth offers some helpful tips from the front seat. He tells Juan to take slow steps to focus on this vision, but he reinforces his earlier warning about not trying too hard to see this vision.

Kendra begins to feel very uncomfortable in the car, and she bends down to her ankles. Malcolm wants to stop the car to check on Kendra, but Thoth decides to keep on driving the car. Thoth advises her to think only about the four of them inside of this car. Kendra does as Thoth tells her to do, and she begins to feel a lot better, so Thoth warns her to not attempt to use her ability on more than one person at a time.

"Thank you," replies Kendra. "I was sensing the feelings of other people in their own cars that it was bringing great discomfort to me."

"Kendra—I know of your attempt, seeking answers to a certain question by reading my feelings, but there are some things better left alone," says Thoth. "You haven't known me long enough to trust me, but it's in your best interests to get out of this city."

Kendra, Roland, and Juan decide not to seek any more answers about his secret feelings. They know in their hearts that Thoth wishes nothing more than to protect them from Seth. Juan whispers to Kendra and Roland about wanting to face this threat of Seth likes heroes, but

Roland and Kendra remind him not to compare this situation to one of his wild fantasies. Juan takes a long breath to get his thoughts together, and he decides to go along with his older siblings' request for now. Kendra puts on her earphones to listen to some tunes on her iPhone, but Roland puts his arm on Juan's shoulder and tells him that he's right in wanting to face Seth like a hero. But Roland tells him to play along with Kendra's request so they don't have to listen to her arguments. Juan quietly thanks Roland for believing in him, and he agrees to avoid anymore discussion with Kendra.

Thoth drives slowly for the O'Hare Airport. Cars are closely together like fish sardines in a can. Thoth waits for the teens to ignore them, and they become focus on playing with their iPhone. Thoth takes this opportunity to talk quietly with Malcolm.

As Thoth waits for the light to turn green, Juan looks at a stranger at a gas station. Juan gets a mild headache, so Roland leans over to check on him. Juan tells Roland to use his powers to turn on the water hose near the gas pump and aim it at a driver who is going to exit the car wash. Roland doesn't understand Juan's request, but he uses his ability to make the water hose release water in the direction of that car. The driver gets an unexpected shower, angering him. Roland sees gas leaking from another car. Roland finally sees the irate driver prepare to toss a partially lit cigarette, which will strike the gas on the ground near his car, sparking a fire. Roland rubs Juan's head, proud that he was able to foresee this event before it caused a major disaster. Juan wants to say something to Malcolm and Thoth, but Roland tells him not to say anything to them for the time being.

Juan concurs with Roland and offer congratulates him on controlling his ability as well. Roland and Juan laugh for their first time as real heroes, since real heroes don't always hang around to accept thanks for doing the right thing. Kendra stops listening to her iPhone and she asks about the laughter. Roland remarks about preventing a fire at gas station.

She shakes her head with disbelief and advices them to stop making up tales. "Why can't the two of you use your brains? A mind is a terrible thing to waste?"

THE OUSIAS

"We were not wasting our time, telling tales," replies Juan. "In fact, both Roland and I are heroes."

"No, Kendra is right," says Roland. "We were playing video games on my iPhone that we were rescuing people at a gas station. But Juan and I promise to work become as conceited—I mean as learned—as our dear sister."

Roland and Juan begin laughing again, and Kendra looks at them with one question in mind: "With all the knowledge in my head, how did I get struck with these two knuckleheads?"

Both Roland and Juan respond to her. "It was your destiny to have two such knuckleheads as your brothers, so don't be jealous over destiny's choice."

Kendra leans back in her seat and wishes that her best friends were here, since they respect her knowledge and intelligence. She turns her head away from them and listens to her iPhone to tune out her brothers. The car starts warming up, so Thoth turns the air-conditioner to its highest setting.

Roland sees Juan looking at him with questions. Roland tells him to turn off his future radar, since he's got nothing to say about it. But Juan refuses to stop inquiring, so Roland takes a deep breath to gather his thoughts. Roland says he was thinking about a friend at school, so Juan knows Roland is referring to his ex-girlfriend who broke up with him this summer. Juan slaps him lightly on his back and tells him that it's her loss. He smiles at Juan and agrees.

Roland reaches into his pocket to bring out his own iPhone for him and Juan to watch some videos that he had downloaded from his Amazon and iTunes accounts. Juan promises to himself to treat Malcolm with more respect, but he hopes to deal with it later. Thoth talks to Malcolm about his assignment to mentor another person and his failure to train her properly against Seth, leading to her death. Thoth relates to Malcolm that he doesn't want to make the same mistake again, so he made the choice to run this time. Thoth blames Osiris and the others for not assisting him in saving her life. Malcolm doesn't want to know the name of this person, but he sympathizes with Thoth. It only increases Malcolm's need to leave the city, though, and as he watches the traffic clearing toward O'Hare, he wants nothing more than to get his kids far away from Seth.

Kendra looks at her iPhone to check the end of afternoon news. The screen shows many tourists and visitors traveling to the THES building to enjoy the radiant blue light shining from the top of the pyramid. Mr. Nicholas O'Reed. Nicholas, the designer of the THES pyramid, stands in front, and he announces to the media about not building pyramid in other cities, to her surprise. Mr. O'Reed wanted pyramids in other cities around the world. But as Seth is no longer a prisoner of the Ousias, Seth orders him not to build more pyramids.

✳ ✳ ✳

Inside of the pyramid, Mr. Tek waits for the interview to end, so he can congratulate him on making a wise decision.

After Mr. O'Reed leaves the area, Tek goes to an empty office inside of the building, and changes out of his police uniform and into a traditional silk black-and-gray silk suit to better go with being a follower of Seth.

When Tek finishes putting on his suit, he travels down the hallway to a door made of gold. Tek opens the door and sees paintings of Seth fighting against Horus and Osiris, and there is also a white Persian rug on the floor. It contains four man-size gold-and-silver statues with the heads of crocodiles, and there are several bronze replicas of Seth's head hanging on the wall nearest the window.

Seth looks intently at the marble triangular-shaped table in the middle of the room and notices two small light-brown canopic jars, each about two inches long, on the table. One jar has the face of Seth on top of it, and the other jar has the face of Anubis. Tek walks into the room, and he enjoys the strong smells of myrrh, frankincense, and cinnamon. As Seth also embraces the different fragrances, he stops to sense something new that causes his mood to turn sour. Two followers of Seth walk in with Aster in their grip, and they place him in front of an enraged Seth.

"Aster, why did you go after Thoth and the chosen ones without my permission?" questions Seth.

"My lord, I thought that I could get to Thoth and those teens myself," replies Aster.

Seth becomes infuriated. "Your failure gave Thoth the opportunity to escape with those brats, but I'm not without mercy toward your efforts."

Seth looks at him like a lion observing his prey before eating it. Aster falls to his knees. "Please forgive me, my lord, but I'm a valuable source of information about this world. You will need to know more about this world, as it is your destiny to rule mankind."

Seth is disgusted by Aster begging for his life. "Yes, your knowledge will be a big help to me, so please accept your fate like a man."

Seth touches Aster's shoulder and bundles of white linens start to wrap over him completely. Aster starts to feel like a mummy being preserved for storage, but Seth has other plans for him. A small piece of the wrapping reaches out to touch Seth's forehead, and Aster begins to scream with great pain. This goes on for several moments until Aster falls to the floor, drained of energy. Seth loves to observe the fear upon his enemies' faces, and he equally loves hearing a certain sound that soothes his dark heart.

"There is nothing like knowledge to make the body feel good," laughs Seth. "Guards, take this person and dispose of it."

Several guards pick up Aster to carry him downstairs to the basement. They find a door leading to the basement, but the guards can't go into the basement without Seth's authorization to do so. They couldn't see anything, since it was dark as night. They open the door slightly and hear a loud hissing sound, as if there's a snake in the room. They toss Aster and close the door. Seth has done this with other persons who failed him. They can hear Aster crying for help, but soon Aster's whimpering comes to a silent stop. However, there is one other sound coming from the basement, and it isn't the voice of Aster. It is the sound of bones cracking in the darkness like walnuts cracking under the power of a nutcracker that Seth is able to hear from far away, bringing an evil, delightful grin to his face.

Tek approaches Seth with caution. "My lord, did Aster give you the necessary knowledge, or do you require more help?"

"No, my powers allow me to transmit knowledge from one person to another, and it worked well with Aster," responds Seth. "Aster is—or was—surprisingly full of information for an idiot. So did you find the location of the other missing pieces to my original pyramid?"

"Sadly, Thoth hid them very well in different locations, but I'm going to find them, along with the chosen ones' bracelets," says Tek.

Seth has a way to track down the pieces of his pyramid, and he reaches into his desk for a magical stone. But Seth doesn't sense any reaction from the stone and concludes Thoth is using some kind magic to block any attempt to find the pieces of his pyramid. Seth doesn't allow this minor setback to anger him, since he knows that Thoth doesn't have the power to deny Seth his destiny.

Seth expresses praise toward Tek for his self-assurance but cautions Tek against failing him. "There is little time left here, and I mustn't let Thoth and his weak chosen ones alter my plans," says Seth. "Besides, if I know Thoth, he will be trying to depart the city to avoid any possible harm to the chosen ones. This is Thoth's biggest weakness, and it will lead to his ultimate downfall."

"What can we do to stop them?" asks Tek. "What if they should leave the city before we can acquire the bracelets?"

"Don't be concerned, Tek. I'm always one step ahead of Thoth," says Seth.

Seth orders Tek to go near the window. He places his hand over the eyes of Tek, which allows him to observe an invisible blue light shining from the top of the pyramid. He sees another light coming from behind the ground, but this light is a dark-reddish color. Tek watches the two light merge together, and the result is a glowing purple effect. Without any warning, the purple light moves into the room, touching a closet door.

Seth can see the curiosity on Tek's face. "You must be wondering about the unique light show and why it lands on the closet door. This light will place a blanket over the city, and it will lead me to them. The light combines with my own powers, increasing its range to cover the entire city. This will prevent Thoth and his chosen ones from escaping us. It is an incredible drain on my powers, but it is only temporary. I want you to get the jar with my face on it from the desk and bring it here. I'm going to get those objects from Thoth and those foolish chosen ones."

A confused Tek does as Seth commanded, and he hands the canopic jar to him. Seth walks over to one of the statues and unscrews the top of the canopic jar like a jar of peanut butter. He pours the dust from the jar over two of the four statues in his room, and there is a slight noise from each statue. The statues begin to move on their own as they come to life, and Tek moves away in fear. But Seth pulls him back toward the statues, so he won't be afraid of them.

The two statues bow in front of Seth in order to honor him as their master, and Tek starts to calm down. Seth tells Tek to wait here for his return while he goes after Thoth and the teens. Seth takes a silver amulet from around his neck, leading the two statues toward a closet. Tek wonders why Seth wants to go into a closet, but he knows Seth must have a reason.

Seth touches the closet door slightly with the amulet, and the light encircles the amulet before it disappears. Soon after, a strong wind can be heard, blowing from within the closet. The wind carries Seth and the two statues through the door, to the surprise of Tek, and the door shuts on its own, leaving Tek curious. He opens the door, and finds nothing but an empty closet. Tek remembers an ancient legend about an amulet having the power to open a doorway into any place. He recalled a dark light that combined with an amulet, helping to guide one to another person's location. Tek follows Seth's orders to the letter, and he gathers the other guards to await Seth's return with the bracelets and his pyramid pieces.

8

NOWHERE TO RUN

Thoth reaches O'Hare Airport in great time and parks the car near the terminal. Everybody gets out of the car. Malcolm doesn't have enough money to help pay for the plane fare, and he wonders about Thoth being able to pay for the five of them. It is as if Thoth was reading Malcolm's mind, because he goes into his pocket and brings out hundreds of dollars in cash, shocking everyone. Thoth tells them that Osiris had given him the secret locations of his treasures and relics, where Osiris had ruled as pharaoh several millennia ago.

"How come archeologists, historians, or even tomb robbers didn't find Osiris's treasures before your return to earth?" asks Malcolm.

"Pharaohs possessed great, powerful magic back then, and they were able to hide their treasures well," says Thoth. "There are still several places of undiscovered treasures around the world to this day. But we will have to wait for another time to learn more about this, since we've got to leave this city."

"We are going to get out of this OK, so don't be concerned." Malcolm says to the teens.

"OK, Dad," says Kendra and Roland.

Juan can't accept running from a fight. "Why do we have to run from Seth, since we have these powerful bracelets to fight him with?"

"Seth is one of the most dangerous people in Egyptian history, and I don't want you to face such a threat," says Thoth. "But you have the power to protect yourself with the power of belief, so don't be afraid to use the bracelets to create a powerful shield for protection."

"Juan, we are out of our league in this one, so please just trust me for once," says Malcolm.

Juan can feel the honesty in his words, so he agrees to keep quiet.

Malcolm is the first one to open the door to the terminal, but they find themselves in the middle of Malcolm's living room at his house instead. Everyone else walks in to discover that this isn't the O'Hare Airport. Thoth orders them to leave the house, and they run outside very quickly like rabbits. Unfortunately, they are right back in their own living room, and they aren't alone in the house. A loud banging sound can be heard throughout the house, and they behold a shadowy figure coming out of the darkness.

"Who is it, Thoth?" asks Malcolm.

"Please allow me to introduce myself here. I've been waiting for all of you to return," says the sinister menacing figure. "I'm the future ruler of mankind, Seth, and you must be the chosen ones of the Ousias. Give me those bracelets, and no one will get hurt here. You have my word on the matter."

"No, don't pay any attention to him!" yells Thoth. "Seth doesn't have a sincere bone in his whole body when it comes to keeping his word."

Seth looks at Thoth with dark deadly piercing eyes, "It has been too long since we last saw each other in ancient Egypt. Did you really think to leave this city without seeing me again? My powers are still strong, and I'm not even a fully corporeal being yet."

Seth brags that he tapped into his magic, predicting their movement. He guessed their plan, boarding one of the planes at O'Hare to escape. But Seth had shown Thoth his amulet, which he had stolen from Osiris's throne room. He had used this power to create a barrier at the airport, forcing Thoth and his friends to return to Malcolm's house.

"I want the rest of my pyramid pieces, Thoth, so why don't you remove your hedge of protection over them," Seth demands. "You can't keep me from my destiny. Maybe the chosen ones can help you to change your mind."

Thoth becomes full of fear and concern for his friends. He yells out to them, "Use the power of your bracelets to make a force field around the four of you here so you can save yourselves from Seth."

Roland and the others don't want to leave Thoth unprotected with Seth in the room, but Thoth yells out to them again to follow his order. Kendra, Roland, and Juan concentrate together, and a strong yellow field forms around them and Malcolm. They watch as Seth walks toward them, and he touches the shield with his fist. But the shield absorbs the force to protect the teens, which makes Seth extremely angry to the core.

Seth tries to get the teens to lower their defense. "Please don't throw your lives away for this pitiful slave of the pharaohs. Thoth bows down to every pharaoh like a dog without a care for his own desires. I offer all of you a chance to give me those bracelets and walk away with your lives. If you don't give me what I want now, then I can't be responsible for the actions of my servants here."

Everyone looks around the room, but they can see no other person or thing in the house. Until, Seth starts to whistle loudly throughout the house, and then loud footsteps begin walking throughout the house. The sound got louder and louder, and everybody look to the kitchen with astonishment and fear. They behold two muscular man-like creatures with the faces of Nile crocodiles with the traditional narrow snout. The creatures move with swiftness toward them. Malcolm looks at the creatures and identifies them in an instant. He can't believe his eyes. These creatures are the dangerous sobeks, the legendary servants of Seth. He notices the sobeks each wear a black linen outfit with a gold belt around their waists.

Roland, Kendra, and Juan become afraid of the creatures, but Malcolm advises them to keep focusing on the shield for their protection. Kendra's concerns for Thoth grows too deep and last long enough for her to lose focus on the shield. The shield weakens in an area large enough for one of the sobeks to attack. The creature reaches inside his belt for a small rectangle glass vial. The sobek grabs hold of this vial in his right hand, and he throws it in the direction of Juan like a pitcher at a baseball game. It moves superfast at Juan, but Malcolm pushes Juan out of the way. It hits Malcolm in his chest, and it bursts into a deadly liquid around his body. The liquid penetrates his clothes to go inside of his body. Malcolm collapses to the ground in great pain and falls away from their shield.

The teens are too concerned for Malcolm to restore their shield. Thoth runs over to Malcolm and uses his own magic to protect him. The sobeks circle around them and Seth takes pleasure at their suffering. He offers one last chance to rescue their father and Thoth.

"No," says Thoth. "Please don't trust him. He won't hesitate to kill all of you."

Thoth is unable to help them, since he is weak from trying to aid Malcolm. The teens are scared beyond belief. They realize Seth is completely evil incarnate to the core. Seth gives them five minutes to obey him, and one of the sobek moves closer to Malcolm.

"What are we going to do now?" asks Juan. "Malcolm is hurt and Thoth doesn't have any strength to fight them. I haven't been so scared in my life since I was trapped in the hall of mirrors at the amusement park two years ago."

"We don't have a choice here, since we can't let Malcolm or Thoth get hurt by these monsters," says Roland. "There is no upside to this situation. We have to give in to Seth's demands."

Kendra thinks about her brothers' comments, and she for a brief second looks upward without anyone seeing her. Kendra motions for the boys to come near her, and she speaks softly about a chance to get out of this in one piece. Neither Roland nor Juan understands her reasoning, and she doesn't want to give away her plan to Seth. Kendra talks about Juan's earlier vision of being trapped in the hall of mirrors, just like four—Roland and Juan interrupt Kendra's thought, since they have finally figured out the connection. Kendra decides to keep Seth focused on her to distract him from Roland and Juan. She falls like a rock to her knees, begging for their lives.

THE OUSIAS

The sobeks and Seth center their attention on Kendra, so Roland takes this chance to use his power to remove the mirrors from their resting places. He slowly removes the mirrors on the ceiling and the wall next to the grandfather clock. Roland successfully moves the screws off mirrors in the air, gently places the screws on the couch. Roland begins to feel weak from using his power too long, and he is losing his focus as Thoth warn him about earlier. The mirrors almost fall to the ground, but his strength returns, and he regains control of the mirrors. Roland magically places two of the mirrors behind him, and Juan shifts his hand behind his back to receive them.

In no time, they had put the mirrors under their shirts to hide them, and Seth hasn't even noticed a thing. Seth is busy enjoying observing Kendra begging him to have mercy on them and taking pleasure in the distressed look on Thoth's face. Seth laughs at Thoth, reminding him about his failure as a mentor. Kendra senses the pain coming from Thoth, so she goes over toward Roland, who gives her one of their mirrors to hide under her shirt. Seth orders the sobeks to move near Malcolm, while he offers to heal their father if they give him the bracelets now. The teens stand next to one another, following Seth's command to the letter, but he shows signs of impatience with their delay. Kendra wants to know that Seth will keep his word about Malcolm, but Seth doesn't offer any guarantees.

"I don't owe any of you anything, but I do promise vast pain and death to Thoth and Malcolm for not obeying my orders," says Seth. "Why don't I give you a demonstration?"

Kendra senses that Seth is preparing to inflict bodily harm on Malcolm. "Wait! You win, Seth, we shall hand over our bracelets. There is no more use in delaying it. Please take my bracelet."

"You can't do it," whispers a weakened Thoth.

Kendra murmurs to both Roland and Juan, and Seth tells them about their time is up. They walk toward Seth with their hands behind their backs. Seth is thinking about the three bracelets and how close he is to gaining control of this world. Seth smiles with evil glee as the teens walk toward him from three directions, but Thoth's face is full of despair as he watches helplessly. Malcolm turns his head down to the ground and fears for their safety. Seth reaches out with his hands to receive the bracelets, but the teens surprise him. They bring out three five-inch-square mirrors. Seth becomes very angry that the teens dare to hold mirrors at him. He starts to develop strong pain throughout his body. Seth observes his reflection in the mirrors, and he realizes too late about the cause of his sudden illness. The sobeks are unable to move as well, since their existence is bound to Seth. The sobeks disappear from sight. Seth moves his body back and forth to regain his balance but falls to the ground instead. Seth tries to reach the teens, but the pain is too great for him to withstand for any longer. He uses his hands to cover his face.

"No!" cried Seth. "You cursed fools. How did you discover my weakness? It is a guarded secret! I didn't even know what it was myself. Your bracelets gave you the powers to foresee it, but this won't stop me from destroying all of you."

Thoth orders the teens to keep those mirrors aimed at him. Seth tries to recuperate his powers, but his face begins to pull away from him in different directions, causing inescapable distress.

Seth can't win this battle, but he offers a final message of despair to them. "Curses it be on the three of you. Your deaths were going to be quick and painless. But I promise nothing now except the fiery, long-suffering deaths of everyone here, and your father shall live long enough to witness this before his own death at my hand. Even the vultures won't pick at your flesh and bones, until my heated fury over your pathetic bodies cools off enough to consume them."

With those last words, Seth transforms himself into a pile of dark-blue sand. He smashes through the window with the force of a powerful storm, and the dark sand appears as a cloud leaving the house. Everyone looks outside as the huge blue cloud travels farther away from the house, and the neighbors who see this weird phenomenon leave the neighborhood.

9

THE AFTERMATH

The alarming blue cloud leaves the area, and the force of the cloud shakes each nearby house. Many of the neighbors look out of their windows and open their doors to investigate. None of the neighbors saw anything out of the ordinary, except for one elderly silver-haired man, Mr. Ted Hardgrove, who leads the neighborhood watch. He is always keeping an eagle eye out for anything usual or criminal on his block. Hardgrove sees the weird sand cloud moving out of Malcolm's house, so he calls the fire department for help.

Back at Malcolm's house, Malcolm is sweating and finding it hard to breathe from the poison. Roland, Kendra, and Juan want to help him, but Thoth tells them to stay away. Thoth touches Malcolm's left shoulder lightly with both hands, and it brings a sense of comfort to him. But Thoth knows this will only last for only a little while, so he tells Kendra to call 911 for an ambulance. Kendra talks to a dispatcher about her adoptive father's condition.

"The dispatcher told me that they will be here in short order," says Kendra.

THE AFTERMATH

"What are we going to tell them about what happened here? No one is going to believe an ancient Egyptian lord attacked Malcolm with magic liquid."

"Where did Seth get this magic poison in the first place? Is there a cure for Malcolm?" asks Roland.

Juan walks toward Malcolm with guilt on his face. "Why did you push me out of the way? Seth was trying to hurt me."

Thoth's magic is helping Malcolm to feel better, but Thoth is losing his own strength in the process. Kendra tells him of the paramedics are on their way, but Thoth doesn't hear her talking to him. He goes into his pocket and pulls out several pieces of wrinkled light brown paper. Thoth tries to read one of the pages but he is too weak to say anything.

"Please read this..."

Kendra takes the page from Thoth and observes Egyptian hieroglyphics on it. Kendra reads the message. It talks about allowing the one to agree with the one in pain that they may give strength and relief to each other. Kendra was reading the message about protection when a tattoo showing a falcon-faced representation of Horus appears on the chests of both Thoth and Malcolm. Thoth stands to his feet and informs them about this tattoo preserving their lives against the poison. The symbol of Horus is able to prevent Seth and his followers from harming them for a period of time.

Fearing his strength failing with every second, Thoth goes into his pocket for his wallet. He brings out a huge load of cash. Malcolm understands Thoth's intention for giving this money to his teens, and he orders them to take it and leave the neighborhood.

"I want you to get out of here, before Seth regains his strength," says Thoth. "Wait a minute," Kendra cries. "I read something else on this page. It says this agreement will last only a short time. It makes reference to the Ousia performing this action and how it can lead to his or her death."

"No, we can't allow anything to happen to you or Malcolm," says Roland.

"Yes, there's got to be another way," agrees Juan.

THE OUSIAS

"I'll make this clear to all of you here, since the needs of the many are more important just me," replied Thoth. "The goal is to thwart Seth from opening up the underworld and becoming ruler of this world. Please forget about me and get out of this area. Seth may be able to keep you from leaving the city, but he can't stop you from hiding in the city. There are enough places here to go for safety where Seth won't be able to locate you."

"Thoth is right. We can't let Seth win here," says Malcolm. "I've done enough research about Egyptian mythology, or what is now fact. Seth was, or is, the most dangerous person in the history of ancient Egypt. You must follow Thoth's suggestion to leave."

"How are we going to explain this to the police? No one is going to believe this, Dad," asks Kendra.

"You can tell them that I found an ancient potion in my travels," said Malcolm. "Thoth and I were crazy enough to open it together, and we both got sick from it. Once you have answered the police's questions, then I want you to leave this area for your own good."

Malcolm borrows a piece of paper from Thoth and writes a note for the police. He explains how they accidentally spill some substance from a bottle on themselves, and it had made them very sick. Once Malcolm has given Kendra the note, Thoth glows brightly like a light bulb. For several minutes, the light radiates the entire house, like a beckon from a lighthouse, which temporary blinds the teens. The bright light fades away from Thoth, and the teens find a comatose Malcolm and Thoth. The protection tattoo of Horus disappears from their chests, which only increases the teens' fears for them.

Soon after, someone knocks on the door, and two paramedics dressed in write come in to check on the two people on the floor. The loud noise of a police siren rings throughout the neighborhood. Roland opens the door and sees the officers parking their car in front of Malcolm's house. Kendra gives the note to the paramedics that Malcolm wrote for the police. The paramedics examine the two people and insist on taking them to the hospital for further testing.

Another police car is heard approaching the house, and two officers head for the house. The teens talk to the officers about the possible

85

THE AFTERMATH

poisoning of the two men, but they say they don't know on what type of poison it is? The paramedics hand over the note to the officers, and Officer Tek takes the note. Officer Ray wants to get a look at the note, but Officer Tek refuses to give it over to him. Tek turns his attention to the paramedics, who are placing each man on a stretcher. A third paramedic comes out of his ambulance. He wants to check on the teens, but Officer Tek whispers that he should remain behind. Office Tek offers the paramedic a ride to the hospital in one of the squad cars.

As Malcolm and Thoth are place in their ambulance, the neighbors watch with trepidation. Kendra, Roland, and Juan look on with concern. The other two paramedics agree, letting their partner stay with Officer Tek. The ambulance speeds off toward Metro Hospital a nearby neighborhood hospital is about two or three blocks from their house. Officer Ray knows these teens because they go to the same school as his daughter, so he goes over to offer his support to them. Ray wants nothing more than to know the truth behind the poisoning, and he gives them a little time to gather their thoughts to explain this mystery poisoning.

Officer Tek corners the last paramedic inside the living room, while everyone watches the ambulance drives off to the hospital. Office Tek discusses their problem regarding the teens. Both men ponder their next move, which doesn't satisfy either the paramedic or Tek.

"I was at the station when I heard the call about the predicament at the Witmore's house," says Tek. "I was looking forward to hearing the news that Seth took possession of the bracelets."

"What are we going to do here?" asks the paramedic. "Seth wasn't supposed to lose to a bunch of children. If he is as powerful as the ancient Egyptian legends claim about him, then maybe the legends are a complete fabrication."

"How dare you speak such lies about our lord?" asks Tek. "If we were alone here, then I would show you the error of your statement. We have no other choice but to acquired those bracelets ourselves."

"How are you going to do this, considering there is no crime here but a simple accident?" questions the paramedic.

THE OUSIAS

Officer Tek thinks about this. "Yes, but what constitutes an accident or intent? It is just a simple matter of how the facts are interpreted. I have a plan."

Officer Ray comes into the room, looking for a progress report. Officer Tek walks outside, asking another officer to drive the paramedic to the hospital. Officer Ray wants to take the teens to the hospital, but Officer Tek knows his main goals—acquiring those bracelets from the teens. Tek can't allow his partner, whom he has to keep in the dark, to ask too many questions.

"You told the dispatcher about your teacher and Malcolm being sick," says Ray.

"Please tell us in your own words about this poison. Where did your adoptive father find such a bottle?"

"Our father went to Egypt and found it a pyramid," answers Kendra. "Malcolm and Thoth were curious about it, since the substance within the bottle was as clear as water. They both open it and breath into it. They began to feel sick. So I call 911 for help, and the rest is history."

Officer Tek tries to appear doubtful of their story. "It a very tragic situation, and I'm going to need some more information about it. Why don't we continue this discussion at our police station?"

Ray wishes to take them to the hospital, but he follows his partner's lead. Officer Tek promises to take them to the hospital when this horrible situation is cleared up. Everyone gets into the backseat of the police car, but Ray finds it difficult to accept this as anything more than a just simple accident.

As they leave the house, many neighbors watch the teens get into the police car. Mr. Hardgrove, Malcolm's best friend, wants to go with the teens, but the officers say no and they drive off. Kendra and Juan can't hide their fear, but Roland whispers to the others to remain calm. Juan rubs his hands very hard, almost ripping the skin off. Roland pulls his hands apart to stop this nervous gesture, and he reminds Juan that Eyeshadow's father, Ray, gives people the benefit of the doubt before jumping to the wrong conclusion. Juan promises to settle down, so he sits back in the backseat to hope for the best.

10

THE WITMORES ESCAPE

At the Windy City police station near the teen's home, the teens make their way into the tan five-story building. None of them could escape their concern for the well-being of Malcolm and Thoth, but they had to focus on answering questions now. As they enter the building, Officer Tek leads them to a dank, isolated interrogation room. Kendra feels sick to her stomach. Tek offers to get her some water or something, but she doesn't want anything to drink. Tek leaves the teens in the room to wait for him to return while he goes to check on the report about the illness.

Roland waits for Tek to leave and moves quickly to Kendra. "Are you OK?"

"Yes, but we are all in terrible danger here, so we need to escape at once."

"Why are we in danger? We're at a safe place," says Juan.

"Juan has a point. Why are you so nervous about being here?" asks Roland.

"I got a bad feeling from Officer Tek, and it's only happened once before, guys," says Kendra. "It felt similar to the feeling at school when we had returned to Thoth's classroom, wearing our bracelets. I thought it was a stomachache, but my gift reacts to Aster. I couldn't seem for some mysterious reason to get any detail from Tek."

As they wait quietly, Kendra tries with all her strength to read the feeling of her brothers. She suddenly finds herself nearly falling to the ground. Kendra realizes her inability is due to lack of energy after trying to protect Malcolm. She relates this to her siblings, which brings only loathing from them. Juan remarks that he sees small drops of water coming down from the ceiling.

"This is normal. This station was built twenty-five years ago," answers Kendra. "In fact, it is scheduled for remodeling at the end of the year."

"It is really a shame that this doesn't help us or Malcolm," says Roland.

"I wish I could do more to protect Malcolm and Thoth, than simply just sense trouble around us," says Juan. "There must be a way to increase our powers but Thoth's guidance."

"I don't know the answer, but maybe things will improve over time for us," answers Kendra. "We just have to learn how to better use these bracelets to enhance our abilities, so we're ready when the time comes to stop Seth."

"I think you're right about these bracelets, Kendra. I remember focusing on those mirrors at the house," says Roland. "My bracelet glowed at the thought of those mirrors, and they helped us to stop Seth. And Juan had a vision about a person in the middle of four walls, and it was right on the money."

"If I can have these visions about future events, then why didn't a vision warn us about this Tek person?" says Juan.

"I don't know what Tek is up to, but we can't wait to find out," answers Kendra. "Maybe we can just sneak out of here before anyone notices our absence."

The teens move slowly to the door and open it carefully. But Tek is standing in front of the door with a malevolent look in his eyes, and the teens become scared as they move back into the room.

Officer Tek folds his shoulder in front of him and closes the door behind him, "Well, well. You three aren't very good guest for trying to leave without saying good-bye, so I can do away with the niceties. Seth wants those bracelets of yours, so why don't give them to me?"

"You can't take our bracelets unless we give them of our freewill," says Roland.

Tek doesn't show any concern as two detectives stroll into the room. Both men are dressed in a two button piece gray suit and they inquire to the cause of Malcolm and Thoth sudden illness. The detectives say that Juan's fingerprints was found on two pieces of glass with an indefinite substance, which matches the substance discovered in the bodies of both Malcolm and Thoth. The teens deny trying to hurt Malcolm or Thoth. But the detectives had discovered several reports from Juan's orphanage, which showed Juan's disregard toward his foster family and Juan's wish for someone else to adopt him. Officer Tek had discovered several incidences of neighbors complaining about hearing argument between Malcolm and Juan.

The detectives claim either Juan acted alone or with the other two siblings' assistance. The detectives offer Kendra and Roland a chance to avoid charges against them as well, if both siblings would admit the truth about their brother. Kendra refuses to answer any other questions without a lawyer. Officer Tek insists on the detectives to leave alone with them so he can get the teens to admit their crime. Neither detective enjoys Tek trying to take over their case, but he is very respected by their supervisor. They walk outside, leaving Tek with the teens.

"Your case is so deep against you that even a lawyer couldn't prove your innocence," says Tek.

"You must have planted Juan's fingerprints on those pieces of glass, because I know his prints wasn't on any of it," says Kendra. "It won't work, Tek, since the paramedic receive our note with Malcolm's writing, clearing us of any wrongdoing."

Tek presents the letter from Malcolm and tears it to pieces in front of them. Tek informs them that the paramedic is a follower of Seth as well. Officer Ray walks in to see the distress on the teen's faces, and Roland wants to use his powers against Tek. But Kendra pulls his arm in the other direction and reminds him not to use his powers against the innocent. Roland argues that Tek is anything but innocent. Juan tells Ray to check the pockets of Tek for a letter written by Malcolm. Tek tells Ray not to believe three criminals over his partner. Ray wants to believe the teens but can't go against Tek. Tek tells Ray to get ready to charge these teens as criminals who tried to injury their adoptive father and teacher.

Ray leaves Tek, and two more officers enter the room. "Can you two officers stand on the other side of the room so I can talk to them?"

The other officers are confused with Tek's request but they realize Tek possess great influence with the bosses at this station. They don't argue with him, and he asks them not to listen or face reprimand from station's supervisor. Roland again approaches Tek with frustration, bur Kendra and Juan grab hold of him.

Tek speaks softly to the teens. "You were wise to stop Roland—since your bracelets would lose their powers—from using them against my innocent fellow officers. Seth told me all about your bracelet's strengths and limitations and about the bracelets drain on your bodies when you continue to use their powers. Seth is still recovering from his injuries at your hands, so my temper is at the three of you. But my master needs your bracelets to rule Earth. This is your last chance to survive this in one piece, so please don't be foolish here."

"You can't force us to give up our bracelets," says Kendra.

"Besides, we can transform our bracelets into simple tattoos," says Roland.

Roland, Kendra, and Juan try for several minutes with no success. Tek informs the teens that is takes more energy to transform those bracelets. The teens are not strong enough to transform the bracelets but Kendra remains determined not to surrender.

Tek agrees with her, but he reminds them about the charges against the teens. "I can't take your bracelets. There is another way for Seth to claim your bracelets."

THE OUSIAS

Kendra begins to develop chills over her body, a sign that her ability is regaining their strength. Kendra tells Juan and Roland to change her bracelet into a tattoo but nothing happen. Their powers is still not enough to change the bracelets. But Kendra is able to read the feeling within Tek, increasing her chills.

"We have a problem here," says Kendra. "The other officer are going to take our pictures, fingerprints, and our possessions, including our bracelets."

"Your officers won't take my bracelet without a fight," says Roland.

Kendra stops Roland and warns him that these officers aren't followers of Seth. She reminds Roland that they can't use their powers against innocents, like the officers, isn't very wise. Kendra knows that they would lose their powers as a result. Tek smiles at the teens, since he knows they're back into a corner.

"There is only one choice, my friends," whispers Tek. "You must give the officers your bracelets and await your court date for trial. There is no shame, spending the next few days in jail. The whole world is going to belong to Seth as he rules the Earth as Pharaoh. I'm going to leave these officers with you, since my supervisor wants to credit me with your arrest."

Kendra is worried about her Malcolm. "Please tell us how they are doing at the hospital."

Tek refuses to answer her question and orders the officers to watch over them. As he strolls out of the room, he tells them that the teens are dangerous criminals who shouldn't be underestimated in the least. He walks out of room smiling at the teens, and the two officers are confused by his action. The other officers don't view these teens as dangerous criminals. However, the officers follow their duty to watch over the teens, and they sit quietly in chairs near the desk. Kendra asks for Roland and Juan to bend their heads so she can whisper to them.

"We have to get leave before those officers can return to arrest us."

"How are we going to leave without hurting these innocent people?" asks Juan.

"It's amazing that we have all these different abilities but we can't use to any without breaking the rules," says an irritated and scared Roland.

"I hate these crazy rules in the first place. I wish that we could get them to move out of the way on their own," says Juan.

Both Kendra and Roland look at each other, and Juan's words offer an idea of escape. They survey the whole room before they begin to talk to each other. The other officers tell them to stop whispering. Roland struggles to concentrate for fifteen minutes, and the officers become concerned as Roland moves his head to the left and right without stopping. Soon after, other officers come in to arrest the teens and ask why Roland is scratching his head. The officers approach Roland; however, a loud noise can be heard in the station. The officers decides to investigate this sound and leave the teens alone. They open the door and see another officer completely drenched. As the officer closes the door behind him, the supervisor remarks the station is being flooded with water, which already appears several inches high. Tek remains outside since he fears the teens, using their bracelets against him.

"We must get those bracelets off the teens at once," screams a frantic Tek.

The supervisor doesn't understand Tek's request but doesn't have time to think it over. A loud pounding sound goes throughout the station from seemingly everywhere. A powerful wave of water smashes into the interrogation room from the window. Roland successfully controls the water pressure for the time being, and many of the officers work to evacuate the station. The other officers figure that the flooded office was caused due to the damaged water pipes underground. The supervisor was told this problem might happen months from now, which is why they were going to shut down the station to remodel. Tek and the other officers try to get back into the room to get to the teens, but the incredible force of the water prevents them from entering.

"You did it, Roland!" shouts Kendra.

"Yes, but it was your idea," replies Roland.

"But I recalled Juan's vision, seeing a room flooded with water," says Kendra. "It gave me the idea."

"Wait a minute," says Juan. "I had the vision of the flooded room. And I came up the idea to avoid, using our bracelets against the officers. Why is no one thanking me for such a great idea?"

"Fine, we are grateful for your excellent idea and your crazy visions," says Kendra. "Now, can we get out of this room before Roland loses his control of the water? Unless you want to go to jail."

"How are we going to get out of here, since the front door is blocked with water?" asks Juan.

Exhausted, Roland tells Kendra, "Please figure something out now, before my head explodes from controlling this water. Plus, the water is beginning to fill the room, so what is your plan?"

Kendra looks around the room and turns her attention to the wall where the water is flowing into the room. She tells Roland to control the water, since Kendra hopes to leave before Tek and the other officers find a way into the room. Eventually, Roland gets his own idea and makes the water tear apart the window. With Kendra and Juan speechless, Roland is able to change the water into a watery stairway that leads to the street below.

"Kendra and Juan, please take the stairs to the ground at once, since I can't hold this for much longer," orders Roland.

"Walk down stairs made of water? But I guess we don't have any other choice here," says an unsure Kendra.

"Oh," says Juan. "I never thought I'd walk on stairway made of water, but I'm not going to complain about it."

Kendra and Juan walk down the watery stairs, and Roland follows them to escape the area. The water continues to flow in and out of the station like a flood, but the water slowly trickles to a stop. Tek opens the door to the interrogation but there are no teens inside. He immediately tells his supervisor.

The police supervisor and Tek look outside to see wet footprints on the ground leading from the station, so the supervisor orders his officers to search for the missing teens. Tek approaches the nearest hallway, and he uses his hand to hit both the left and right sides of his head in frustration. But he vows to get those teens for Seth. Tek goes into an empty office where Ray finds him. He is now questioning his belief in their innocence after all. Tek pretends to share in his partner's disappointment, since this escape now leaves no doubt about their guilt. But Tek laughs within himself at Ray, and he hopes his partner never discovers the truth. Ray leaves the hallway to look for clues to find the teens, but he suddenly reflects on his daughter. Ray thinks about his daughter, who is probably concerned for her friend, Kendra, and he wonders about Eyeshadow's willingness to help her in spite of the evidence against the teens. Ray runs out of the station and heads for his car to return home.

Tek thinks to himself about the teens, and how they are probably very weak from using their powers to escape. Tek brings out a two-inch glass bottle. He opens the bottle to release a swarm of deadly black scarab beetles. They move around Tek like they are circling a meal. But Seth has given him the power to control the beetles, so they stop in front of him like ants following the command of their queen. He doesn't care about trying to take the teens alive anymore, since they dared not only to wound Seth but to make him look bad with their getaway.

Tek prepares to release the scarabs. "Don't stop searching for those teens, and consume anyone who tries to protect them," he says. "If they try to run away, I want you to treat them like the food on your table. We can gather the bracelets from their bony arms, and Seth won't lose any sleep over their remains."

He unlocks the window, and the beetles fly out in search of their next meal. Their wings sound like tiny buzz saws growing louder, reflecting their overwhelming desire for food. The beetles are ravenous meat eaters who want nothing more than to consume anything in their path. Tek hears his supervisor calling for him to return. He hopes that the teens suffer a painful end at the hands of those beetles.

11

THE EYES ARE UPON THEM

As the teens leave, they hear a loud special alert on the afternoon news as they pass a popular, eighties-themed tavern, the Hot Spot. The teens get overly curious about the story, so they move closer to the window of the tavern to hear.

The anchor says, "The police have issued an alert for the arrest of three offenders. Kendra, Roland, and Juan Witmore in the poisoning of their adoptive father, Malcolm Witmore and their teacher, Mr. Thoth Hermes. These criminals must be considered extremely dangerous, so don't attempt to a citizen's arrest on your own. Please call the police with any information for the capture of these criminals. An anonymous friend of Malcolm's is offering a reward of $3 million for any information that it lead to their capture."

The report finishes with saying that $1 million will be paid for each of the teens. This is going to lead to the ultimate hunt for them. A great dread grows upon Roland and Kendra, but Juan doesn't seem to have any reaction to it. In fact, he looks like an inanimate object with no emotions. Roland notices Juan's emotional state at the window, and he waits for Juan to snap out of it. But Roland doesn't get a chance to wait, because they soon hear an ear-shattering scream. They turn to see many people on the street, and one of the them has spotted the teens and is yelling out their location to the crowd.

Soon after, the crazy fortune-seeking crowd comes within range of the teens, each one of them savoring the idea of becoming an instant millionaire. Roland wants to use his ability to block the people from reaching them, but he's too weak from using his powers to escape police custody. The teens begin running away from the tavern, but several more people start to chase after them. They run into an alley to shake off their pursuers, hiding behind a large blue Dumpster. The crowd has stopped to look around when they hear someone else talking about finding the teens. Everyone runs over to see for themselves, and the teens wait for the crowd to leave.

"Great—we're now more wanted than any other criminal in the country, so where do we go from here?" questions Kendra.

"Hey, we did beat Seth, so there's got to be a way out of this for us," says Juan.

"Everybody sees us as a winning lottery ticket. I don't have any other way out with the whole world searching for us," says Roland.

Kendra is the first one to complain about the odor of garbage. A flock of seagulls rummages around the garbage bins in their endless search for food. Roland and Juan see even more seagulls, sitting on top of telephone wires. Juan and Roland ask Kendra why the seagulls remain so still on the wires. Kendra, who tries unsuccessfully to ignore her brothers, looks to the flock of seagulls. She prepares to tell her siblings when Kendra remembers her need to use her iPhone. Kendra takes out her iPhone and prepares to dial out. But Roland snatches the iPhone out of Kendra's hand, preventing her from dialing out. She informs them not to worry, since Kendra could scramble a cell phone signal. Rose was one of the leading cell phone engineers, and she shared her knowledge with Kendra.

Juan peeks around the garbage bin and observes more people moving back and forth in search of the teens. Roland wants to know on why she would need to scramble a phone signal in the first place. Kendra would only say it was a secret just for the ladies. Roland and

Juan sarcastically speak out about developing their own secret code language for guys only. Kendra stops readjusting her phone to stare at her brothers for a second, before she gives them a smirk. Kendra thinks, "As if either one of them could create a secret code message on their own."

As Roland and Juan observe Kendra, they see her sending a text messages similar to Morse code. But the message is a combination of dashes and dots that are mixed together with letters and numbers. Kendra had designed this special code as a way to talk privately with her closest friends. Roland is insisting to know the meaning of her message, and Kendra translates the message as follows: "We are completely innocent of these false charges against us, and I'm going to need a big favor for tomorrow."

Juan wonders why Kendra would need a secret code. "Do you believe that Kendra created this code for simple chitchat?"

"No, I don't believe that Kendra had been using this code for private chitchat," says Roland. "Kendra can't keep the truth hidden forever—I intent to find out the real story."

"I have found a special place for us to hide, but I saw our picture with us, wearing these clothes," says Kendra. "The police delivered the video from the station to the media, and everyone is looking for us. I don't know how to get us there without being discovered."

As they ponder their next move, Roland sees an opportunity to conceal their reappearance. He points at a sidewalk sale of clothing and other items two blocks down. One at a time, they slowly move out of the alley and travel toward to the sidewalk sale. Kendra takes the lead in getting the items since she is a pro at quick shopping. She picks up three sets of blue jeans, black sunglasses, and red, white, and gray shirts, which the cashier places into the bag. Kendra notices a restaurant near the sidewalk, and they find men's and ladies' restrooms. Roland and Juan sneak into the men's, while Kendra walks causally into the ladies' restroom. They hastily change out of their old clothing and into the new clothing.

After several moments, they come out in their new disguises, Kendra speaks to Juan. "OK, we've got to act normal, and I mean you, Juan."

"I can act normal, so don't treat me like some child," replies Juan.

Kendra gets an idea and rips the left side of her jeans. Roland and Juan figure out her plan and begin tearing at the right side of their jeans. They put on their sunglasses to hide their faces and finally regain enough strength to transform their bracelets into hieroglyphic tattoos. Kendra tells them about this special place that they can go hide for the evening, but she says they have to wait awhile before they go to this place.

Over the next few hours, they travel on several trains and buses to stay away from people, journeying through many neighborhoods in every direction. They sit in different seats to keep from being seen together, but this doesn't stop people from recognizing them. People begin to look at the other passengers on the train and some passengers start grabbing at each other for the money. Fighting and arguing commuters desiring to become instant millionaires soon cause riots and injuries aboard the train.

The teens speedily walk from one train to another. They eventually left the trains and buses to walk silently to places like Millennium Park, the House of Blues, the Shed Aquarium, the Alder Planetarium, and the Field Museum, where people are enjoying too much to notice anything else for a while. That is, until people hear word of possible sighting of the fugitives, which makes some people turn their focus away from the experiences to search for these teens.

But after running around the city for the last few hours, the teens wish for a place to rest. However, it isn't easy. Not only the people of Chicago, but tourists and visitors have gotten wind of the reward money as well. Just like any resident of the city, Roland, Juan, and Kendra can easily spot tourists, and they recognize several such people walking the street. This increases their level of stress to the breaking point. Roland and Juan, both frantically sweating like a pair of joggers on a humid day, worry about people viewing them as the winning lottery ticket.

"I can't stop this stressful feeling of us being behind bars or worse," says Juan.

Kendra concurs with their concerns over the wild manhunt for them, but she knows this won't prevent more and more people traveling to Chicago from different parts of the United States to find them. It reminds her of people going to California during the eighteen hundreds to find gold.

Meanwhile, the police department tries to get people to stop this crazy hunt for the teens, since it is causing people to treat every young teen as a suspect or as a million-dollar check. In fact, people begin flooding into Chicago from other nearby places to seek their fortune, and the teens watches people crowding in cafes, restaurants, or other Internet-friendly places to use their laptops, iPhones, iPads, and Blackberries to go online to Twitter and Facebook to find out more information about them.

Meanwhile, Roland wonders nervously on about their next move. As the sun sets to signal the evening, Roland and Juan yearn to know why Kendra doesn't want them to go to her special place yet. They choose to follow her suggestion, though, and the moving helps to keep their mind off Malcolm and Thoth. However, Kendra can see the unease in their eyes over the fate of Malcolm and Thoth, and she shares their concerns.

Kendra hopes to calm their nerves, so she bring up memories of the North Avenue Beach to relax them. Roland and Juan listen to her to a point, since they love going to the beach next to the skateboarding area at the park. It helps to relax them a little to hear about these places, but they can't wait to get some rest. She looks relaxed with no worry, until the sound of a click and a clack on the iPhone brings a smile to her face. Kendra insists that they ride the bus. Juan doesn't want to argue with Kendra, so he trusts her judgment. But Roland is little more caution and he wants Kendra to explain her happy attitude. She tries to avoid his question, when some people on the bus take notice of them. They get off the bus at the next bus stop, but Roland notices them getting off the same stop as well to get their attention. Kendra, Juan, and Roland start running away and the people begin chasing them, but Juan stops running when a strong headache starts banging like a drum in his head.

"Are you OK? Those people aren't far behind us," says Roland.

"Yes, what is wrong with you? They're going to catch us soon," adds Kendra.

Juan holds his right hand in the air with horror. "No, those people aren't the problem—those flying creatures are the real danger."

Roland and Kendra look upward, and they witness a small, dark swarm of flying beetles approaching them. Juan insists on leaving with posthaste, but Roland doesn't understand why they should run from some simple bugs. Kendra asks Roland to borrow his iPhone, so she can zoom in and get a closer look at the cloud of insects flying toward them. Kendra watches the insects for herself, and she can't believe her eyes. She looks at their dark-brown, circular bodies topped with yellowish spots, and notices two sets of eyes separated by two antennae.

"They look like beetles, but there is something wrong about them," says a stunned Kendra. "Since beetles don't have four eyes, and they don't go attacking human beings."

Roland scratches his head. "Seth must have used his magic to turn these peaceful creatures into deadly flesh eaters." She doesn't want to believe him, until Kendra sees someone drop his bag from the meat market. The beetles surround the food and go through the plastic to devour every bit of the meat like sharks. Kendra is a believer now and starts running along with the others for safety. But the crowd chases them as well. The teens discover other people seeing this pursuit and joining the hunt. Roland, Kendra, and Juan run for several blocks, but they turn the corner to become trapped with people on all sides. No one notices the beetles until they hear the buzzing sound. It sounds like bees confronting a threat—or lunch, in this case.

As the sun is about to set, the beetles begin to surround the people, and everyone runs for safety. Kendra gets an idea, and she asks Roland if he is able to open a nearby fire hydrant on the people. Roland has regained his abilities and opens it just in time. The beetles begin to bite the people, causing them severe pain, but a sudden flood of water washes the bugs off the people. Everyone goes for cover, but the beetles redeploy their attention on the teens. The beetles fly with great speed to get their revenge, Kendra and Roland fear for their flesh becoming a tasty meal. Roland wants to use his powers to move those beetles away, but Kendra worries Roland will use too much energy.

"We can form a shield around us," says Juan.

"It won't work for long, since the shield will make us extremely weak," answers Kendra.

"You have to think of something fast before the beetles leave nothing but bones," replies Roland.

The teens run like the wind as the beetles come upon them. Kendra observes the approaching sunset and tells her brothers to follow her. She leads her siblings across the street, with the beetles flying in hot pursuit. Roland recognizes Kendra is leading them back to the alley where they hid from people trying to turn them into the police for the reward.

"Have you gone crazy, Kendra?" asks Roland.

"There isn't any time to argue," replies Kendra.

Kendra notices the Dumpster is covered with more sea gulls than earlier, looking around and within the Dumpster for food. Roland can't wait for the beetles to attack and seeks to use his powers. Kendra tells Juan to help her open the Dumpster, and she relates to Roland to tosses the contain of it into the air at her signal. Roland doesn't understand his sister's plan but agrees to follow her orders. The beetles circle them for a millisecond and make a loud buzzing sound comes from the beetles. It is a signal that a potential feast is at hand.

As the beetles swarm the teens, Kendra announces to Roland. "Now! You must throw every bit of food into the air."

Roland magically tosses tons of thrown-away food at the beetles, but it doesn't stop the beetles. The beetles continue their pursuit of the teens, and both brothers question their sister's wisdom. But the beetles suddenly become the prey themselves—of seagulls that consume every bit of food and the beetles as well. As if an alert was broadcast, another group of seagulls arrives to join in the banquet. Before long the seagulls take pleasure in the consumption of every piece of garage and beetle. The teens enjoy the show and watch the seagulls finish off the last of the beetles. As the sun finally sets, the seagulls fly away from the area, and the teens wave good-bye. Kendra decides to leave a message on her iPhone and asks her siblings to trust her.

"I don't like this but I'm going to trust you for now," says Roland.

"Hey," says Juan. "How did you know that the seagulls were still waiting here? And why are there so many seagulls on land anyway? I thought sea gulls are birds of the sea, right?"

Kendra recalled her last experience at this same alley several months ago. She came home from school and walked through this back alley. She saw her neighbor, Mr. Hardgrove, waiting near the Dumpster. Kendra watched him, observing the sunset. Kendra was curious about his behavior when he opened up two bags filled with popcorn and nuts. He tossed the bags into the air. Kendra related this to Juan, amazed with the appearance of many seagulls who had eaten every piece of food before flying away.

Hardgrove notices Kendra outside of the alley and told her that he had been coming here for many years. It was always near sunset and these bird had gotten used to seeing Hardgrove coming there. The seagulls waited for him to appear every day at this same time. Hardgrove told Kendra that he had never missed feeding the seagulls every day for almost twenty years. Strangely—Kendra notices that Hardgrove weren't here to feed them today, which Kendra found his behavior very bizarre. Hardgrove had mentioned to Kendra that more and more seagulls are moving away from the sea.

"The seagulls are finding more food on land, going to landfill and garbage bins," says Kendra. "This is part of a new trend, in which seagulls are finding more foods on land and fewer predators to threaten their eggs. I hate the way that seagulls fly around like scavengers. But after today, I have gained a new admiration for the seagulls."

"I'm glad that my sister has such a big brain," says Juan.

"I love all this stuff on seagulls, but how are we going to get out of here safely?" asks Roland.

"I know that we can't remain here forever, since the smells, from the Dumpster, are getting harder for me to breathe," replies Kendra. "But things are about to change in our favor."

Roland demands an answer. Before Kendra can tell him, a yellow cab pulls in front of them. Roland and Juan want to run away, but Kendra stops them from leaving. They observe a stout individual with bushy black hair and a large mole on his right cheek, and Roland worries about this stranger recognizing them until they see Glitter sitting next to him. She jumps out from her hiding place under the front dash, dressed in a sparking multicolor designer miniskirt and pink high-heeled shoes. Glitter and Kendra hug each other, but the taxi driver tells them to get inside quickly. They climb into the cab. Kendra squeezes herself into the front seat next to Glitter. This left Roland and Juan to share the backseat.

"Don't take this the wrong way, but the three of you really stink," says Glitter.

"I'm sorry—the aroma from the Dumpster left it mark on us," replies Roland. "But we couldn't find anywhere else in the city where people weren't looking for us."

Glitter takes out her perfume and sprays it within the cab. Juan and Roland smell Glitter's perfume and both of them want another whiff of the Dumpster. Kendra tells Glitter to ignore them; she does it all the time. Kendra reminds her siblings of Glitter's kindness to help them, refusing to call the police. Roland worries that they shouldn't talk in front of the cab driver. But Glitter introduces her most trustworthy Uncle Karl, and he mentions his refusal to believe the news story about the teens. Uncle Karl trusts his niece, especially when Glitter strongly believes in their innocence.

"I'm surprise to see you helping us, but Kendra told us that you've become a less selfish person," says Roland.

Glitter made no comment, since she loved treating Roland with no respect at school. Roland and Juan give her the benefit of the doubt, but Glitter admits to Kendra that she wants to stop off at a beauty salon. She wishes to help improve Kendra's sloppy looking hair. Roland mumbles to Juan, reversing his opinion of Glitter's new attitude, and Juan speaks out for a place to stay for the night.

"Relax, our safe house is at hand, so please leave the driving to Uncle Karl," says Kendra, much calmer now.

As the night sky appears, strangely brighter due to the increased number of sparkling stars. Karl drives around different area of the city for some time—to ensure no one is following them. He looks directly at his watch to see the time is a exactly ten o'clock. He drives steadily down Cicero for a while, and then he turns toward an out-of-the-way motel, the Lance Motel. Karl hands them some black plastic bags containing some more clothes and other necessities. Glitter hugs Kendra with tears in her eyes. Glitter also gives a brief hug to each of the brothers, and she tells them to be very careful, as virtually the entire city is looking for them. Kendra agrees and thanks Glitter's uncle, who also gives them some money for a rainy day.

Karl literally drags Glitter into the cab so he can drive her home. As Karl drives speedily down the road away from the motel, Glitter waves one last good-bye at Kendra. Kendra hopes to see her again soon, when she doesn't have to hide anymore.

The teens walk into the lobby, and a plump, wrinkled old man, Mr. Lugg, the doorman, greets them. He knows Kendra's name, and she introduces him to her brothers. He moves like a snail to shake their hands and Lugg tells to them he talked to Glitter about the teens staying here. He tells them not to worry about being referred to as criminals on the news, adding that he refuses to believe Kendra would hurt anyone.

Lugg leisurely walks with a limp to their room, giving Kendra the key to enter for the night. Lugg inquires if anyone wants something to eat but everyone is too exhausted for food. After everything that happened today, they are happy just to get some sleep for the night. Lugg accepts their choice, and he closes the door. As he does, he mentions to Kendra about it being good to see her again. Roland takes this chance to ask Kendra what Mr. Lugg means. Kendra tries to ignore his question, but Roland asks the question a little louder. Juan sat back in his chair to watch the show.

"I have no comment to make now or ever," says Kendra.

But Roland wouldn't stop repeating his question to Kendra, so she decides to answer him. She admits to them about sneaking off to go to a rock concert in Washington DC, last year, since Malcolm wouldn't allow her to go. A school trip had been planned to visit the nation's capital, but the officials had cancelled the trip a week before the scheduled time. Kendra had tapped into Malcolm's computer to erase the message about the trip being cancelled to use this opportunity to go to the concert instead, and Roland feels vindicated in his suspicion that Kendra was using her secret code for more than just conversation.

Kendra says she had stayed at the Lance Motel last year, before she had gone off to Washington to enjoy the concert with Glitter and Eyeshadow. She sees the judgmental look in her brother's eyes, so Kendra counters with some information about Roland. She recalls Roland asking Rachel to drive him and Rachel's younger sister, Dawn, who is Roland's ex-girlfriend, out of town so they could attend a skateboard tourney in Crystal Lake.

Kendra remembers how they had looked on the weather channel to notice a delay in Malcolm's return bus trip home. Roland had taken this opportunity to slip out of city, since the storm wouldn't come near Chicago or Crystal Lake. Roland had gotten Kendra to fool their babysitter, covering his sneaking out of the house. Kendra reminds Roland how he never told Malcolm about his deception either.

Roland starts to get angry, but Juan turns his attention to something more important to him. "I want to see Malcolm and Thoth at the hospital tomorrow, but the police will be there in full force to catch us."

Roland and Kendra know Juan is right about the police being at the hospital. Roland tells Juan not to give up; he's working on a plan to see them tomorrow. Juan begins to yawn with exhaustion, so he moves lethargically to his room for some rest. Juan tries to look into the future with no success, so he decides to trust in his brother to work out the plan for the morning. Kendra wonders how is he going to fulfill this plan, but Roland promises to have something ready for tomorrow.

Kendra chuckles at Roland softly, but he doesn't let her laughter slow his belief in his words one bit. They hear the sound of raindrops falling steadily on the ground. Kendra tells Roland she's proud of him for helping Juan, and they each retire to their rooms for the night.

12

THE UNIQUE MAP

The next morning is seasonably humid today with temperatures predicted to reach in the nineties. Treasure hunters are traveling to the city from every part of the country, hoping to get rich with the capture of these wanted teens. Watching the TV, Kendra listens to reports about sighting the teens throughout the city, but the officers find no credibility in any of these sighting.

The police announce a massive hunt for the teens, promising to search every car, train, and truck on the main roads. Kendra runs out of her room in a panic and goes into her brothers' room. Kendra sees Juan sleeping like a baby, but Roland isn't anywhere in the room. Finding no sign of him, she begins to worry. A soft crackling sound near the door almost stops her heart, but Roland walks in calm and cool, like nothing was out of ordinary. He is holding several bags from a clothing store down the street. Roland sees Kendra in the middle of the room with her arms folded across her chest, and he can't miss the enraged look on her face.

"Why didn't you tell anyone about your leaving the motel?" shouts Kendra. "In case you aren't up on current events, the police are going to begin searching cars, trucks, trains, and buses for us."

Juan grows tired of hearing Kendra's yelling at Roland, so he runs off into the other room for some peace and quiet. Kendra says she isn't very hopeful about seeing Malcolm and Thoth. Roland shakes his head disagreeing with her, and then they hear the sound of an ambulance wailing toward this motel. Kendra carefully opens the window to find out the direction of the ambulance, and it stops in front of the motel. Two paramedics get out. Juan returns to the front room at the sound of the ambulance. She tells them to prepare to leave, since this must be some kind of a trick to catch them. Roland moves to stop Kendra and asks her to trust him this one time. There is a knock on the door, bringing some discomfort for Kendra, but Roland opens the door to allow a slender, fair-haired, middle-aged woman with brown eyes to enter the room.

"Hello, Rachel," says Roland. "To the others, he says, "I used to date her younger sister, Dawn, and she's willing to get us into the hospital."

"What?!" shouts Kendra. "There isn't any other explanation for your actions. I used my skills that Rose taught me to scrambled all our cellphones. The police won't be able to use the GPS to track down our locate too fast."

Kendra tells Roland that the scrambled cellphone signals won't work if he continue to use the phones. Roland waits for Kendra's anger to die down so he can explain his decision. Roland says he used a nearby public telephone so he could talk safely to her. Rachel tells Kendra that she doesn't believe the lies about them, because she knows Roland would never do such a thing. Kendra decides to believe her, with some reservation, since she wants to check on the status of Malcolm and Thoth. Rachel and Roland come up with the idea to get through the police barricade and into the hospital. She says she'll disguise them as patients who were in an accident. Juan looks out of the window at the heavy set older man with little hair and grey eyes who is standing next to the ambulance. Roland introduces Mr. A.R. to Kendra and Juan. Roland tells Kendra and Juan that Mr. A.R. and Rachel have worked together as paramedics for years.

"Are you really sure about trusting them?" asks Kendra.

"As positive as you were about telling Glitter and Eyeshadow," says Roland.

In fact, Roland tells Kendra and Juan that Mr. A.R. helped him on getting this summer job. Kendra didn't feel convinced of his goodwill, but Juan tells her there's no other way to get into the hospital. Kendra swallows her pride to go with Roland's plan, and Rachel uses her phone to send a text message to her partner. She goes outside to take two stretchers, and Mr. A.R. helps rolls them toward the teens' room.

In the meantime, several people, including Mr. Lugg, and the hotel guests run toward outside to discover the identity of the sick individuals. Mr. A.R. speaks soothingly about getting some sick people to the hospital. His words don't impact the teens or Rachel, but the hotel workers and the hotel guests appear to accept his answer at face value. The teens observe this behavior with astonishment as the guests return to their rooms, and the hotel workers resume their jobs. Not wishing to look a gift horse in the mouth, Kendra climbs onto one stretcher, while Roland and Juan share the other stretcher. Mr. A.R. and Rachel wheel the stretchers out of the motel and secure safely in the ambulance. He takes the wheel of the ambulance and turns on the siren to get them to the hospital faster.

As the ambulance speeds down the highway to the Metro Hospital, a weary Juan moves from the stretcher toward the front seat with Rachel and Mr. A.R., who welcome his appearance. He doesn't seem to be enjoying the trip. He thinks about how Roland and Kendra have friends who support them in such times.

A low tranquil voice speaks to Juan, "Don't compare your worth to your siblings. There is a friend who believes in you. Don't sell yourself short. You have an inner strength that will help out in due time."

Juan looks at Mr. A.R. to thank him for his kind words, but he insists he did not say anything to him. Rachel didn't hear anything, and Mr. A.R. suggests he's hearing things due to the intense pressure of everything around them. Juan doesn't agree, but he keeps his mouth shut for now, knowing the truth will come out sooner or later.

Rachel hears the siren of a police car approaching them, so Juan climbs hastily back on the stretcher with Roland. The officers stop the ambulance and want to look inside for the fugitive teens, but Mr. A.R. convinces the officers of the importance of getting these very sick people

THE UNIQUE MAP

to the hospital. Kendra and Roland are afraid of being discovered, but Juan doesn't show any fear at all. The calmness of Mr. A.R.'s voice makes the officers decide against looking in the ambulance, and the teens are relieved to hear the officers telling them to drive on. Roland wonders why the officers didn't wish to search anymore, and Juan tells him that someone is looking out for them.

A confused Roland asks, "What person would be watching over us?" He looks at Juan, seeking an explanation. Juan doesn't have the answer, so Roland decides to forget about it. In the other stretcher, Kendra takes out her iPhone to text Eyeshadow about something. As they relax during the journey to Metro Hospital, the teens think about finally getting to see both Malcolm and Thoth.

At Higher Learning it's close to lunchtime. There is nothing new on the teens running from the law, but many students use their phones to check the Internet for possible leads. Some students believe in their innocence, but they are in the minority. As the lunch bell rings. Chuck and Drake talk for several moments in the hallway, and their conversation doesn't give any comfort to Drake. Chuck believes he has a way to find them, so he may possibly become the richest guy at school.

"How are you going to find them, when even the police don't know where to look?" asks Drake.

"I talked to one of Kendra's former friends, Molly Gets, and she is checking out places where Kendra can be hiding at after school," says Chuck. "I'm going to get some buddies of mine to help out."

"Are you a 100% sure about doing this? There may be another side to this story," says Drake. "Besides, it is bad enough to use Kendra's former friend but involving other students in this chase? This could get out of control here. I think we should take a step back to get a fresh look at this."

"What's with your weak attitude here? They are escaped convicts who fled from a police station," Chuck reminds him. "In my mind that makes them guilt. Your need to start accepting them as criminals. I'll talk to you later, when I get a lead on Kendra and the others. So cheer up, Drake—we will all be millionaires soon, and those losers will be going to jail."

Drake tries to talk to Chuck, but he runs away. He scratches his head and wonders about this being the right thing to do. Drake sneaks out of school, and he rushes several blocks back to his house. Drake is one of the faster runners on the football team, so he doesn't have a problem getting home in a hurry. Drake gently opens his front door, and he treads softly inside to avoid his father, who is home on vacation. Drake's footsteps are as quiet as a mouse crawling silently across the floor, and he hears his dad snoring upstairs. He continues to the kitchen, where Drake sees a group of keys hanging on a hook.

He uses the keys to unlock the garage, and Drake ponders taking his father's red Firebird without his permission. His father promised to give him his own car. Drake has recalled an instructional permit for the past year without any traffic violations. Drake knows he's going to get his license next year, so he doesn't want to jeopardy it. However, Drake can't just stand there in the face of this injustice toward Kendra and her brothers. Drake doesn't know where to look for them, though, until he receives a call from Chuck on his iPhone. Chuck agrees to inform him about the location of the Witmores, and Drake promises to be there. Chuck doesn't want to miss a call from Molly on the teens' whereabouts, so he hangs up the phone. Drake decides to look for Kendra and her siblings on his own and avoid his father catching him. Drake climbs into the front seat of the car and drives the car out of the neighborhood.

Meanwhile, the ambulance arrives at the Metro Hospital, but Kendra wonders how Roland's friends are going to get them through the security to see Malcolm and Thoth. Rachel and Mr. A.R. go into back of the ambulance and bring out the stretchers, getting some assistants from the other workers. They don't let anyone remove the white sheets hiding the teens from the two stretchers. Rachel tries to wheel them straight to their adoptive father's room, but she spots a police officer coming toward them. Roland and Kendra sneak a peek from beneath the sheet, and they sees Eyeshadow's father, Ray, searching every person coming into the hospital via ambulances. As Ray heads for Rachel and Mr. A.R. to search the stretchers, Juan looks with Roland anxiously. But Ray hears a familiar voice calling his name—it is his daughter, Monica.

"What are you doing here? Why aren't you at home?" asks Ray.

"Father, my name is Eyeshadow, not Monica, so can you please call me that?"

An unyielding father looks her directly in the eye. "As long as you are my daughter, then I'm going to call you Monica. Please answer my question. I want to hear your reason for being here."

A quick-thinking Eyeshadow answers, "I wanted to see Malcolm and Thoth, since I fear for their health, Dad. You can't believe Kendra, Roland, and Juan caused their injuries, father."

Mr. A.R. and Rachel use this opportunity to move the stretcher around in another direction, and they are successful in avoiding Ray. Kendra holds out her thumb from under the sheet to signal Eyeshadow, who nods her head to acknowledge Kendra as they move to Malcolm's room. Roland and Juan watch Kendra's thumb in the air and laugh at her cleverness. Ray tells Eyeshadow that the evidence clearly points to the guilt of her friends, but Eyeshadow reminds him about not believing in just the evidence alone, since Ray always tells her there are two sides to every situation.

Ray guarantees that he will look at every piece of evidence, and he offers to let her to see Malcolm another time. Eyeshadow agrees to wait until next time to visit Malcolm, and he tells her to stay near his squad car so he can take her home. In her haste to leave, she runs smack into Tek, who falls. Eyeshadow expresses her apology to him, but he doesn't show any emotion because he is focused on finding the teens.

Ray goes over to check on him, and he motions with his hands for Eyeshadow to leave at once. Eyeshadow moves quickly away from Tek, as he inquires about Ray's daughter sudden appearance. Ray tells him about her desire to visit Malcolm, adding that he doesn't have any more news about the teens. He wants to take his daughter home in the patrol car, and Tek agrees to let him do so after he gives the hospital one last hunt for the teens. Ray follows his request and begins another sweep. Tek's phone rings, and he answers it. A follower of Seth asks for a progress report. Tek goes off to talk on the phone, while Mr. A.R. and Rachel continue toward the elevator to Malcolm and Thoth's room.

"How are we going to get into the room without anyone seeing us?" asks Kendra once they were inside of the elevator.

Rachel hits the red stop button on the elevator, and Mr. A.R. reaches under the stretcher to pull out three red student volunteers uniforms. Kendra goes under one stretcher to change her clothes, and both Juan and Roland switch into their hospital clothes. Rachel restarts the elevator again, and the doors open on the seventh floor. Mr. A.R. and Rachel stay on the elevator so they can return the stretchers to the basement. Roland leads Kendra and Juan to Malcolm's room. He is familiar with the layout of the hospital since he worked there this past summer. Rachel whispers something to Roland in secret. Roland sighs but he focuses on something other than Rachel's message. He promises to find a way out of the hospital when they are finished seeing Malcolm and Thoth. Rachel tells Roland to call her if they need any more help. As the elevator's doors close behind them, Mr. A.R. and Rachel wish them good luck.

Roland lightly moves down the floor with Kendra and Juan until they come upon room 701. Kendra and Juan feel out of sorts in these uniforms, but Roland tells them to walk naturally, like they are teen volunteers. Roland grabs one of the charts from another room, and they make their way to the Malcolm's room. They notice a police officer guarding the door, but Roland takes the lead in fooling the guard into letting them inside to check on the patients. However, the police insists on examining their ID. Then the officer hears his name being called on the loudspeaker, and the officer runs over to check on outside call. Roland recognizes Rachel's voice speaking the message, so Roland, Kendra, and Juan take this chance to sneak into the room.

A nervous Kendra grabs Roland's arm. "I'm so afraid of what is in the room. I probably won't be able to handle it."

"My fear temperature is going higher and higher," says Juan.

THE UNIQUE MAP

Roland reminds them that Malcolm and Thoth are alone in there, and how they would fight to see them in their time of need. Kendra and Juan get strength from their brother's words and go into the room. Roland hides his own fears.

"Roland, I'm impressed. I guess Kendra isn't the only genius in this family," says Juan.

Everyone walks into the room, and they see a scary sight. Malcolm and Thoth are sleeping in different beds, attached to monitors, with tubes in their arms. Kendra and Juan run over to Malcolm to check on him, but he doesn't even respond. Roland looks at Malcolm with fear in his heart, since he, based on the knowledge he had gained last summer, recognizes that Malcolm's vital signs are very unstable at the moment. Roland says that the poison is going through their systems, but the doctors are probably unable to stop the poison. Juan reaches over to hold Malcolm's hand. Juan wishes that it was him in this bed instead of Malcolm. Roland looks at Thoth, who seems to show no more improvement than Malcolm, until he feels a tap on his arm. Roland looks down to observe Thoth holding onto his arm, bringing a smile to everyone's faces.

A fatigued Thoth is able to sit up in bed. He smiles at the teens. "Please don't be afraid for Malcolm. I've promised to watch him. But you shouldn't have come here on your own. Seth doesn't have much time left. If he can't get your bracelets before the seventh day begins, it will be the last day for Seth on Earth, so please find a place to hide for the next few days."

"My friend, Rachel, told me privately in the elevator that your vital signs are fading with every passing hour," said Roland. "You two might not be able to hold out forever, and we couldn't help being afraid for both of you."

"The power of Horus's tattoo protects us both, so please don't worry about our safety," Thoth answers.

Kendra notices Thoth's skin is changing color to almost completely pasty, and she confronts him about it. Thoth tries to hide this from them, but he sees the concern on their faces. Thoth admitted that he has felt his powers draining like water from a faucet. He has come to the conclusion that Osiris and the rest of the Ousias didn't restore his powers. He regretted lying to them earlier but didn't want to alarm the teens.

Thoth gives his word that the power of Horus's tattoo will protect both him and Malcolm. None of the teens believe Thoth, so he agrees to allow Kendra to use her ability on him. Kendra stares at Thoth for a moment, and she is able to read the truthfulness of his words. Kendra learns the tattoo's power isn't going to last forever. It is causing a drain on his life energy to maintain the tattoo's powers. She says this could lead to their possible…death for both Thoth and Malcolm. But Thoth tells them not to fear for him, since he guarantees it will hold out for the time being. They struggle to believe Thoth, but he orders them to leave this place for their own good.

"No!" cries Juan. "We aren't going to leave either of you, so what can we do to save both of your lives and stop Seth?"

"I'm sorry for choosing to resist being your mentor, but I couldn't knowingly involve the three of you in this," answers Thoth. "It is too dangerous for words, and I still managed to mess things up."

"You were trying to protect us, like any adult in your position would, but we care too much for both you and Malcolm not to do something," says a determined Kendra. "Now, what can we do to help out here?"

Thoth knows nothing is going to change their minds, and he rubs his hands together to create friction. Before long, a piece of old, wrinkled paper appears in his hand, and he gives it to her. Kendra thinks this might be another paper like the one that Thoth used to protect Malcolm at their house. She also sees something appearing on the paper, which didn't show itself to her at their house. Kendra observes a slight image of a woman's face on the paper, but the image fades mysteriously, as if it was never there.

"Thoth, I could have sworn that there was a picture of a woman's face on this paper," says Kendra. "Since I think this is the paper from which I read those words of healing to you at the house, can you tell me about this mystery person?"

"I've no comment on this mystery person. This isn't the time for solving the identity of mysterious people," says a bewildered Thoth. "There is a way to cure both of us and destroy Seth at the same time."

THE UNIQUE MAP

Before the teens can speak, they observe the paper turn magically into a unique map of the earth, much to their amazement. He fights for every breath to talk about how this map contains a very strong magic.

"How can a magical map help us to defeat Seth and cure both of you?" asks Kendra.

"I took the three pieces of Seth's pyramid and magically hid them," says Thoth. "The magic was too powerful within these pieces to destroy so hiding them was my best option. You see, Seth must have these pyramid pieces and your bracelets prior to the seventh day. It is upon you to find these pieces before Seth, so Malcolm and I will be cured."

I don't understand how can Seth find something that is hidden from him?" asks Kendra.

"It would take some time to explain it," Thoth says. "Suffice it to say, those pyramid pieces can't remain hidden forever, but there is a place that even Seth couldn't retrieved the pieces from."

Thoth tells the teens that the map is a guide to the missing pyramid pieces. The map contains information about what to do with the pyramid pieces once they are in the hand of the teens. He warns of consequences of choosing to do this, and Thoth asks if they wish to continue in spite of the danger to them and the world.

They agree to do it together, so he passes the old wrinkled map to Kendra. She looks at him for a real answer to her question about the woman, but he ignores her inquisitive look. Thoth doesn't wish to answer her question or explain his reasoning to her. Kendra can see the expression of pain on his face and doesn't want to add to it. Roland and Juan are ready to stop Seth, but Juan begins to have an excruciating headache.

"Are you all right, Juan?" asks Roland. "Did you get another vision? What was it about?"

"Yes, but I saw something very confusing in the vision, and I don't understand it, Thoth," says Juan.

"What did you see in your mind, Juan?" asks Thoth.

"I could see Kendra running from something chasing her, and then I saw a huge fireball coming down on me and Roland," says Juan. "I didn't see anything else in my vision—so does this mean an end for us?"

THE OUSIAS

Thoth uses his failing strength to sit up again. "No, your visions are of a future as it *may* come to pass. All of you have the power to change the future, since the greatest power exists within each of you."

"The bracelets are the only reason for our power," says Kendra. "And they don't always work when we need them to work. How can we believe in something in ourselves being greater than the power of three magical bracelets?"

Thoth speaks to the teens with assurance. "As I have told you earlier, these bracelets may not always meet your wants, but your inner strength will help to increase the powers of the bracelets to do great things. It will help out in a time of need."

Everyone takes Thoth's words to heart, but they still wonder about their hidden powers. Kendra inquiries about going to places that may be out of the city. She refers to Seth's magic, which kept them from leaving the city earlier. Thoth feels his strength failing him again, so he discusses their chances of escaping the city. He tells them about sensing Seth's lack of power, when he saw his reflection in the mirror. Thoth tells the teens that Seth won't have the power to stop them from leaving the city. Juan is standing over Malcolm and hoping for his speedy improvement, when he develops another headache. Kendra and Roland look at him with worried eyes toward Juan, and they hear someone knocking on the door. Everyone becomes silent until they identify the voice of their neighbor, Mr. Hardgrove, at the door.

Hardgrove speaks softly through the door, "Hello, is there someone in the room?" Oh, I can see Ray and Tek, coming this way."

"This is just great," says Kendra. "How are we going to get out of here before Tek can catch us?"

Thoth raises his hand to perform one last magic trick, ensuring them not to be afraid. Thoth says that he's sensed Malcolm's feeling of love and faith in each of them, and he wishes nothing less than their complete success in this adventure. In the hallway, Tek yells at the officer for leaving his post as he and Ray run for the room, where Mr. Hardgrove stands in the doorway. Tek orders him to move out of the way, and he bursts into the room like a rhino. A petrified Roland, Juan, and Kendra see Tek forcing his way inside, and they, barely able to breathe, expect for him to grab them. But instead, he looks intently around the room to see only Malcolm and Thoth. The teens conclude that Thoth made them invisible, and it gives the teens a peaceful sense of calm.

"Mr. Hardgrove, you were shouting at someone in the room. I want to know the identity of this person," says Tek.

"I was talking to myself—I'm growing old, you know," said Hardgrove. "If I do remember the name of this imaginary person, then you will be the first to know."

Hardgrove turns to leave, but he takes one last look around the room. Tek motions for another officer to take over guarding the room, while he takes this moment to have some choice words with the officer who left the room unguarded. Ray walks his daughter toward his car so he can take her home. Kendra and Roland take this opportunity to slip out of the room, but Juan feels too guilty to move. Finally, Juan runs with them to the stairway.

"Where are we going to now?" asks Juan.

"We need a place to look over this map. We could go back to the motel," says Roland.

Kendra stops in midstep near a traffic light with a solution. "We can go to the public library two blocks from here—there is a private viewing room."

"Please explain this to me: we have the police looking for us, along with most of Chicago," says a worried Roland. "Is the public library really the best place to hide?"

"If Seth is too weak to stop us, then we should try to leave town, going to either the airports or the bus stations," says Juan.

"I don't want to panic anyone here, but I could read Tek's feeling in Thoth and Malcolm's room," says Kendra. "Tek was thinking that police are covering the airports and bus stations, hoping we would try to leave town that way. Seth relates to Tek—he is too weak to maintain the barrier, preventing us from leaving the city. Thoth was right about Seth's weakness. And before we decide to try to leave town, I want to examine this map. I also read Ray's feeling. The police have pulled most of their officers from places within the city. They want more officers to cover the airports, bus stations, and all the Metra trains—the police think we may use them to leave the city. I have made my case for the library, so do either of you have another place in mind?"

"No," says Roland. "I guess it time for us idiots to follow Kendra to the library, so we can learn something for once in our lives."

"You two are lucky to have me as your sister. You'd be lost without me as your leader," answers Kendra.

"Don't say anything but just nod your head," Roland whispers to Juan.

Juan and Roland laugh together, but Kendra is too focus on this mystery map to even notice. They walk the couple of blocks down the street to the public library, where they hope to get some answer.

As the afternoon sun starts setting, Tek finishes yelling at the officer for leaving his post and calls Seth at his pyramid. Seth is becoming more familiar with the technology of the modern world, but he is less than pleased with Tek's effort in catching those teens. Tek tells that the police is trying to find their iPhones, but they are having a hard time, breaking through a jamming signals.

"I believed in your ability to catch these three young children on your own, so I offered to pay a $3 million reward for them," roars Seth. "But I don't see any results on my investment here. Clearly, I have either overestimated your abilities or underestimated the teen's resolute. On the other hand, the fact that most of the people are searching for those teens. This will cause them to use most of their energy trying to hide, and it will make them weak and vulnerability. I want you to monitor every call regarding those teens and allow the greedy—I mean some good citizens to catch them."

Seth hangs up the phone in frustration. Two of Seth's followers walk in to offer their help, but Seth ignores them. Seth begins to get an idea to remedy this situation, and he runs toward the basement.

✶ ✶ ✶

Ray returns home with Eyeshadow, thinking about the teens. Ray decides to revisit the hospital. He can't stop thinking about his daughter's faith in her friends' innocence. Ray takes a shortcut to avoid the rush-hour traffic and arrives in no time at Metro Hospital. He gets to Malcolm and Thoth's room and insists that he be allowed to enter the room.

Ray walks in to see a quiet room with two people on life support, but then Ray observes something strange happening to Thoth—Thoth's face is turning into an ibis. Ray is horrified, and he's about to call for someone to help him. Thoth's face turns human again, only adding to his confusion, and an unknown voice speaks to him from within the room: "Your daughter is correct about her friends. They are innocent of this crime." Ray looks around again to a silent room with the exception of Thoth and Malcolm. He concludes that his imagination is working overtime. Ray leaves the room and goes off to find Tek.

Kendra and the others make it to the city library down on Belmont Street, and they go through the turnstiles to the elevator, where they head to the third floor. Kendra leads Roland and Juan to a private viewing room where people can view microfilm of old documents. She picks the last door at the back of the room.

Unknown to the teens, one of Kendra's classmates, Molly Gets, recognizes her Kendra's behind her sunglasses, and she texts Chuck about them. Chuck listens to Molly's description of the young woman she believes is Kendra, and he asks her for the quickest way to the library.

The teens enter the viewing room. "OK, Kendra," says Roland. "What are we going to do with this thing?"

Kendra looks at the map and doesn't observe anything unique about it. Roland was the next to scrutinize this map, with no results. While they try to figure out the map, Kendra's former friend, Molly, watches them talking to each other in the private room, until her iPhone begins ringing with a low tone. As the tone becomes louder, Molly runs to the stairwell to avoid being discovered. Roland and Kendra look toward the door, and Roland goes out to look for the source of the noise. Roland doesn't hear or see anything, so he goes back inside to further observe the map.

"This is so annoying! There is nothing on this map to see," says Kendra. "Juan, I wish you could have one of your visions. I'm out of ideas."

Juan and Roland move closer to the map, and the images on the map begin to move. Juan starts to walk away, but Kendra tells him to come closer. When all three of them approach the map, new words appear on it with a message.

Kendra uses her iPhone to take a picture of the words to translate. "I, Thoth, leave this message to the ones who wish to stop the Seth. I tried to get revenge on him when he took something from me long ago. But I wasn't powerful enough to stop him or strong enough to save... I went to the THES pyramid in the River North area, and I saw Seth's followers, who used the famous Rosetta stone to locate pieces of Seth's pyramid in Cairo, Egypt. They also found the remaining pieces of Seth's pyramid in a British museum. I took three pieces of the pyramid and hid them in different locations. I tried to get rid of them in the only place where the pieces would be out of Seth's hands. But I couldn't overcome the obstacle that protects this place from intruders. You may be able to succeed where I failed. This map will aid in your finding these pieces."

"What obstacle could be powerful enough to stop Thoth?" asks Roland.

"Excuse me, but what is the Rosetta stone, Kendra?" asks Juan.

"It is a stone that allowed people to translate the Egyptian hieroglyphics so everyone could understand their meaning," answers Kendra.

"How could they understand something in another language, since there wasn't anyone to help translate?" asks Juan.

"One day, someone found a stone with words written in Egyptian, Greek, and another language. It was known as the Rosetta stone since it was found near a city called Rosetta. People could understand the Greek," says Kendra. "They were able to use this to help translate the Egyptian languages for everyone. I don't know what kind of obstacle could have prevented Thoth from getting rid of Seth's pyramid pieces."

THE UNIQUE MAP

Kendra reads the rest of Thoth's message on the map. It says the abyss, the only place on Earth where the pieces could be kept safe from Seth to end his threat to mankind. There were people who followed Horus when he defeated Seth in the great battle for Egypt. Horus's followers tore down Seth's pyramid, but the pieces couldn't be destroyed by anyone. So the people hid the pieces in different places around the world, and the Rosetta stone was magically enhanced with the ability not only to translate languages but to act as a compass for the pieces from Seth's pyramid to better hide them. Then Seth's followers discovered the secret of the Rosetta stone, and they used the stone to find the pieces of Seth's pyramid.

"Wait—how does tossing some broken pieces of a pyramid stop Seth, since his power doesn't come from these pieces?" asks Roland.

Kendra calmly places her hands on Roland. "Don't you remember what Thoth told us about Seth getting our bracelets and having his pyramid back together in seven days, or else, he will expire on the seventh day? So we can get those pieces before Seth. Then we can throw them into the abyss, before the abyss closes. According to this map, the abyss will be closing soon for another thirty days."

Roland screams out with excitement. "Yeah, we got two things in our favor. One is that Seth has five more days to get all of these pieces, along with our bracelets. Also, we must throw Seth's pyramid pieces into the abyss in order to help Malcolm and Thoth. So everything is in our favor to beat Seth and save them."

"Wait a minute—was Thoth referring to something or someone that he couldn't save in the message?" asks Juan.

Kendra thinks to herself about Juan's question and how she had seen an image on the map at the hospital someone from Thoth's past. But she didn't want to think about something that might be best to leave alone. Right now, Kendra realizes they need to focus on finding the pieces of the pyramid and saving Malcolm and Thoth. The hieroglyphics and the pyramids of Cairo, Egypt, disappears off the map, and a picture of a museum in Chicago materializes on the map like a hologram.

Outside of the viewing room, Molly listens through the door but can't hear much of their discussion. Molly presses her ear against the door and is able to learn the location of this museum. Kendra brags that she enjoys this museum. Molly reflects this is Kendra's last trip to a museum, or anywhere else, since she is going to jail for a long time.

Kendra hopes this will guide them to Seth's pyramid piece in Chicago. Unexpectedly, water flows out of the map like a flood, engulfing them, and eventually the water drags them inside of the map. The teens try to use their bracelets to stop this with no success, and they go through the map like riding a waterfall at Niagara Falls. Molly hears their voices through the door for some time, until she can see water underneath her feet. She goes inside to see an empty room with water dripping off the table and onto the floor. Molly couldn't figure out on how they escaped from here, so she calls Chuck to tell him that she'd lost the teens. Chuck wasn't very happy with her, but Molly tells Chuck to relax, since she knows where they're going. The news brings great delight to Chuck's heart, and he promises to share his reward with her. Chuck disconnects his iPhone with Molly and starts calling some of his friends.

13

THE CHASE IS ON

After traveling through the watery map, Kendra, Roland, and Juan find themselves at the back of the Art Institute of Chicago. Everyone shakes their clothes but none of them are even wet. They move to the front of the Art Institute where two bronze lions stand on either side of the main entrance to the museum. Everyone looks at the map carefully. They don't want to get sucked into the map again. They start to move closer to the front entrance of the museum, and the map begins shining as they approach the doorway.

"How are we going to find this missing piece? This place is full of art exhibits— sculptures of ancient figures from ancient to modern times," asks Roland.

Kendra directs them to the front door. "We can start looking in the most obvious place—the Egyptian exhibits. I know it's been a while since the two of you have been here. So I will be your guide through the museum. It won't take anytime to get there."

"How much are we going to have to pay to get in, Miss Tour Guide?" asks Juan.

THE CHASE IS ON

"You two are very fortunate today, since we don't have to pay for anything," says Kendra. "Dad made me a member of the Art Institute last week, and he gave me two passes for each of you, too. But I kind of forgot to give them to you, and this whole situation didn't help me to remember until now."

She reaches into her pocket and gives Roland and Juan their tickets to the museum. Roland and Juan take the tickets and present them to the ticket agent at the main entrance as they walk up the grand staircase to the exhibits. Everyone attempts to avoid the small crowd of people there. Luckily, everyone is too busy enjoying the sights of the museum to give them a second thought.

The teens walk through the Asia exhibit and they observe several statues and figurines from both the Asian and Himalayan cultures dating from the second century to the tenth century. Roland and Juan become intrigued with looking at these historic sculptures, but Kendra keeps them focused on their goal. They stroll through the Asian gift shop until they find themselves in the Egyptian exhibits. Kendra and her brothers look around for any clues to the location of Seth's pyramid piece.

"Kendra, I don't have any idea about the location or even the hiding place of the missing pyramid pieces," Roland says.

"Why don't we just look at each exhibit with our bracelets, and maybe the bracelets can lead us to the missing piece?" Kendra suggests.

Roland and Juan stare at the large Egyptian wooden boat with excellent figures of Egyptian people, and Juan wishes he could sail in one of those boats. Roland becomes focused on the statue of a jackal, while Kendra looks at the mummy Paankhenamun resting in a gold leaf case.

She notices of a hieroglyphic inscription with a painted scene of the hawk-headed Horus introducing Paankhenamun to Osiris. Kendra doesn't pay any attention to anyone passing her, since she is lost in a daydream for several moments looking at the mummy case of Paankhenamun. She is about to walk away from the mummy when the map starts to radiate with a bright golden light. A small group of people begin to get curious about the light; Kendra places the map inside of her shirt to hide it from them.

Kendra softly calls Roland and Juan to her. "Hey, the map began glowing near this mummy case, so I think a missing pyramid piece might be inside of it."

"OK," says Roland. "How are we going to get it out of the mummy case, which is behind glass, without this crowd noticing us or setting off any alarms?"

The teens are considering the problem, when the people at the museum become frozen like statues. Roland, Juan and Kendra are the only ones able to move. Kendra takes this chance to move closer to the mummy case with the map. She could see a three-inch-high piece of a triangle in front of the glass case. Kendra carefully approaches it. Her brothers don't notice her: they are watching the lifeless crowd. A strange, overwhelming feeling comes over Kendra like a fever. She can't ignore the desire to reach for the triangle.

Her brothers finally notice Kendra's weird behavior, but before they can react to stop her. She is able to put her hand through the glass as if it weren't there, and Kendra immediately touches the small brown triangle. Her brothers are speechless. They nervously wait for the alarms to ring, but everything is silent. Since it defies all rules of physics, even Kendra can't explain what had just happened.

"How were you able to get your hand through glass?" Roland asks.

"I don't have an answer, but I have a feeling my bracelet gave me the power," Kendra replies.

As Kendra grabs the triangle with her hand, she notices that the piece is as light as feather. She places it swiftly in her pocket. After several minutes, the crowd of people starts moving again at the museum. Roland, Kendra, and Juan warily leave the Egypt exhibit and walk toward the grand staircase.

"I could feel this irresistible wave of energy upon me when I got near the mummy case," says a dazzled Kendra.

"I think it's time for us to get out of here, so we can help Malcolm and Thoth," stated Juan.

Roland, Kendra, and Juan make their way down the grand staircase, and they walk out of the museum. Their moment of glory is cut short with the surprise of seeing Chuck and seven of his buddies from school, and all of them are carrying a baseball bat. They surround the teens.

"What are you doing here, and how did you find us?" asks Roland.

Chuck smiles at them, holding his iPhone in his hand. "We're here to make a citizen's arrest, but it's thanks to your former friend, Molly, who called me after seeing you at the library. She overheard your discussion about going to the Art Institute. Now, I just need to call the police, so we can collect our reward."

As Chuck talks to the police, many people walking by are intrigued to witness kids being surrounded by other kids with bats in their hands. Chuck speaks loudly about making a citizen's arrest of the three fugitives from the news, and the crowd maintains its distance. Juan turns to Roland to use his bracelet's power to get them out of this mess. But the bracelet won't change out of its tattoo form, so he can't use his powers to aid them. Kendra recalls Thoth's warning about not using the bracelets' powers against the innocent, although she knows their goal is to capture them. Even though there is a greed factor with Chuck and his buddies, they are still innocents.

"What is our next move here, since there isn't a way out for us?" says Juan. "Also, if these jerks don't get us, then this crowd of justice-minded people will get us for sure."

"Thoth should have given us a rule book on these bracelets," Roland adds, "It was so nice of your ex-best friend to find us at the library, since no one was supposed to find us there."

"Seriously, you pick this moment for I told you so," says Kendra.

"Can you two save the arguing for later, since we are going back to jail," says Juan.

As they argue about escaping, Chuck tells a 911 dispatcher about holding the teens for the police. Drake, who had received Chuck's call to come here, parks his dad's car in front of the museum. Chuck finishes his conversation with the dispatcher, and the message is picked up by Tek, who is listening in on all 911 calls in hopes of catching a lead. Tek hears the message with great delight and makes a telephone call of his own to Seth. As Chuck waits for the police, Drake jumps out of his car heading to Kendra, but Chuck's friends prevent him from reaching her.

"It's good to see you finally made it here," says Chuck. "The police are on their way, so we can all prepare to become rich and famous."

Roland confirms his doubts to Kendra. "I told you about a leopard not changing his spots. I always knew not to trust Drake, and my suspicious was right."

Kendra boldly looks back. "No, I was right about him, since Drake still believes in our innocence."

"You're completely out of your mind, Kendra. Drake, please tell her why you're here," says Chuck.

"No, Kendra is right about me, and I think you should let them go before the police get here," demands Drake.

"Your feelings for Kendra are clouding your good sense, so you need to put them in a closet," replies Chuck angry.

"But I'm a changed man, and this is the new and improved Drake," says Drake.

"Well, you just pick the losing side, Drake, and this leaves us with no other option," replies Chuck.

Chuck tells two of the teens to point their bats at him, and Drake is about to fight alongside of Kendra, Roland, and Juan. The enraged Chuck aims his bat at Kendra, but he falls mysteriously to the ground. Within moments, he manages to get to his feet with a stunned look on his face. None of Chuck's friends can explain what force knocked him to the floor. Roland and Juan's tattoos change back into the platinum bracelets, and they move over toward Kendra, along with Drake.

"It looks like you aren't trying to stop some criminals, but rather all of you are hoping to injure some people for your own cowardly and greedy purpose," says Roland. "You guys are in some much trouble now. So what are you going to do, Chuck?"

Chuck taps his hand against his bat and gnashes his teeth. "We're in trouble? So you think one freaky event is going to stop us? I don't know why I fell but my buddies and I aren't going to walk away from million of dollars."

As Chuck and his friends move to attack them with their bats, Juan falls to his knees with another headache. Roland and Kendra shift over to Juan along with Drake, but Juan remains unable to get to his feet even for a few seconds. Drake suggests to Chuck to stop this action against them, but he just laughs. Juan finally gets to his feet and impresses the message to move away from here. Roland echoes the same message to Chuck.

"Do you really think that some fake fainting spell is going to prevent us from becoming rich?" Chuck asks. "I expected better from you, Roland, so why don't we hit a home run with your heads as the ball?"

Chuck prepares to swing his bat at them, but then they hear a loud yelling comes hastily toward them. They don't see anything at first, but everyone is soon alarmed with the presence of several brawny men in leather outfits. These men consider themselves as fortune hunters, and they want to collect the reward money.

As the fortune hunters hold out several layers of chains and wooden clubs to the crowd, since they don't anyone to interfere with them. Chuck and his friends are at a loss for word and refuse to let someone else steal their reward.

"You've got to leave here at once, before these people hurt you, Drake," pleads Roland. They only care about hurting us."

"Are you trying to scare us to runaway?" answers Chuck. "This is our reward and no one is going to steal it from us."

Kendra talks to Roland and Juan for a minute, and they start walking backward toward the main entrance. Drake goes along with them, while Chuck and his friends swing their bats at strangers.

These strangers are determined to capture the teens, and they pick up two of Chuck's friends like a twigs. They throw the teens across the sidewalk. Some people in the crowd tries to help them, but the strangers chase most of the people out of their way without breaking a sweat. Chuck strikes his bat at one of the strangers, but he misses him. The stranger picks up Chuck with one hand and tosses him in the air, where he lands very hard onto Drake's father car. The remaining strangers chase Chuck's friends from the area. People fearfully runaway to escape the onslaught of violent.

"I've got to use this power to help them, but there are too many of them to move around without weakening me," says Roland.

"What are we going to do to keep them from catching us?" asks Juan.

"I got an idea," says Kendra. "We were able to use our combine power to form a shield around us, so maybe we can do it again."

Roland stares at the bronze lion statues in front of the museum. Drake fears for their safety. Kendra looks at the statue and finally figures out Roland's plan.

"I don't think this is going to work, since I can't maintain this power forever," says Roland.

"You won't have to sustain it, if we combine our powers together," says Kendra. "Besides, we don't have any other choice."

Drake is the one who is confused. The remaining crowd leaves the area, Drake doesn't understand why Kendra and her brothers are standing around in a circle. Then he sees something remarkable. Roland focuses his bracelet to create a powerful glow around him. Kendra and Juan use their bracelets to help strengthen Roland.

Chuck is slowly able to move himself from the hood of Drake's father's car and runs for his life. A loud voice yells out to the strangers from behind, and they turn around to spot Roland, Kendra, and Juan. All of the strangers run at them with their clubs, but a powerful claw strikes the clubs, shattering them into pieces. The remaining strangers look to see one of the bronze lion statues from the museum roaring with the might of a real lion as the creatures move on their own with the power of the bracelets. This makes the strangers flee in fear, and this leaves the Witmores and Drake, who shakes his head in amazement.

"OK—are you three going to explain what I've just seen? Bronze statues shouldn't be able to move on their own," says Drake.

"You really don't want to get yourself involved in this. It would be best to walk away from us without looking back, for your own sake," says Roland.

Kendra agrees with Roland for once: Drake should leave the area. However, Drake doesn't want to simply walk away, and he refuses to accept her suggestion. Roland and Kendra seek to change Drake's mind, but then Juan grasps his head and tells them that more trouble is coming their way. Juan tells them that they will have to take Drake with them.

"Take Drake with us? We don't want to get him mixed up in this mess," Kendra says.

"It's too late to leave him behind. They're coming for all of us," says Juan.

Roland and Kendra think Juan is having another vision until they turn their heads. More strangers like the others are coming down the sidewalks of Michigan Avenue, and they are riding motorcycles. They have several more chains, and clubs in their hands.

"I think that maybe we were wrong to leave you out of this. Can we get a ride in your father's car?" asks Roland.

Drake runs over to the car to check on it, but the hood of the car is as flat as a pancake from where Chuck fell on it. He tries to start the car with no success, and the strangers are within minutes of attacking them. Roland and Juan see mountain-climbing rope in the back seat that Drake's father had left there.

Kendra shows her fear at them, but Drake places his hand on her shoulder and whispers that he is confident in her. Kendra takes a deep breath and tells Roland to be ready to move out. Roland and Drake take out meters of thick, gray ropes stacked together. They tie the mountain-climbing rope together to form the reins for the lions.

They make two big holes for the lions' heads and attach each one gently to the lions, planning to ride them like horses. The teens jump on the lions' backs to run for it. Kendra would rather ride on top of a real horse, but Roland explains there isn't any choice. Drake tells Kendra not to worry, since he is going to be riding it with her. This helps her relax, but not a lot. Drake takes control of the reins with Kendra holding to him. Juan mounts behind Roland. They start traveling swiftly away from the approaching bikers. The strangers wonder that those lions are the same ones from the Art Institute. But one of the stranger refers to it as some kind of trick or something.

The chase commences with the lions running down Michigan Avenue and the strangers pursing in their motorcycles, reminding Kendra of drawings from the ancient days of Egypt and Rome where chariot races was the event. The teens come upon people walking down Michigan Avenue to enjoy the great shopping area, but their hopes of fun are disrupted by the sights of teens riding on top of two bronze lion statues running from crazy fortune seekers creating panic among the people. This chase goes down several streets until they careen down Lake Street. Roland and Juan strangely aren't afraid, but Kendra isn't so fearless. "This is so totally awesome!" yells Roland.

"Awesome," says Juan.

"Seriously?" replies Kendra. "There are crazy people chasing us here, and my crazy brothers think this is cool. The city squirrels could feast on these nuts for the next five winters."

The pursuit runs in the middle of rush hour with people on the sidewalks jumping away. Drivers swirl their cars out of the way to avoid a possible crash that causes a huge traffic jam. Most people get their phones out to take pictures, some thinking with excitement that this is a stunt for a movie. As the streets and sidewalks fill with people watching them, Roland and Drake shout about trying some maneuvers to lose them. They get the lions to make a sharp turn toward Lower Wacker Drive to lose their pursuers, but the strangers turn their motorcycles to maintain the pursue. Drake asks Kendra if she is OK, since she hasn't said a single word for a while.

"Yes, I'm fine here. I'm starting to get used to these crazy situations," replies Kendra. "Drake, save me!"

Kendra screams with fear as one of strangers throws his chains at her, and the chains grab ahold of her waist. Kendra tries to fight against the pull to no avail, since the stranger is very strong. Drake reaches out to pull Kendra back, but another stranger uses his chain to wrap around him. As both struggle to break free, they call out to Roland for help. Kendra and Drake are about to be snatched away when Roland uses his powers, having their lion rip the chains apart with his long sharp claws. Drake and Kendra nearly land on the ground, but the lion catches both of them in midair. The lions begin to slow down, and everyone can see the strangers gaining momentarily.

"Kendra, I'm getting tired here, and the lions are losing their strength," says Roland.

"What does Roland's weariness have to do with the lion's energy, Kendra?" asks Drake.

"Our bracelets are able to meet our needs in times of troubles but they are a drain on us physically," answers Kendra. "There may be a solution to this problem. Just give me some time to find a solution."

Kendra pulls out her iPhone and finds the RTA transit tracker website. They head out of Lower Wacker Drive, where more people observe them with shock on their faces. Two of the strangers toss their clubs like missiles in their direction, but everyone ducks, and the clubs fall to the ground. Kendra tells Roland to head down State Street, and she points out a nearby subway. But they find themselves in the middle of rush-hour traffic. Everyone moves out of the path of the approaching lions and the strangers following them. Roland notices the subway is closed for repair and shouts to Kendra, but she tells him and Drake to push their way through the barrier.

Roland and Drake aren't positive about going into a damaged subway, but they choose to follow her directions. The bronze lions smash their way through the sealed entrance, and everyone lowers their heads to avoid the broken wooden barrier. Unfortunately, this doesn't stop the strangers from following them through as well, and they travel swiftly on the empty track. Kendra notices the track to the right of them is where the trains travel through the tunnel. She insists on going this way, but both Roland and Drake fear running into a train as well as being electrocuted on the third rail. Even so, Kendra gives them a firm, unyielding look, and this means nothing can change her mind.

Both boys scratch their heads in confusion to understand her plan but they trust her enough to follow her directions. Roland and Drake direct the lions to move onto the busy track, and they follow her directions to go on the train heading southward. Kendra tells Roland and Juan to focus their bracelets' magic along with her bracelet to keep them from being electrocuted, but Roland worries whether they can maintain this protective shield. They proceed onto track, traveling into a crowded station. People are awestruck when they see the teens riding bronze lions on the track.

"Can you at least explain your idea to me, since I'm getting more exhausted with every second?" asks Roland.

THE OUSIAS

Kendra is about to tell him when a loud reverberating sound can be heard up ahead. She looks at her tracker and advises Roland to begin moving more rapidly for the exit. Juan thinks about Kendra's plan, and he starts to freak out as he grips onto the lion. The strangers fear that they are traveling on an active track. They turn their motorcycles around and head back in the other direction.

"Why is Juan so nervous, since the so-called fortune hunters are retreating?" asks Roland. "We are safe. What is that sound ahead of us?"

"The sound is the train that is moving toward us," replies Kendra. "So we have to get out of the tunnel before it crashes into us. By the way, the train is running express."

A fearful Roland yells, "By the way, you have gone absolutely nuts! So we can either get hit from an oncoming train, or get electrocuted. The magic of these bracelets isn't going to shield us from the three rails forever, since I'm too tired to use the bracelets' magic to keep everyone safe from electrocution."

"At least we have choices here. We can get out of this, right?" says a worried Juan.

"We can do this, so don't give up here," answers Kendra.

"OK, but if this idea doesn't work—" says Roland. "Oh, never mind."

"I know that I'm the new guy here, but I say go for it," says Drake.

Roland uses his remaining strength to increase the magic in his bracelet, so Kendra and Juan focus with their bracelets as well to help give strength to Roland. Roland calls upon some last bit of energy that helps to increase their speed. They progress with almost supersonic speed through the darkened tunnel. Soon they can see a light ahead of them, and everyone heads for the exit. The train moves within seconds of entering the tunnel, but Roland gets enough inner strength to get the lions through the tunnel.

As the teens travel out of the tunnel, the train conductor hits the brake. The train comes to a high-pitched stop and causes people to hang on to their seats. Roland and the others smile with relief about surviving their ordeal, but they are not out of the woods yet. First, they need a place to stay for the night. Drake suggests they could stay at an apartment complex near the McCormick Place, where his uncle rents a place there. Drake tells them that his uncle is away on vacation. Drake also mentions that he found his uncle's keys on the same keychain as his father's car key. No one has the energy to argue, so they go with his idea. The lions travels so fast that many people saw only a flash of an undetermined object moving down the street. Eventually, the teens come to an apartment complex, and the weary teens climb off the lions. Roland falls to the ground like a rock, and he uses his last bit of energy to magically guide the lions back to their resting place at the Art Institute.

Kendra and Juan run over to see him, but he doesn't want anyone to touch him.

Roland needs to keep thinking about those lions, so they don't fall to the ground in pieces. Several officials from the Art Institute call the police when they disappeared. When the police appear to investigate, they find the statues return in their proper places, leaving the officials completely confused. Roland feels extremely weak from the entire adventure. Drake carries Roland to the apartment. He wants to know everything, and Kendra promises to give him the whole crazy story.

Drake uses his uncle's code to deactivate the surveillance devices. Kendra uses her bracelet, disabling the video cameras for a few seconds. The security guards try to fix the problem, and the teens slip past them unnoticed. Kendra restores the video cameras to normal as Drake uses his key to get into his uncle's room. Everyone walks in to see three fancy black-and-silver leather couches and two light wood chairs in the living room and one silk-covered bed in the bedroom. An incredible, rich smell of lavender fills the room. Roland is the first to inquiry about his Drake uncle's job, and Drake says his uncle works closely with his father who is an executive at X-Gen Games, a company that designs the best action games in the world.

"If I don't say it now, then I'm going to hate myself later," says Roland. "But I want to thank you for helping out with Chuck and saving our sister's life."

"Yes, thank you," says Juan. "Even though you were a no-good creep at one time."

Roland hits Juan on the back of the head, and Juan tells that Roland used those exact words not too long ago. But Drake doesn't mind it, since he was a no-good creep. Juan whispers to Roland if Drake is a friend or someone waiting to turn them into the police. "We'll give him the benefit of the doubt but lets keep an eye on him," Roland tells Juan.

"This is all so amazing for me, that people are risking so much to help us," says Kendra. "First, Roland's friends Rachel and Mr. A.R. help sneak us into the hospital to see Malcolm and Thoth, and then Drake risks everything to stand with us."

"Especially since I wasn't worthy to go to the dance with, but you were right about not wasting your time with such a loser," says Drake.

Kendra accidentally uses her powers to look within Drake and stops herself short of seeing too much of him. It causes her to grab her stomach in pain, and Drake goes over to examine her. She tries to explain her powers to him, but her words come to a stop like a car at a red light. Instead, she tells Drake about regretting her description of him as a loser, since she sees him now in a different light. They look closely at each other with strong feelings, and they are ready to speak their minds. Juan shouts out that he's tired from everything, and he wants to sleep. Roland also wants to go to sleep. Drake and Kendra stare at each other, deciding to talk another time, and Kendra walks past Juan to accidentally step on his foot. Juan screams in pain, and she bents over to him to pretend to be concern.

"Your timing is utterly the pits," whispers Kendra. "Oh—I'm so sorry."

Juan doesn't understand her anger at him, but he figures it must be some girl thing. Kendra turns her attention back to Drake, and he turns back toward her. Roland tells Drake about talking more in the morning, and he pulls out the beds within the leather couches for them to sleep on. Drake tells Kendra to sleep in his uncle's room. Kendra goes into the bedroom, while Drake, Juan, and Roland get comfortable on different couches for the night. Drake is the last to go to sleep, and he comes to the undeniable conclusion that he is involved with either a team of lunatics or the most amazing friends he'll make in his life.

14

DRAKE IS ONE OF US

As a full moon shines ever so brightly over an eventful day in Chicago, the teens awake at the apartment. They were able to regain their strength that the bracelets had drained earlier. Juan is the first to notice that Drake is nowhere to be seen. Kendra doesn't express any concern, and she tries to convince her brothers. But Roland and Juan refuse to listen to her since they believe Drake is turning them in for the reward money. The soft sound of a key is heard opening the front door, and everyone experiences fear racing over their bodies. Drake opens the door.

Kendra is relieved to see him. "I'm so glad that it's you instead of somebody else." "I never doubted your return, but reassuring my brothers was another thing."

"You were expecting somebody like the police or the F.B.I?" says Drake. "I just went out to get some fresh air and check my messages. Chuck reported me to the police for assisting you three, so I'm a wanted person as well. The police found my car at the museum, and they asked my father about my involvement. My father left me a text message about not telling the police anything, and I should return home."

"Did you contact him or respond to his message in anyway?" asks Roland.

"No, I didn't leave any text message on my phone, which could be tracked back to us," says Drake. "I watch a lot of cops' show. "Unfortunately, phones can be tract to the exact location—even if the phones are turned off. That is why I had removed all the phones in the apartment. I smash them including mine to pieces before I tossed the phones into the trash."

"What!" says Roland. "I loved using that phone. But I can't argue with your choice to protect us from Seth's followers like Tek."

"This wasn't easy for me either, having to deny myself the pleasure of talking to my best friends," says Kendra. "But Drake did the right thing."

"I was able to toss them in a private garbage company that picks up late at night," says Drake. "I've seen them many times in the past when I would stayed overnight. These private garbage companies travel throughout the city before the trucks return to their main office several miles away. It will take them time to track down our location, so we have brought ourselves some time, but not very much. I read the rest of my father's message: 'I'm extremely disappointed in you, choosing to disgrace your family like this.' I don't regret my decision in the least."

"Maybe, we should get out of here, since the police will eventually think to check at your uncle's place," says Roland.

"I was going to bring this up earlier, since the police were here a little while ago," says Drake. "The police were waiting to storm into the apartment, and an Officer Tek was with them. But another officer, who Officer Tek refers to as his supervisor, came down the stairs. The supervisor mentions that he searched the apartment with no sign of the teens. I thought for a second that his appearance turns into Mr. A. R. It was probably just my imagination out of control. Then another officer reported the teens at the airport, so Tek and the rest of the officers left the building. A real lucky break."

Roland and Juan find it hard to believe him, but there have been so many close call. Juan hasn't stopped wondering about this Mr. A.R., and this only adds to Juan's questions. Roland can't discount anything at this point, but Kendra uses her ability to read his feeling to learn the truth. "I believe him," said Kendra. "You know I can tell if someone isn't being honest with me, and he didn't lie about anything."

"I'm sorry, dude," said Roland. "It's going to take me some time to get use to the new Drake, since the old one was so rude to people. I was correct about Chuck, though."

"Hey, it's all right. I was a jerk," says Drake. "But that's all in the past, and we need to be focusing on the future. Besides, my head is still spinning around like a yo-yo from seeing bronze lion statues moving. I want to learn the whole truth about everything."

Roland wants to leave, but he figures that it isn't likely for the police to return to the same place too fast. Drake sits down on one of the chairs. Kendra and Roland tell him about everything from the Ousias, Thoth, and their mission to stop Seth from taking over the world. Drake nearly falls out of his chair. As he hears the rest of the story, Drake is surprised to learn about their different abilities, which includes Kendra's talent of reading other people's feelings to discover their most private thoughts. She tells Drake that she won't use her ability to read his secret desires, but he isn't too sure about believing her.

A dumbfounded Drake tries to soak up all of this information, willing himself not to lose his mind. Kendra and Roland tell him about feeling the same way upon learning this for themselves, but they know Seth mustn't be allowed to rule mankind.

"I wish there was an instruction book on these bracelets," says Kendra. "Since they only work in a time of need and are unpredictable. Speaking of time, it is two minutes past midnight according to my watch. Can one of you turn on the TV? I'm wondering if our adventure made the late night news."

Kendra's thoughts were right on the money. The leading news story of the evening was definitely about them. A fresh-out-of-college female reporter discusses the reaction of people who had seen bronze lions moving around at the Art Institute, and how these bronze lions—now with ropes attached to their bodies—were ridden by four teens throughout the city.

Most of the police refuse to support these claims of moving lion statues and creatures running throughout the downtown area earlier today. People show fuzzy pictures of something being chased in the city, but all of the video evidence is either erased or mysteriously too fuzzy to provide proof. However, there is enough witness testimony and fuzzy video to allow the news station to run with the story.

The news reporter finishes with their story and moves on to another story. As Roland and Juan watch with interest, they see Officer Tek and Officer Ray being interviewed, since they were the first to question the teens, and Kendra wishes that she could read his thoughts through the TV. But Kendra knows her power isn't powerful enough to do this. She tries to force her mind, hoping to activate her abilities. Kendra grabs her head and falls to the floor. Drake runs over to her, but she recovers. Kendra admits she was trying to read the mind of the Tek, but she found herself overloading on the minds of the nearby tenants.

"Don't you remember what Thoth told you about misusing your ability?" asks Roland.

"What was this warning about, Kendra?" asks Drake.

"I can only read one person at a time, but I tried to push my ability to read the TV news reporter," says Kendra. "It causes me to tap into the other tenants and security people within the apartment building. But I promise I will never do anything like this again."

"I'm going to hold you to that," says Drake.

Back at the police station, Officer Tek returns from following several false leads. He reassures the reporter that these teens are most dangerous criminals. He insists they used some kind of poison to incapacitate their adoptive father and teacher. Officer Ray hears this description of the teens from Tek. Ray recalled his conversation with his daughter, Eyeshadow about her friends. Ray didn't want to let his instincts as a police officer be influenced from by his daughter's personal feelings. But as Ray listens to his partner, Tek, speaking to the reporter. Ray thinks about the voice that he heard in Thoth and Malcolm's room.

It only adds to Ray's doubts about the teens' guilt and the truthfulness of his partner. The reporter finishes her questioning Officer Tek, regarding the Witmores, and she wants Tek to answer more questions. Tek's refuses to answer her. He moves the reporter out of his face in an impolite matter and orders Ray to continue their search. Ray goes into the public restroom for a second and uses his phone to call his wife. She senses the worry in his voice on the phone and inquires about the reason for his fear. Ray tells her about owing their daughter an apology, since he didn't respect or even trust her belief in the Witmores' innocence. She questions him about his next move, but he isn't sure what to do at the moment.

Mrs. Hightowers wants her husband to talk to his partner, Tek. Ray fears discussing this with him, since he isn't sure that he believes Tek about anything. They both discuss the idea of taking their daughter out of the city, since he feels enormous fear for their safety. His wife doesn't want to share in Ray's worries, but he convinces her of the danger. Mrs. Hightowers prepare to get her daughter and leave the city.

At the apartment of Drake's uncle, Kendra finally recovers from her stupor, and everyone starts to relax. She grabs her head and asks for some water. Juan runs into the kitchen and returns with a glass of water for her. Kendra takes a sip of water, and then she takes a little more with ease.

Drake asks if they have other abilities. Kendra says they are able to form shield around themselves and others within their range. Roland steps in to mention about Thoth's promise that other talents will come forth in their times of need. Juan doesn't want to be left out, so he demonstrates how the bracelets changes into a tattoo on his left arm, to Drake's amazement. Drake asks that the bracelets must be on either the left or the right arm. Roland responds, "It doesn't matter which arm it goes, since the magic works on either arm." Roland takes his bracelet off his right arm and places it on his left. He focuses on his bracelet, and Drake watches it turn into a tattoo.

They continue the conversation for some time, and then Kendra wants to get some more sleep. As Roland and Juan finish talking with Drake, Kendra runs into the bathroom first with the promise to be out in a few minutes. Roland and Juan begin immediately pounding the bathroom door with their fists, since a few minutes for Kendra is several hours for everyone else. Drake grins at the nonstop banter between them, and he marvels at how they manage to work as a team. Juan stops walking around for a few seconds and develops another headache like a hammer striking a nail. Roland dashes over to Juan who looks at Drake with dread in his eyes. Juan tells Drake about seeing his father talking to the police. The police suspect them of releasing some kind of gas to give people hallucinations.

"OK, we don't have to fear them finding us tonight, so we can locate the rest of the pyramid pieces in the morning," says Roland.

"I'm so glad that my father didn't tell the authorities about me," says Drake.

"You can tell him the story, assuming he would even believe it," says Kendra.

"You told me that Seth needs to have all of the bracelets and these pyramid pieces to complete his plan," says Drake. "Why can't we just throw those pieces into a garbage can or just set them on fire?"

"These pieces are too magical to be destroyed so easily, and Seth has the legendary Rosetta stone in his control," says Roland.

"I thought the Rosetta stone was just used to translate languages," says Drake.

Kendra tells Drake that the Rosetta stone was magically altered to locate Seth's pyramid pieces. She explains Seth would be able to find the pyramid pieces too. Roland mentions Thoth hid the pyramid pieces with his magic. But Kendra admits that Thoth and Malcolm are getting weaker with each passing moment. She admits her fears that Seth will locate the pieces to his pyramid.

"We wanted to stop Seth but didn't wish to lose Malcolm in the process," says Juan.

Kendra takes this moment to sneak away, and Drake insists he wants to see this pyramid piece. Roland and Juan run into the kitchen and find

THE OUSIAS

the map there. Drake is astonished to see this pyramid piece. Drake tells Juan that his uncle has some video games in his room. Juan doesn't hesitate to go look, and Kendra takes this chance to talk to Drake.

"You were right about me being a jerk, and I'm ashamed for refusing to see it for this long," says Drake. "People have told me for a very long time that I was the most athletic person at school. Unfortunately, it got to my head and caused me to treat people with disrespect. Does this mean you would be willing to go on a date with me, or is it too soon to hope?"

"I knew there was more to you than meets the eye, but I couldn't let myself see the truth," replies Kendra. "It's nice to be wrong about something for once, but don't tell my brothers. They would never let me hear the end of it. It would be an honor to go on a date with you."

"OK, I can show you the new and improved Drake," says a jovial Drake. "If you're willing to go out on a date with me, then I promise to give you the best date of your life. After this whole situation with Seth—after we have saved the world, of course. Now, was your bracelet able to help you to read my inner feelings again, or did I surprise you with my statement?"

"Drake, there are some things that a girl doesn't need a magic bracelet to figure out," says Kendra. "But the bracelet is a big help, so don't ever lie to me."

Kendra and Drake laugh together, and Roland approaches them like a big brother protecting his little sister. Kendra sees Roland staring at the two of them while Juan stands behind him, with hopes of witnessing a fight. Drake goes up to Roland with a no-backing-down attitude of his own. Kendra has seen enough of these two and prepares to end it. But Roland offers his hand in a gesture of friendship.

"Hey, I used to think of you as a jerk, but if my sister believes in yo2u, who am I to say different?" answers Roland. "I'm proud to be your friend, so you better not hurt my sister or else."

"I wanted to say this since the day you kicked my butt in grade school," says Drake. "Thank you. You gave me a chance to take a long look at myself, and I didn't like it."

"As far as I'm concern that person never existed," says Roland.

Roland and Drake shake hands with each other, and they finish it off with a high five for good measure. Kendra goes over to congratulate them for being so mature at last. Juan tries to sneak away from Roland, wishing to play the video games before Roland. But Roland stops Juan to demand to play the games first or, he promises, there will be a fight. Juan hands over the game remote to Roland, and Kendra tells Juan to give his approval to Drake or else.

"No, I'm glad to welcome my new buddy to our group," says Juan.

Just then, Juan gets another of his piercing headaches, and he jumps up and down like someone on a pogo stick. Roland wants to know what he sees, but Juan can only say it's time to leave this apartment. Kendra demands to know why they should leave at this late hour, and Juan tells them that Homeland Security wants to check Drake's uncle place themselves. Everyone begins to share their brother's anxiety to leave, and Juan informs them that they are getting a search warrant to check Drake's father assets as well as those associate with him. Juan says they will arrive with the police within the hour.

"Excuse me." says Kendra. "Did you just say Homeland Security?"

"Yes, they have placed us near the top of the most wanted criminals list," says Juan.

"I don't understand a powerful group like Homeland Security, wasting their time on minor criminals," says Drake.

"You can thank our pursuer, Tek," says Juan. "In my vision, Tek traced our damage phones to a landfill. Tek had no other way left to find us. He told the Homeland Security agents in my vision that we used some kind of gas to cause illusion among the people. He gave the agents some of the liquid from our house, relating to Malcolm and Thoth's illness. They think we developed some chemical mixture to make the people hallucinated. They believe our genius sister, Kendra is smart enough to create this."

"I'm so glad that my sister is such a genius and not a regular knucklehead like us. Then no police or federal agents would ever consider you brainy enough to do this," Roland replies.

"You are so funny, Roland," says Kendra. "We are being hunted by the police, fortune hunters like those strangers at the museum, Seth and his followers, and now federal agents. Plus, we were given magical bracelets that don't always work. I miss my normal life as a teenage girl, spending her time with her best friends, talking about boys and parties, and shopping at the malls."

Roland waits for Kendra to snap out of her delusion and says it's time to escape. Drake tells them about his uncle buying clothes for his cousins' birthdays. The cousins are their ages. So Drake suggests looking for something to wear, and they go in the bedroom closet to search. Kendra grabs some clothes out of the closet, and she runs speedily back into the bathroom. Both Roland and Juan begin complaining about her time in the bathroom again. Neither can wait for her, so they go into Drake's uncle's room to try on some clothes for themselves. Kendra comes out of the bathroom, voicing her concern over Drake getting into trouble for taking his cousins' birthday presents.

"It can't be any worse than assisting three fugitives to escape the law," responds Drake.

Everyone comes out dressed in the new black outfits, so they won't draw any attention. They're happy with Drake for doing this, and they prepare to leave the premises at once. Drake offers to pay for the bus and train fare, but they inform Drake that it's not necessary to take any transportation. Roland tells her to use the map to seek the next piece of the pyramid. Juan warns Drake to get ready for the ride of his life, but he doesn't fully grasp how they will travel to find this pyramid piece without riding anything to get there. Drake stares at Kendra touching the map. The map begins glowing again with the same dazzling light, and an image appears on the map. He looks at it with amazement, but the real fun for Drake is about to commence.

The image on the map is a three-dimensional picture of the Willis Tower in Chicago. "So the second piece of Seth's pyramid is somewhere in that tower?" asks Drake.

"Yes. We have to get it before Seth locates it for himself," replies Kendra.

"I'm ready to go. What are we waiting for here?" Juan asks. "We should be able to get there in no time, and Seth is going to lose another piece of his pyramid."

"It is nearly one o'clock at night, and it's going to take some time to get there," says Drake. "What does Juan mean about getting to the Willis Tower in no time and getting ready for the ride of my life?"

Roland grabs hold of Drake's shoulders and begins to grin at him. "Kendra, I think you should inform him about our little travel plan, since he is part of our team now."

"There is a way of traveling to this place, but it is an unusual method for us to get around," says Kendra. "You may want to find another place to hide."

"I'm part of this team to the end, so I insist on going all the way," says a bold Drake.

15

GREAT FIERY ONE

After reading Thoth's earlier message on the map, Kendra brings out the first pyramid piece from her pocket and places it on the map. She touches the map with her bracelet. Drake notices the map glowing with the brightest light to illuminate the room and a wave of water appearing out of the map to engulf everyone in it. Before anyone can react, they are sucked into the map once again.

Within seconds, the wave of magical water sets them in front of the Willis Tower.

Drake examines his clothes in order to dry himself, but he discovers to his surprise that his clothes are totally dry. Drake and the others look up to see the 1,729-foot high building. Including the antennas on top, it is the tallest building in Chicago.

"You guys weren't kidding about an unusual way to travel. So what are we going to do now?" asks Drake. "This building has one hundred and eight stories, and this piece could be anywhere in this huge place."

"I'm impressed with your knowledge of the tower. How did you know that so fast without looking online?" asks Kendra.

"I went on a tour of the Willis Tower this past summer, and the whole experience stayed with me," says Drake.

"It looks like we've got another bookworm in our group. Guess you can never have enough bookworms in this group," jokes Roland.

"If you two comedians are done with your weak jokes, then we need to find the next piece." insists Kendra.

Roland notices the glowing again, and the energy moves out of the map like an arrow aiming at the top of the antenna. Everybody is getting ready to go to the top floor to retrieve the second pyramid piece when they hear Drake yelling in pain. Everyone turns their heads around to see Seth with a tight grip on Drake's neck. Kendra, Roland, and Juan are horrified to see a Seth in his true form. He appears as a jackal-like person with two gray, flattened horns similar to the horns of a giraffe. Roland plans to use his bracelet to find and make a mirror like before, but Seth places more pressure on Drake's neck and promises to snap it in two.

"I order you, Roland, to keep your hands in front of you at all times. I'm tired of playing around here," commands Seth. "My Rosetta stone was able to track down the location of my pyramid piece, but I couldn't get a fix on its location at first. A little while ago, my Rosetta stone was able to track the second piece. Thoth's magic wasn't strong enough to hide my pyramid piece. He must have used up the last of his magic to protect himself and Malcolm. So once I knew where my pyramid piece was placed—I just had to wait here for your appearance. You have one minute to give me the first pyramid piece and your bracelets, or I'll break his neck. Don't try to use your trick with the mirror again, since I brought these along as insurance."

Seth pulls a pair of black sunglasses and places them over his eyes. Seth begins to crack Drake's neck. Drake cries out in extreme pain. Kendra tells everyone to take off their bracelets, and she brings out the first piece of pyramid as well. Seth smiles with an evil, delighted smirk as he mocks the three without mercy.

"The Ousias chose the three of you to stop me from rising to power again, and it was a very foolish choice for them to make," says Seth.

"Don't give in to this wicked creep. My life is nothing compared to the lives of everyone else on earth," gasps Drake.

"You dare try to talk tough to me? You are nothing more than a pawn in my subjugation of this world!" shouts an incensed Seth.

Kendra expresses her terror and panic over Drake's plight, which does nothing more than give delight to Seth's callous heart. Seth tightens his grip on Drake's neck as they are ready to toss their bracelets and the pyramid piece. But a powerful, unseen force moves between Seth's hand and Drake's neck, and he is unable to get ahold of Drake. Drake takes this opportunity to judo toss Seth in the air, and he lands hard on his rear end. Drake quickly runs to Roland and the others, and they put their bracelets back on their wrists.

"I don't know how could a teenager could flip me to the ground with no power, but it doesn't change a thing here," says an astonished Seth. "Those bracelets are mine to use, so don't be stupid enough to challenge me."

Seth realizes to his shock that his sunglasses are missing. Seth refocuses his attention to Drake who nonchalantly clings to the glasses. As the angry Seth seeks revenge on him, the three teens run within a few feet in front of the Willis Tower. The teens form an invisible shield around them and hope Seth's image would be caught on the tower like a mirror. Seth figures out their plan, but it doesn't scare him Seth in the least.

"Your bracelets can't maintain your current shield for long, since they depends on the energy of the three of you," says Seth. "I'm sorry to disappoint you, but there isn't enough light shining at this tower to reflect my image. I can just wait for your feeble strength to grow weaker."

Seth approaches them with victory in his heart, but a sudden light as bright as the morning sun shines brilliantly on them. Seth's image appears on the glass of the Willis Tower, and he sees his reflection, which brings unstoppable pain spreading over his body like a sickness. Seth is a creature with the darkest heart, so he doesn't have to feel any sorrow or guilt over his victims. When Seth is forced to watch his

GREAT FIERY ONE

image, he feels the pain of every person he has brought untold damage or death to.

Seth is unable to bear the intense, agonizing pain, so he falls to his knees. "No, this can't be possible—it is nighttime. You don't have the power to change night into day."

"The reason for this sunlight doesn't matter. You are now at our mercy," says a self-confident Roland."

"No, it is not over, child. I've got one more trick up my sleeve, so to speak," Seth says.

As they watch Seth try to stand up, there is a strong force moving the ground from several blocks away. No one knows the reason for the upheaval, but the sound gets louder and closer to them. They see some people trying to drive their cars down the street, but the ground begins swaying, forcing the drivers to slow down. None of the drivers is hurt as it moves quickly from them, but the drivers park their cars away from the shaking, and they wait for a safe moment to drive away.

The teens get ready to run away, but the quaking stops. The ground collapses under their feet, and the teens go flying toward the front entrance of the Willis Tower. Everyone recovers to find Seth on the ground, and they look at a massive hole near the tower.

Roland gradually gets to his feet first, and he goes over to check the others for injuries. Everyone is surprised, but they have no serious injuries, except for a few scratches and pieces of concrete on their bodies. Kendra peers into the gigantic hole, which appears deep enough to reach the center of the earth. She keeps her distance from the sharp pieces of concrete and steel, and the wide electric wires to avoid electrocution.

"We can't remain here. Something cause the ground to come apart," she says.

"Wait, we can't just leave Seth behind, especially after what he did to Malcolm, Thoth, and all of us," says an angry Juan.

The once powerful Seth stands to his feet and laughs. "You are worrying about Thoth? Then you are truly a weakling like him. Thoth tried to stand in my way as well, but it cost him more than what he bargained for. Please allow me to introduce my pet. Great Apophis, come forth to show your awesome might to these weaklings, since they will never see another day."

A loud hissing comes out of ground, and it gives way to the most powerful snake in the history of Egyptian mythology. A seventy-foot-long serpent, weighing over one thousand pounds, rises out of the ground. They stare with horror in their hearts at the sight of this golden snake with several black circles along his back. The creature's eyes are the personification of true darkness, without an ounce of light. The teens stare into the creature's face.

Many people arrive to investigate the crash, and they behold the colossal snake, terrifying them. Apophis hypnotizes the crowd with his mesmerizing eyes, and they go back to their normal routine like nothing happen here. The snake refocuses on the teens, and they are unable to look away from the snake's spellbinding eyes. They find themselves moving toward the snake like people walking in their sleep, but Kendra's bracelet allows her resist the power of the snake's evil eyes. She releases a powerful light to act as a shield against the snake's mesmerizing gaze and frees the others in the nick of time just as they are walking into the mouth of Apophis.

"Hey, what happened to us? I feel like I've been sleepwalking," Roland says.

"Yes, Apophis enthralled us, but we've got a bigger problem right now," says a fearful Kendra.

Roland, Kendra, Juan, and Drake move together to stand united, but this increases Apophis's mounting rage. It rushes the teens with great fury. Their bracelets are able to keep the creature back for the moment with an invisible shield, but the effort drains their own diminishing strength.

"I got an idea to push the shield in front of the creature," says Drake. "Kendra and I will run inside the Willis Tower, and Roland and Juan will dash in the opposite direction."

"I don't like it, but there is no other choice here," says Juan.

"We shall come back for you and Drake before this snake can turn its ugly head," Roland promises Kendra.

GREAT FIERY ONE

Apophis runs into them with the power of a battering ram, but the teens use every ounce of their willpower and concentration to force the shield against the snake. Apophis falls backward toward the great hole and nearly into it. Everyone takes this chance to runaway from the scene. Kendra and Drake head for the front entrance of the Willis Tower. Roland and Juan race away from the tower in the opposite direction, but Apophis slithers across the ground after Kendra and Drake.

Kendra uses her bracelet to open the front entrance, and they make it inside. They run past the works of the American artist Alexander Calder, who designed sculptures of objects of different shapes, sizes, and colors referred to as mobiles, an exceptional design of the varieties of different elements in the universe. As they rush along the polished granite flooring and transparent walls with steel columns, two husky security guards stop them from moving to the elevator. One of them asks how they entered a locked building without a pass, but Kendra can't come up with a quick answer for them.

"Please, you have to get out of here, and I don't have time to explain it in full detail," says Kendra. "Don't tell me that neither of you heard the noise outside a moment ago."

"They're probably under the spell of the snake," says Drake.

The guards are about to detain them when something comes crashing through the door. Apophis forces his way into the front lobby, but the security guards aren't under the snake's power this time. Apophis knocks one of the guards against the mobile sculpture and consumes the other guard. Kendra and Drake race for the elevators, and Kendra employs her bracelet to override the security barrier. Before long, Kendra and Drake board the elevator, pressing the button for the top floor.

"Oh my goodness," sighs Kendra. "I just saw a man get eaten by a giant serpent."

"We can't do anything about it. We have to leave," says Drake.

"OK," replies Kendra. "You are right. I'm going to try to stay calm and—"

The elevator mysteriously stopped moving. Kendra frantically pushes several buttons to restart it. The elevator remains immobile for a few seconds, and then the floor gives way to the force of Apophis. He hisses at them and uses his dark-red tongue to grab hold of Kendra. Drake tries to pull her out of the snake's tongue with no success. Meanwhile, outside of the Willis Tower, Roland and Juan see its tail and begin striking it with some concrete rubble. Apophis's scaly skin is as hard as rock, too hard to feel anything, but they use their bracelets to increase the strength of their blows.

The bracelets raise their might to another level, so this time their blow is powerful enough to give a mighty jolt to the snake. The creature cries out in pain, releasing Kendra and discharging the security guard from its belly, leaving him covered in slime and comatose. Drake and Kendra take hold of the guard, getting some snake slime on them as well. The guard is as slippery as ice on a cold day, and Drake struggles to maintain his hold on him. Apophis releases the elevator, so they are able to regain a better grip of the guard. Kendra's bracelet makes most of the slime disappear. But Apophis's grip on the elevator is so strong that it snaps every steel cable line holding the elevator. The elevator begins to fall like a rock to the bottom. Kendra stands near the elevator button and uses her bracelet to slow down the elevator. But the elevator is traveling fast, which makes it difficult for Kendra to delay its acceleration. Drake moves toward the nearest wall to avoid the huge hole in the floor from Apophis's attack.

As the elevator continues to accelerate, Kendra regains some measure of control of the elevator, delaying it for a moment. Drake mentions the elevator's buttons are still working, and he realizes they are at the 103rd floor.

"I don't know what you're thinking, Drake, but please hurry up," says Kendra. "I can't hold the force of this elevator forever."

"Maybe you can move the elevator to the lobby, giving us the chance to leave the building," Drake suggests.

"No," says Kendra. "We can't allow Seth to get the second piece of the pyramid. I know you were thinking earlier that we can place the guard here to keep him safe from Apophis."

Kendra concentrates with all her might, and the elevator doors open. Drake grabs ahold of the guard, and they immediately jump out of the elevator, landing hard on the ground. They recover and observe a glass box with a transparent floor. It extends over the street, a popular viewing spot for tourists. Drake places the guard near the box for his own safety. Kendra remains far away from the glass box. Drake asks about it, and Kendra admits her fear of heights. Drake talks about the view from the box and how he enjoys standing in midair to see the street below. However, Kendra doesn't wish to experience any of it in the least.

They can hear the sound of Apophis, so they decide to try to reach the top floor to get the second piece of Seth's pyramid, resting on the highest floor. The elevators are too damaged to use, and they prepare to run for the stairwell. Kendra worries they shouldn't leave the guard behind, but Drake reminds her that Apophis will be too focused on the two of them to think about the guard. They run to the stairwell, and there is some concrete on the ground. But the stairwell isn't completely destroyed, and they run up the stairs to the top floor.

At the front entrance of the Willis Tower, Apophis refocuses on Roland and Juan, swinging his tail in the their direction. It tosses them in the air, and Roland nearly falls into the hole. Juan holds out his hand to pull him up, but Roland is too heavy for Juan.

"Roland, I can't get a good hold on you. Why won't these bracelets work?" asks Juan.

"Don't give up now," says Roland. "I'm going to try to get a grip on part of this hanging piece of concrete, so I can get a foothold to climb out of this hole. Can you hear me? Please say something here."

"Roland, do you remember my vision of Kendra running away and a huge fireball?" asks Juan.

"Yes, I do," says Roland. "You didn't just say a fireball, right? Since we don't have enough problems right now."

Roland turns his head toward the night sky, and they see a huge, burning, yellow fireball heading toward them. Neither of them is able to retreat, and the fireball completely engulfs them like a blanket.

✳ ✳ ✳

When Kendra and Drake reach the top floor, they are in awe that they are so close to the antennas on top of the tower. Kendra doubles up in great pain, and Drake goes to her.

"What is the matter?" asks Drake.

"I don't know why, but it feels like something struck my heart with a fist," says Kendra. "Maybe Roland and Juan are in danger, or something worse."

"We must stay positive. We don't know anything for sure," says Drake.

Kendra feels a warm glow inside of her pocket, and she takes out the map to see a yellow arrow pointing toward the antennas. Drake notices the arrow. Kendra realizes the second piece must be at the top of one of the antennas, but she refuses to climb onto the antennas. She is quivering, since she's petrified of heights. Drake asks Kendra to use her bracelet to bring the second piece toward them. Kendra concentrates, but she doesn't seem able to bring the piece from its hiding place.

As they wonder what to do next, a powerful noise like an explosion crashes through the ground, sending small specks of glass to land on their heads. They use their hands to block the flow of glass and debris. They have barely recuperated from the falling glass when they hear the hissing of Apophis from below, amplifying their fears. To their relief, the sound stops. An angry Apophis forces its way through the ground, using its powerful and destructive tail like a crane to destroy more of the tower. Drake leads Kendra to the ledge, hoping to escape Apophis. But Kendra can't get her body to move. Drake refuses to leave her behind and gently holds out his hand. Kendra relaxes enough to take his hand and strolls onto the ledge.

Apophis hisses with the sound of a million rattlesnakes at them. Drake tries to stand in front of Kendra, but she steps in front of him instead. Kendra forms an invisible shield of her own for protection. Apophis takes a piece of the building's damaged antenna in his mouth, and the creature strikes the shield over and over with the antenna.

"If this banging keeps up, I'm going to lose control of this shield." Kendra sounds weary and worn-out.

Apophis successfully pushes his way through the shield and forces Kendra and Drake to mover closer to the edge of the building. Kendra makes another barrier, but it's too weak to stop the snake. She loses her energy to maintain the barrier, and Apophis takes advantage, moving toward them like a cat stalking its prey. Kendra doesn't have enough time to regain her strength, and the barrier starts to vanish. As Apophis prepares to attack, a small part of the antenna falls toward Drake. Drake uses quick reflexes to seize it, like a wide receiver catching a football. Apophis opens his mouth, covered in slime, to engulf the teens.

Drake looks over the ledge and swiftly gets an idea. "We should jump off before the barrier disappears for good."

"Are you nuts? I can't use my bracelet to fly," says Kendra.

The barrier soon fades away completely. Apophis is within swallowing distance. Drake fears the thought of becoming a meal for the hungry snake, but Kendra isn't willing to even consider his idea. So he carries her to the edge of the building and leaps off the Willis Tower with Kendra screaming at the top of her lungs. They find themselves not falling to the ground at a rapid speed but landing on the back of an eighty-foot flaming bird. This creature is known to some as the phoenix, but many refer to it as Ra. Kendra and Drake can't believe their eyes. They are sitting on top of the great legendary bird from mythology. Drake asks if she summoned this creature with her bracelet, but she denies it.

Kendra marvels at the phoenix's red-and-gold plumage, but the plumage isn't feathers. The plumage appears as red-and gold-flames that cover the creature's whole body with the exception of its red-and-purple tail. They aren't able to relax, because they observe Apophis and the Ra staring at one another with hatred. Kendra and Drake become concerned about falling off of Ra's back as the mighty creature flaps his wings to create the impression of a hurricane. They soon find that they are not only able to stand firm on the phoenix, but neither teen feels the intense heat of the phoenix's flaming body. Apophis uses his mouth to rip another piece of the tower's antenna and launches it at Ra. But the fiery bird, as powerful as the sun, increases the intensity of his flames to completely annihilate the antenna. Then Ra bellows an earsplitting shriek at Apophis that brings terrible pain to the creature. The shrieking sound shatters much of the windows at the tower and several other buildings.

Drake and Kendra cover their ears to protect themselves from Ra's devastating shriek. Apophis spits out a wave of slime at Ra, but Ra launches another flaming fireball to destroy the slime. In a great panic, Apophis hurries to escape Ra's attack and burrows through each level of the tower to reach the underground. The snake uses his mighty tail to grab ahold of an immobile Seth and it burrows his way through the streets to escape Ra. Drake looks on the creature's back and notices Roland and Juan both unconscious on Ra.

Kendra examines her brothers, placing her head on each one's chests to listen for a heartbeat.

"They are alive and well, and I'm so happy about getting away safe and sound from Apophis," says Kendra, relieved. "I can't explain it, but I feel safe with Ra, like this creature is a friend somehow."

"How are we able to sit on a flaming creature without feeling the flames?" Drake asks.

"Ra is a creature who stood for the protection of Egypt in Egyptian mythology, and those fighting on the side of good will not feel the wrath of its flames." Kendra explains.

"OK," says Drake. "What was with the stare-down between the two of them? They were acting like bitter enemies."

"Yes, Ra and Apophis fought against each other during the ancient time of Egypt. Apophis was—or is—one of the creatures of chaos who wanted to destroy the order of Egypt. He attacked Ra in the underworld many times for control, but Ra was a powerful creature. The battle ended with Ra enlisting Seth to fight Apophis. Seth thrust a great spear into Apophis, but Seth didn't kill the snake, as many thought he did." Kendra finishes.

"I get it," says Drake. "Seth got control of Apophis, so he could use the snake for his purpose." He adds, "I enjoy listening to you talk. I always learn so much."

"Thank you, Drake," says Kendra. "But I still owe you for tossing me off this building."

"Yes, but I knew I wasn't going to get a word in with you, so I took the chance of facing a flaming bird rather than being swallowed by a giant snake," says Drake.

Kendra hits Drake in his chest with humor and a smile on her face. Drake moves over to her brothers, planning to wake them up from their naps, but Kendra draws his hand away from them.

"You can't wake them up, since this is the most peaceful moment I've had around those two idiots," says Kendra, laughing. "I'm not going to allow you to spoil my time of happiness, and I can sense Ra wants to go wherever we want him to go."

Kendra and Drake look each other in the eyes again. Kendra knows Juan won't able to interrupt this time. She apologizes for misjudging him as a loser. Drake tells her about the pressures being the best athlete and student in the school. Drake was able to win several school championships that created an image of superiority in his mind toward others.

Drake asks her again about using her powers to learn this about him, but she gives her word about not seeking these answers. Drake says he felt that he was better than everyone else. Drake enjoyed bullying others like Roland and being look upon like a king for a long time. But Drake admits that his attitude started to change, when Roland had the guts to stand up to him at grade school. "But the real impact came from you, telling me about myself." Drake says. Kendra tells Drake that she was equally impressed with him this summer. When he stopped the other students from making fun of her, because her father embarrassed her at school. But she couldn't see past Drake's mistake to appreciate him until recent events changed her opinion of Drake.

"Hey," says Drake. "I did, however, fulfill my promise of a first date, since I chose to travel on Ra," says Drake.

"I don't think that jumping off a building and landing on the back of Ra counts as a date in my book," says Kendra. "So you need to come up with another plan, since I've got high expectations for you. There is one thing that you forgot to do on your so-called date, though."

"What?" asks Drake. "Did I forget to do else?"

"Is it no wonder that girls mature faster than boys?" Kendra asks.

Drake still doesn't know what Kendra is talking about, and she shakes her head at him. Ra shifts his huge body to bring Kendra and Drake together. So she takes the opportunity to kiss him gently on the lips, since she couldn't wait for him to make the first move on his own. Drake returns the kiss, but she soon feels something too strong to ignore. Then she looks at him with a shocked expression on her face, since she has discovered his trickery into getting her to kiss him first. He laughs at her, and they chuckle together about who is the so-called mature one.

Drake feels something piercing his chest, and he looks down to see a small three-inch piece of enriched, highly conductive metal. Kendra observes this unusual piece of metal, which is shaped like parallelogram. It doesn't appear to have come from the antenna. It's too different in its shape. Kendra touches this metal with her hand for a closer inspection. It changes form like a chameleon altering the color of its body to protect itself from predators. However, the piece doesn't change colors. Instead it transforms into the second triangular piece of Seth's pyramid. Kendra smiles at Drake for discovering it. He places his arm around her, while Ra spreads out his wing like the wings of an airplane. Ra's wingspan is actually ninety-five feet, and he could hold several passengers.

Ra leisurely flaps his wings in order to prevent causing a major windstorm, since the force of his wings could easily destroy apartments and other nearby homes below. The heat of his fiery body causes the temperature to go up in nearby areas, so people wake up feeling extremely hot, as if it's summer. They turn on their air conditioners or fans for some cool air. As Ra silently move through the city, people near the tower come out of their stupor to see the damage around the area. Soon after, everyone else recovers to hear the screaming sirens from the police and ambulances heading toward the tower.

The security guard who was knocked across the front entrance talks about witnessing a giant python taking his fellow guard. Other people tell of the sighting of a giant flaming bird in the sky, but no one believes them. One person was able to get a picture of this bird on his digital camera, but the police find no clear image on the camera. But no one thinks much about it, since they're more focused on the giant hole in the ground, the destroyed building, and the shattered windows. Everyone wonders what could have caused this devastation and how no one saw or heard anything out of the ordinary.

Kendra and Drake finally fall asleep in each other's arms, while Roland and Juan remain still on the left and right sides of Ra. Ra moves at low speed through the air to prevent the teens from falling off and to avoid damaging any of the neighborhoods. As Ra flies over the city, the light of Ra appears like the light from the morning sun, attracting people's attention. Some people think its some kind of technology trick, but many others see this creature as the real thing. Many try to get a picture with their cellphones, but Ra uses his own powers to place everyone in a daze, ordering them to return home. Everyone walks back to their homes for the evening, and Ra continues to carry the teens, like a plane heading for its next destination.

16

A TRUE FRIEND IN A TIME OF NEED

After the incredible events at the Willis Tower, reporters wait for answers about the cause of the damages. The Willis Tower closes for repairs while the police and Homeland Security inform reporters about a massive gas leak and internal electrical malfunctions that caused explosions. The agents, wearing their jet black three piece suits and sunglasses, examine samples of unusual slime and a large quantity of snakeskin, placing it in plastic bags for further study. They privately don't believe this was some simple gas leak, but they're using it as a cover story to avoid scaring people.

As the heat of the sun shines brightly through the windows, the teens begin to wake up from a long sleep to find themselves in four separate rooms at a stranger's house. Everyone calls out to one another, and the boys run into Kendra's room. Roland and Juan are still buzzing with excitement over Ra, who had rescued them from Apophis. Kendra tells her brothers about finding the second pyramid piece and how they are now one piece closer to stopping Seth, which makes them happy.

Kendra and Drake are happy for another reason as well, since they have discovered their true feelings for each other.

"This is so awesome!" shouts Juan. "Thoth is a genius. No one would have thought to look inside of the antenna of the Willis Tower for a piece to a pyramid."

"Weren't the two of you scared about being on Ra? Why didn't either of you wake us up to enjoy the moment?" asks Roland. "Or maybe there was another reason for allowing us to sleep."

Juan doesn't understand Roland's line of questioning, but he doesn't need her Kendra's ability to sense something new between the two of them. Roland decides not to question his sister further, since she wouldn't give him a straight answer anyway. Juan figures out the meaning of Roland's question, but he pretends not to know anything to keep from getting upset with him again. Everybody focuses on their current location. Juan looks around the room like a hawk, and then he goes back out of the room for a quick peek. After several minutes, Juan notices something familiar about this place, but he can't put all the pieces together. Roland and Drake fear this is part of some trap of Seth's, but Kendra isn't so sure. Kendra, who apparently has sharper eyesight than Juan, sees a small framed picture next to a clock radio on an oak desk. She sees their neighbor, Hardgrove, in the picture. Right then Hardgrove calls up to them to wash up and get ready to enjoy some mouth-watering food downstairs in the kitchen.

Drake, Kendra, and Roland wonder about how they got here, but Juan wishes to eat first and asks question later. Kendra heads straight into the bathroom first, to the dismay of her brothers. Roland tells Drake that this may take some time, and he turns on the TV. Hardgrove says there is a second bathroom downstairs in the basement, which makes Drake, Roland, and Juan clap and cheer for joy.

Juan is the first one to speak out. "Yes, with Kendra as a guest, every house should have an extra bathroom." They grab some towels and facecloths and dart to the basement. When they are finally clean, dressed, and ready to eat. Hardgrove tells the teens that it would a nice idea to straighten out their beds. After some time, their beds are folded neatly, appearing as if no one had ever slept on them. They walk into the dining room to find Hardgrove who is wearing a red-and-white polka-dot apron. He welcomes them to a delicious breakfast at his large dark cherrywood Chippendale table surrounded by six cherrywood chairs.

Everyone tries to relax and enjoy a decent meal instead of running for their lives. Drake is the first one to sit at the table and Kendra, eager to value every moment, throws herself in the seat next to Drake like someone playing a game of musical chairs. Roland and Juan sit on the opposite side. Juan, with the speed of a race car, moves over to get a plate, but Roland snatches his arm.

"Mr. Hardgrove, it is great to see you, but how did we end up in your house?" asks Kendra.

"I don't know. I was sleeping soundly," explains Hardgrove. "I heard a loud shrieking sound outside of my window and saw a light bright enough to be the sun. I went outside, and there were the four of you sleeping in the yard. I had to carry each one of you into my house. I had to move quickly, so no one would call the police to collect the reward. So I put each one of you in a different room. Incidentally, what made you all return to your own neighborhood? You must know that the police will be checking here. That was either two or three days ago."

"Excuse me, Mr. Hardgrove," says Roland. "But what day is it?"

"It is Monday, September, 12, Roland," says Hardgrove. "I was worried about all of you when none of you woke up. I thought about calling someone, but I decided to give it one more day."

Kendra and Roland whisper softly to each other. Kendra tells them that Seth escape on Wednesday, September, 7. Kendra laughs that Seth has only two days left to get their bracelets. They all think about finding the last piece of Seth's pyramid, so the teens can throw the pieces into the abyss out of Seth's reach forever. Hardgrove smiles at seeing them feeling better after their long sleep. He is curious about their welfare under the circumstances.

"We're indebted to you for not turning us in to the police or Homeland Security," says Kendra. "In spite of what the police and media have said about us being criminals."

A TRUE FRIEND IN A TIME OF NEED

"I didn't believe what the police or the news media are saying about any of you," says Hardgrove. "You can all stay here until the truth comes out about your innocence. In the meantime, I've fixed an excellent breakfast, and I don't want it to go to waste."

Juan grabs a decorative plate and places two pieces of bacon and two cheese omelets in the middle of two pancakes, and then he joyously puts some maple syrup on it. Roland and Drake couldn't wait to try Juan's breakfast sandwich for themselves, and they quickly fell in love with the combination of bacon, omelets, and pancakes.

As the boys enjoy eating their breakfast sandwich, Kendra stares at them with dismay. But Juan doesn't pay any attention to her, and he continues put away the food into his bottomless pit of a stomach. Kendra can't resist the aroma of the crispy bacon along with the flavorful cheese omelets, and she enjoys a little of each. It was like eating at a four-star restaurant that specialized in serving Chicago-style food. Kendra recalls watching a show on the Food Network about Hardgrove, who had cooked for some of the city's top restaurants until he chose to retire some time ago.

Drake isn't in a talking mood, and Roland is trying to keep up with Juan's eating. Kendra doesn't desire to appear greedy, so she eats very little. While Roland and Drake finish their food, Juan continues to eat more than his share. Kendra is embarrassed, and she can't take it anymore. But Hardgrove tells her not to hinder Juan's eating habits before she can get the words out of her mouth. He says Juan is a growing young man and tells for her to be patient with him. Kendra thinks about Juan being three growing young men. Juan finishes his pancake sandwich, dripping with more savory maple syrup. Kendra wonders how Hardgrove had known her thoughts prior to her saying anything, and this leads her to get suspicious about him. Hardgrove notices Kendra looking strangely at him.

Hardgrove looks directly at Kendra. "I want to know what I have done for you to be watching me like an eagle."

"I was just wondering why you chose to live in a such a large house, since you are the only person living here?" Kendra says.

"Kendra, why are you being so rude to Mr. Hardgrove?" demands Roland.

"No, it is OK, Roland," replied Hardgrove. "I acquired this house twenty years ago, when it was available for cheap. It was my hope to share this house with someone that I would marry someday. I don't have any regrets about buying this house. If you will excuse me, I want to clean up the dining room first and then the kitchen."

Roland offers to help clean up their plates, since they helped mess it up. But Hardgrove insists they are his unexpected guests, and he tells the teens to go play on his computer in the room upstairs near the bathroom. Drake insists that they are going to straighten out the beds and clean up the bathroom. Roland and Juan agree with Drake. Everyone leaves Hardgrove, so he can start cleaning up the kitchen. The teens walk into in the living room and they turn their attention to Kendra.

"Why did you treat Mr. Hardgrove like a criminal?" asks Roland. "He saved our lives from being discovered."

"I know he is risking going to jail, aiding accused criminals," says Kendra. "But with everything going on, I was just being cautious. Besides, there is something about him that I can't put my finger on."

"With your ability to read another person's feeling, you couldn't get any information from him," says Roland.

"I tried reading Mr. Hardgrove's feelings but I got a bunch of jumbo information," answers Kendra. "One moment, he was a simple neighbor who is concerned for our well-being, but there was another moment when he was thinking about someone from his past. Just then, my ability was blocked somehow. But I didn't sense anything evil or dangerous, so maybe I just overreacted."

"It is a special day when my sister admits being wrong about something," says Juan. "I would like to hear more, but I'm going upstairs to play some of Mr. Hardgrove's games on his computer. Hopefully, there is a sword-fighting game on his PC."

"Are you challenging me again?" Roland asks. "You were beaten so badly that I had to forfeit our last game due to your poor performance."

"This time is going to be different, since I've been practicing for a while," says Juan. "Even though Malcolm allowed Roland to take actual fencing classes, which has given him such an inflated ego."

"That's it," says Roland. "I want to take this upstairs, and after we straighten out the beds. Then I'll show you what real fencing is all about."

Roland and Juan run upstairs to prove their skills. Kendra can hear her brothers yelling from downstairs and turns to Drake. "I hate to admit it, but Roland is right."

"I can't imagine what it is like to have the whole city wanting to turn all three of you in for the reward," says Drake. "I still can't help thinking about Ra."

"This whole thing is the most unbelievable thing that has ever happened to me," answers Kendra. "But Ra is definitely in its own class."

"I don't understand something here. You say that the Ousias can't interfere," says Drake. "How come Ra isn't worried about facing the judgment of the other Ousias who choose to help us? Ra must have been the one who moved Seth's hands off my throat."

Kendra wonders why would Ra risk some much for them. Kendra recalls being helped by many people, but she couldn't accept Hardgrove finding the teens outside of his house. However, Kendra knows there are too many dangers from Seth and his followers to ignore. But she accepts the fact that they aren't the only ones who want to ensure the end of Seth. Drake tells her that it would be better to accept their help rather than question their reasons. Drake barely finishes his statement when Kendra hit him on his shoulder.

"Why was it necessary to hit me on the shoulder?" asks Drake.

"I didn't want to read your thoughts but I can feel your fear," says Kendra. "You want to leave us so Seth can't use you as a pawn to get our bracelets."

"It isn't right to tell another person's thought before that person can even speak their mind," says Drake. But it might be better if I wasn't around—"

"No, Seth is too dangerous. We can't separate from one another," says Kendra. "This is what Seth wants most of all—to divide us and make us vulnerable to him."

"Is that the only reason for your decision or could there be another reason?" asks Drake.

"Well, there might be another reason or not," Kendra answers.

Drake smiles at Kendra and watches as she strolls upstairs to Hardgrove's room. Drake goes off to clean up the bathroom. Drake wants to finish it quickly, so he can take another look at that magical map. Kendra notices a bright light shining under the crack of his door, and she closes her eyes against the blinding illumination. As Kendra knocks on the door, Hardgrove opens it and apologizes for the bright light, saying he is testing a special security light for the backyard. Kendra says she regrets her earlier rude behavior to him. Hardgrove accepts her apology and tells Kendra to hold onto her cautious attitude.

Their conversation is interrupted by Drake, calling Roland and Juan to come into the guest room. Hardgrove tells Kendra to remember this message: "Each of you contains a level of inner strength and power that will help out in your most terrifying moment." Kendra asks Hardgrove to explain himself, but Drake calls Kendra from the other room. She excuses herself and goes into the room. Roland is holding the map. The map begins to glow again to indicate the location of the third and final pyramid piece.

"The yellow arrow on the map is spinning in all directions, so I don't know where we are going next," says Juan.

Kendra places her bracelet on the map along with the first two pieces of the pyramid. The arrow spins around for a few more seconds, but it finally stops on the most unlikely place to their surprise. They look at each other, and then they start to laugh out loud like hyenas. Just then, a knock comes at the front door downstairs. Drake and Roland run downstairs to find out who's at the door, listening closely as someone speaks through the front door.

Roland recognizes the person knocking, to his great uneasiness. "Officer Tek is knocking at the door, and he's got a search warrant to search the house for us," mutters Drake to Hardgrove, who had just walked into the room.

Hardgrove calmly offers a way out. "Try to climb down the window, I will keep Officer Tek busy while all of you get out of here. If you ever need a place to stay for next time, then please feel free to sleep on my front lawn, OK?" he jokes.

They agonize for the safety of Hardgrove, but he insists there is nothing to fear. The knocking on the door increases, and Hardgrove yells out that he's getting dressed and to give him a minute. He moves to the door, leaving his friends. Drake moves over to the window and cracks open the drapes a little to see the lawn full of police and Homeland Security agents.

"There is nowhere to run," he says.

"Don't be afraid. We can get to the next location from here," says a relaxed Kendra.

Hardgrove opens the door, and the teens hear him talking to Officer Tek and the other police. Tek mentions that they had searched the house two days ago, but they need to search again. The teens wonder how the police didn't find them during their first search and where Hardgrove had hidden them from the authorities. They start to come around to Kendra's way of thinking about who this Hardgrove really is. Tek orders his fellow officers to search the house from top to bottom, but Hardgrove remains as cool as a cucumber.

Kendra places her bracelet on the map, and once again they're immediately dragged into the map like a person sipping water through a straw. Officer Ray opens Hardgrove's room to find no one inside, except, a floor covered in water and every other law official returns with the same empty house story.

Tek and the other officers leave his house, stopping by other houses, including Malcolm's house, to check for any signs of the teens. Hardgrove prepares to close the door, when he notices a red large feather near the door. It is in the exact spot that Hardgrove found the sleeping teens. As Hardgrove locks the door behind him, he places the feather inside his pocket. Hardgrove thinks about the teens and hopes no one catches them.

17

GO WEST, YOUNG TEENS

As the map appears outside, the water-like waves drag each person onto the street. Everybody looks around and upward to see the night sky filled with evening stars. Drake looks at his watch, and he realizes several hours have gone by in the blink of an eye. The teens are standing underneath an escalator, and everyone walks around it to discover many hotels in another city.

Roland, Juan, and Kendra laugh with excitement over the significance of it. Drake is very confused, since this whole magic thing is something completely new to him. Kendra walks over to Drake and tells him about Thoth's message at the hospital. She tells him how Seth's power had stopped them from leaving the city before, but now Seth must be too weak. He couldn't stop them from coming to Las Vegas. Drake finally understands their excitement, and he follows them to a strip mall. Fortunately, the people are focused on Las Vegas' entertainment options rather than the fugitive teens. Juan wants to go over to the roller coaster at the New York, but Kendra, with her fear of heights, doesn't even entertain such an idea. She brings out the map to get another look at it, and then they find the next location of Seth's third pyramid piece.

"We must have been moving in the map for hours, since it's nighttime here," says Roland.

"OK, so where do we go from here, so we can find the last piece of the pyramid?" asks Drake.

Kendra looks at the map carefully. A yellow arrow materializes wildly on the map like a compass pointing toward north, but the arrow isn't pointing near any of the hotels near them. Ultimately, the arrowhead points across the street, and everyone strolls straight ahead for a few minutes. They look to see Excalibur, a medieval-style hotel, and Juan hopes this is the place. But the arrow moves west of the hotel, and they proceed on foot for a few more blocks. They approach an Egyptian-type hotel, the Luxor. The arrow on the map stays centered on the hotel without moving in any other direction.

"I should have figured on this being the place. Where else would you hide a piece of Egyptian history?" says Kendra.

"I guess we should go looking for it and get out of here with the piece," says Roland. "So where do we look first, Kendra? The piece could be anywhere in this hotel."

They wander around the hotel, watching the crowd moving back and forth from the casino to the different shows. Kendra notices the Egyptian statues and artwork throughout the hotel, and Juan catches a glimpse of the glowing arrow on the map. They all take a peek at the map, and everyone sees an image of the Luxor hotel from the inside. Kendra leads the way, and it takes them into the casino.

After following the map in the hotel, they travel swiftly through a busy casino. They observe people moving around from one slot machine to another, while others are playing at the poker tables, the blackjack tables, and the roulette wheel, hoping to win the big prize. None of the teens sees anything unusual until the arrow points to a new game of images of the pharaoh's throne room dating back to ancient Egypt. As the teens approach it, they see hieroglyphics on the front.

Kendra translates the symbols. She nearly drops to her knees. The signs says, The Return Of Seth. The boys comfort her, and she tells them her translation. The game also shows the jackal-headed Seth battling the falcon-headed Horus, and the player must play alongside of Horus to stop Seth from rising to power.

"This could be a trap of some kind. It's very weird that Seth's followers have not discovered this game." Kendra sounds nervous.

"We can't leave here yet. The game allows one player to side with Horus against Seth," says Roland optimistically. "The person must travel through the underworld in an Egyptian boat and survive to win the game. But they'll have to maneuver around dangerous traps and pitfalls in order to succeed. Seth would never put a game that favors Horus against him."

Kendra goes around Roland so she can get a closer look at the game. Kendra notices the financial reward for winning the game, but suddenly some more words become visible on the game as well. The game offers to give a piece of the pyramid of Seth to the winner, and it concludes with reference to its designer, a mysterious man named Hermes. Kendra clears her throat, but she recovers to admit Roland is probably right about this game.

"What was I right about?" says Roland.

"When we first met Thoth at school, he told us that Hermes was his last name. He must have created this as a place to conceal the pyramid piece from Seth," says Kendra.

Drake observes the message on the game, and he reminds them that Thoth believed that the best way to hide something is in plain sight. Roland, Kendra, and Juan come to agree with Thoth, because none of them could see hiding pieces inside of a giant antenna in Chicago or in a casino game in Las Vegas. Kendra reads about how Thoth kept the part about winning the pyramid piece from materializing on the game, until he or the chosen ones decide to end Seth's plan forever. The message disappears from the screen.

"Once I win this game and get the last pyramid piece," says Kendra. "We are one step closer to ending Seth's plan and curing Dad and Thoth."

Roland stops Kendra. "There is one major problem to your plan. We're too young for the casino people to allow any of us to play this game, so what is your plan now?"

Kendra looks around to see casino workers watching them, and Drake, who had once visited this place with his uncle, informs them that the casino is under surveillance to protect the casino from cheaters or underage players. Things seem hopeless for them, until Kendra notices a young man who is standing near the stairway to the buffet. He looks to be about thirty years old. She begins to get an insight into this person, and Kendra leaves the others to check him out.

Roland looks around for Kendra, but she is nowhere in sight. Roland begins to worry about her, but soon she returns with a young, husky man with blue eyes dressed in torn blue jean shorts and a ripped blue-and-white torn T-shirt. He comes across as someone with a heavy burden on his shoulders, and Roland isn't pleased about Kendra bringing a stranger to them. He pulls Kendra to the side while Drake and Juan keep an eye on her new friend.

"Are you out of your mind bringing some stranger here? This guy could be a follower of Seth!" Roland says.

"My ability didn't pick up on any deception in him," responds Kendra. "Besides, I could read the fear upon him, for good reason. He wired himself some money for a down on a house in North Las Vegas. He placed the check in his pocket, but now he can't find it. He's going crazy trying to retrace his steps with no success, and there isn't any easy way for him to tell his wife about it."

"Your friend is in a lot of trouble. So what can we do to help him?" says Roland.

"His name is Hank. He is one of the best players in Las Vegas, and I told him about playing this game," answered Kendra. "Hank wasn't too sure about doing this, but he believes that he can beat this game We can help each other out with just one game, so if you have a better idea, then I'm all ears."

Roland can't think of anything. There is no other option for Hank, so he agrees to play the game. The others doubt this guy can win anything, since he managed to lose his money. Kendra believes in Hank, though, and she offers to guide him. Hank doesn't want to get them into trouble with security, so he asks them to trust him. Kendra can feel the radiance of confidence inside of him. The others are not thrilled with this idea, since there is so much on the line. Nevertheless, they put their trust in Hank and Kendra, and he is able to progress through each level with ease for the next hour. Over the next half an hour on the game, Hank fights his way through Seth's sobeks, snakes, and other terrors with speed, and soon he defeats Seth, marking the end of the final level to exit the underworld.

The game sounds with cheers and trumpet sounds. An automated voice speaks of someone winning the grand prize of $100,000 and receiving a three-inch triangular piece of an original pyramid. Several people cheer for Hank, and he proposes to give the teens something for encouraging him to play. But Kendra and Roland want only for the piece of the pyramid—to the dismay of Juan, who desires the money as well. Hank hugs her with gratitude and thanks the others for their support. An official of the hotel comes over to give him his money. They say their good-byes to Hank, and he wonders about the identity of these teens. Hank uses his Blackberry to text his wife about the good news. Juan observes people walking back and forth out of the casino, and he sees something shiny on the ground. People don't even notice it as they walk on the object, but Juan moves to pick up the object for a closer look.

"Hey, I found this gold coin on the floor here. There is a human eyebrow and eye on one side," Juan is excited. "There are also words on the other side, and it is a very weird message: This coin will become visible to one who sees the truth without using his eyes, but the true holder of Horus's power will belong to another."

Kendra examines the coin, and she observes a distinctive brassy sheen to it. Kendra bites the coin slightly to feel its hardness. Kendra tells Juan not to accept this gold as real, and she insists that Juan throw it in the trash. She tells him that the casino workers were probably giving these fake coins to the tourists. Juan refuses to believe her, but Kendra doesn't back off. "This isn't real gold, but it is actually fool's gold," says Kendra. "Real gold is very soft, and this so-called gold coin was hard enough to break my tooth. Wait a minute. I can prove it to you right here, so keep your eyes on this."

Kendra notices a middle-aged woman wearing a pink dress with an elegant pink flamingo-looking hat on her head. This lady reminds her of her friend, Glitter, who is a lover of all things pink. Kendra sees the woman using a small rectangular magnet to hold her keys. She taps the woman gently on her shoulder and asks to borrow her magnet for a science experiment. The lady gives Kendra her keychain, and Kendra moves Juan's gold coin toward the magnet. The coin becomes attracted to the magnet. Kendra returns the magnet to the woman, who tips her flamingo hat to say good-bye. Kendra tells Juan that real gold isn't attracted to magnets as other metals would be. Roland wants to believe Juan, but he agrees with Kendra about the coin being a fake.

Juan places the coin in his pocket. "I'm not going to believe either one of you, since this coin is real."

Roland and Kendra prepare to begin their search for the abyss, but Drake calls out to everyone. He points out several men wearing either a solid royal blue or light gold suit, and Kendra reads their feeling. They are another group of fortune hunters that recognize the teens from the news. Several men approach the teens with greed in their hearts, and Kendra gets a senses of Tek nearby. She doesn't see him anywhere, and Drake pulls Kendra away to avoid those fortune hunters. Several security guards see the teens and prepare to arrest them. Roland tells the others to back slowly toward the exit, but as they move through the crowd of people, a slender striking lady gazes at them, and she remains strangely hidden in the background with Tek. Tek wants to get the teens, but she grabs hold of Tek. The woman orders Tek to stand quietly and do nothing. The casino security guards take out handcuffs, and they hold the handcuffs out slightly to signal an arrest. The security guards tell the men to move away from the teens. But the men are fortune hunters that recognize the teens as the escaped fugitives from the news. They want the reward money for themselves and refuse to leave. Soon after, more and more people circle the teens with desire to claim their fortune, and they surround the guards with the intention of getting the teens. Roland wants to use his power to move the guards and the fortune hunters away. Kendra fears the crowd would overrun them before they could get away.

Drake whispers something to Roland, who whisper something of his own to the others. Tek observes them looking at people at several slot machines. Tek begins to get very nervous, and Roland yells out, "Now!" Before the people and the guards can react the machines begin spinning out of control, releasing winning tickets along with coins on the floor. Soon after, the crowd runs over to the machines and starts to grab every ticket and coin.

Roland and the others are able to make their way past the crowd, but the guards are unable to get through the rush of people. It's like being on a crowded train or bus during rush hour. The teens run out of the casino and head for the escalator, and some of the fortune hunters chase them. Roland brought some of the winning tickets from the casino with him, and he throws them in the direction of people walking toward the Luxor.

Many of the people dash over to grab some of the tickets, and Roland tells them about free winning tickets all over the floor of the Luxor casino, making them run like cheetahs. The teens travel to the escalator that connects the Luxor with the Excalibur hotel. As they continue to run, Juan catches a glimpse of the medieval show. Roland promptly takes out some money and purchases tickets for the show. They run downstairs to the show, with some fortune hunters in hot pursuit. They find themselves looking cautiously at being on the third level, with the medieval show below and no other way out.

"We are trapped," says Kendra. "How are we going to escape from these fortune hunters? Not to mention, Tek is somewhere in the area. At least, we can enjoy the show as they are taking us away in handcuffs—thanks to Roland's brilliant sense of direction."

"I know this is going to sound crazy, but I suddenly got this irresistible idea," suggests Roland. "If we jump from here, then we can make it to the stage. I can't explain it, but we've got to trust in the strength of these bracelets to land safely."

Kendra gets a sense of déjà vu. "Mr. Hardgrove told me about trusting in our hidden strength, but I wonder if he had this in mind," she says "But Drake doesn't have a bracelet to protect himself."

Roland tells everyone to take hold of each other's hands, especially Drake, and they look downward to the stage where the medieval show is taking place. They watch the last round of the jousting match, and the crowd begins cheering for the knights who climb down off their horses to take a bow for their great performance.

The fortune hunters doesn't want to give up on being rich and run over to catch the teens. However, the teens leap into the air and land without any problem on the stage, to the shock of the crowd, and the performers. To add to the weirdness, an eye-catching and dazzling slender red-haired lady, with dark raven like eyes, stands next to Tek and watches as she opens a small calcite canopic jar with the wooden head of Seth on top. The jar releases a powerful white mist into the air and rests in the direction of the fortune hunters and other security guards. They breath in the mist, and it increases their desire to capture the teens at any cost. Several security guards and the fortune hunters rush on stage to move toward the teens.

The teens begin to run and try to avoid the guards and the fortune hunters. Kendra tells them that something other than the money is driving the entire group. Juan think that it must be Tek who is doing this to those people. Drake wonders if they should use their magic to escape, and the teens try with no success. Roland fears they are too tired for their magic to work.

Many in the crowd start cheering with excitement, since they think this is part of the show. The performers don't know what to do about this, but Roland shouts out for them to get out of the way. They follow Roland's suggestion to leave the stage. The performers find themselves in the unusual position of being part of the audience, as they witness the teens climbing onboard horses to escape them.

"We can make a run for the exit, before the guards and the fortune hunters can catch us," says Roland.

"Are you all right, Juan?" asks Kendra.

"Yes. Don't worry about me—this isn't my first time riding a horse," says Juan.

The fortune hunters and the guards climb onboard horses and catch after the teens. The teens are caught in the middle between the fortune seeking men and the security guards. Roland and the others are to weak to create even a shield to protect them.

THE OUSIAS

"I know you can't keep running forever in your weaken condition, but I've got an idea," says Drake. "Maybe the key isn't to defend against them. My father tells me all the time that sometimes the best defense is a good offense, so this could work for us. Can you use a tiny bit of your magic for something?"

The teens admit being strong enough. Drake tells Roland his idea, but Kendra doesn't agree with using some sport strategy to escape these creatures. Roland refuses to listen to her on this one, since there isn't any other way to avoid them. Juan pumps his fist in support of his brother. Juan reminds Kendra that they supported her ideas. Kendra agrees with Juan, so she goes along with Drake's plan.

After Roland explains the plan, they each split of their approach to these creatures. Roland and Juan make a run for the security guards, and they are able to use a their bracelets to blow dirt in his face. At the same time, Kendra and Drake go straight ahead at the fortune seeking men, using her bracelet to do the same thing as Roland.

The crowd and the performers, who doesn't what to make stand out of the way, enjoy the show. The fortune hunters and the guards find it difficult to see the teens. They continue to approach the teens on either side at top speed and come within inches of smashing into them. At the last moment, Roland and Drake nod their heads, and they move their horses to the side. They hit head-on into each other. The crowd cheers when they see this crash, and they give the teens a standing ovation for their performance. Juan, Roland, and Drake take a bow for the next few moments.

"I don't want to interfere with your ovation, but those fortune seeking men are starting to recover again," says Kendra annoyed. "So we should leave now or let your new fans watch you being arrested."

Everyone agrees with Kendra, so they run toward the backstage to escape. Tek and his associate, in particular the one woman look on with anger, and they rapidly walk out of the show, leaving the performers to acknowledge and accept the applause from the crowd. The performers decide not to seek any answers about the teens or anything else. Tek go outside, wanting to pursue the teens, but the mysterious woman tells him to go to the airport. Tek knows Seth can find them with the Rosetta stone that led him to Las Vegas. She mentions Seth wants Tek to return to Chicago. Tek reluctantly agrees. The mystery woman walks outside and finds an isolate area. She then transforms into a raven and flies in the direction of the teens.

After running around for some time, everyone makes their way to the front entrance of the hotel. They look around for away out, and Roland sees several cabs waiting to pick up people. Drake calls for one of them, and the cab driver pulls up.

But before they can get into the cab, the fortune hunters catch up to the teens. They prepare to arrest the teens, until the street begins to crack around them. Two of the men are lifted off the ground, and the teens see Apophis using his tongue to swallow the men. Bearing witness to this, the cab driver leaves his cab behind in terror, and the remaining men forget about the reward to hightail it out of there. The teens are alone in the presence of Apophis.

As other people walk down the strip, they begin to scream and run in horror from the giant snake. Roland looks curiously to Kendra for answers, but she is too afraid to think of anything.

"Who is going to drive this cab, since we don't have a driver now?" asks a frightened Kendra.

Drake motions for them to get in the cab. "Don't be afraid. You're all in good hands."

As Apophis reaches out to attack the cab, Drake drives speedily out of creature's path. Apophis catch after the cab. Everyone hangs on as Drake makes a sharp turn, going west to avoid the giant snake, but Apophis is able to keep up. Apophis's scaly body knocks every vehicle out of its way. Kendra takes the three pyramid pieces and places them on the map with her bracelet to find the abyss. The map glows again with the yellow arrow, but the arrow isn't pointing west like they had expected. The arrow is pointing east toward Arizona, and the famous tourist spot nearby.

"Drake, we have to turn around now—the arrow on the map is going in the other direction," yells Kendra.

"You have got to be kidding me here. Does the map know a huge snake is chasing us?" shouts Drake.

Drake gives an angry look at Kendra before making a U-turn to the rage of the other drivers. But as they witness a giant serpent coming toward them, many drivers ignore drake's driving to swirl their cars out of the way.

"We have to go the Grand Canyon. That is located in Coconino County, Arizona," says Kendra, looking at him cross-eyed. "So we can get to the abyss."

Roland taps Drake on his shoulder. "Dude, I have an idea of my own here, and it begins with us going real fast toward the Grand Canyon. Do you recall that movie with the race car drivers and how they escaped their pursuers?"

"Dude, I get it now. I'm going to push it to the pedal," agrees an eager Drake.

"Do you know what these two geniuses are talking about?" asks Kendra.

"Yes, I can translate the dude language," says Juan. "But you're not going to like the answer."

"I don't know what scares me more," says Kendra. "Roland and Drake found some new type of dude language, or the prospect of being a meal for Apophis."

Juan tells Kendra their plan, and she develops strong anxiety. Drake makes a sharp turn for the Exit 48 at Craig Road. Apophis doesn't give up the chase, and he uses his long tongue to force cars off the road. Drake begins swerving the cab from left to right so Apophis can't take the cab with his tongue. Apophis starts to gain momentarily and is about to take hold of the taxi, but Drake strikes a bump in the road, and Kendra's hand fall onto the wheel, somehow increasing the taxi's speed. Kendra, Roland, and Juan have regained some of their strength to use their bracelets, and Drake is happy about it.

"Whoa, how are we going so fast? We were going sixty, and now we're going eighty-five miles per hour," says Drake. "Wait—the speed of the cab increases with the touch of your bracelet. This is what I call living life on the edge! Apophis can just eat our dust."

Everybody waves good-bye. Kendra doesn't want to chance hitting a car at such an uncontrolled speed, so she asks Roland and Juan to focus their bracelets together with hers to prevent this. They follow her suggestion to the letter, and the cab becomes transparent, moving through other vehicles like air without hurting anyone. The taxi goes from eighty-five to almost on hundred miles per hours in seconds. The driving distance from Las Vegas to Coconino County is a little under five hours, but it quickly changes to less than an hour with their speed going higher every minute. Juan wishes this taxi could actually fly in the air, but his thoughts cause the teens to lose focus. It makes the taxi solid again, and Apophis smashes the cab's windows with his tongue.

Apophis grabs hold of Juan for a second with his slimy tongue, and Roland, panicking, looks for something to help him. Apophis pulls even harder on Juan, but he is able to hold on to the backseat with Roland holding Juan's arms. Drake feels something under his feet, and he uses his left foot to move the object toward the front. Drake sees a battery-operated nail gun, and he bends over with his other hand to take it. Drake motions for Roland to take the nail gun, and Roland uses it to attack Apophis' tongue. Apophis screeches out in pain and loses its hold on Juan. This only increases the rage of Apophis, and he travels even faster to catch them. Drake finally is able to make a turn onto Highway 67 and finds them within striking distance of the north rim of the Grand Canyon.

"You have to get the map working to take us to the abyss, but it's got to be time just right," says Roland. "The key is for us not to lose Apophis but to let Apophis catch us."

"I get your great plan now, and it isn't bad for two dudes," says Kendra.

As they speed for the Grand Canyon, they come upon the Bright Angel Point near the north rim of the Grand Canyon. Tourists gathered there see a speeding car with a huge snake chasing it. People begin running away although some visitors move just far enough to get a picture with their camcorders or digital cameras. Kendra sticks her head out of the cab window to see Apophis, before checking the map that will take them to the abyss.

"OK, we are within range of the north rim near the Colorado River, so I'm ready to begin this scary plan," says Kendra uncertainty.

Kendra, Roland, and Juan stop using their magic on the cab, and it comes to a halt. Almost immediately, Apophis gets ahold of the cab, and Drake tells them to use their bracelets to increase the cab's speed at once. The map starts to magically pull them into it. Apophis can't slow his momentum and falls thousands of feet over the rim. Apophis lands very hard into the Colorado River, splashing vast amounts of water in every direction, leaving startled hikers soaking wet.

18

THE DECEIVER

At the THES pyramid, it is now the sixth day from Seth's escape from his prison. Seth has only one day left to gain his items, or he faces the prospect of death on the seventh day. He is contemplating the thought of losing his goal of conquest when he looks in the sky at a raven. It is dark; the sky has no stars or moon. But the raven flies in the window and lands on the floor of Seth's room with no problem. It transforms into a striking young woman wearing a black headdress and a long white shawl. The shawl is covered with a gold beads and a turquoise necklace, enhancing her outer beauty.

An angry Seth smashes his fist on the desk with rage. "How can those brats get away from Apophis and evade those greedy fortune seeking humans so easily? There is only a little time left until the seventh day. They are now beyond the borders of this country, and I'm too weak from their last attack to force them back here."

The mysterious lady speaks of her charms. "I'm the embodiment of love and beauty, and it is my fate to succeed for you. After all, you didn't bring me back from my imprisonment so I can fail you. There is a way to get your pyramid pieces and their bracelets so your rise to power will happen once again. I have found a weakness in those chosen ones. Tek gave me some background information, and I saw them in action today. I'll go after the weakest one of the three and use my powers of persuasion."

Seth doesn't put up any argument against her solution; instead, he thinks about his real enemy. And he knows the powerful creature known as Ra must die in great pain, since he figures Ra will interfere with his plan again. He moves closer toward the mysterious lady so he can hear her plan. But two sobeks come into the room, holding two women in their arms like prisoners. Seth demands an explanation especially since one woman is Ray's wife and the other one is his daughter, Eyeshadow.

The woman explains how she was doing some research on the teens, but she became suspicious of Tek's partner. So she gave the order for the sobeks to kidnap Ray's family. Mrs. Hightowers and Eyeshadow look at these horrible creatures with horror, and they approach Seth with fright in their hearts. But the sobeks push the women's heads down to show respect for their leader. Mrs. Hightowers begs for her daughter's freedom; however, this doesn't matter to Seth.

"No, your presence will help ensure my rule of the world, so you are both now my guests," says a desperate Seth. "But don't fear for your daughter's safety, since you are both my special guests. Once this world is under my control, then I will deal with the professed Ousias living in Utopia. My dreams rest in your charming hands, so don't fail me, my enchantress," he says to the mysterious woman.

Seth refuses to call her by name until she holds his missing items. He cares only about reclaiming his pyramid pieces and the teens' bracelets. She presents her plan to him. Seth nods his head in approval, and he motions for the woman to hold out her hand. He puts a silver ring on her left hand and whispers about how to use it at the proper time. She accepts his ring with pleasure and opens a small hatch on the ring to find an ounce of Apophis's slime inside. She strolls into one of the offices in the pyramid and rubs some of the slime onto her arm. She falls into a dreamlike state on the brown couch.

✺ ✺ ✺

As everyone prepares the pyramid for Seth's triumph, Officer Ray is looking for his wife. He calls his daughter with no result as well. A strong fearful chill goes down his back, and he remembers seeing his partner earlier with a very attractive woman, whom he has never seen with Tek before today. He recalls Tek leaving for a mysterious reason. Ray knows Tek wants nothing more than to catch the teens at any cost.

Ray remembers this woman staring at him for several minutes, and it had left him extremely uncomfortable. Tek had introduced the woman as an old friend of his from high school, but he never told Ray her name or anything about his leaving Chicago. Ray hits himself on the head. He now realizes something very wrong with this picture. This only adds to his concern about Tek's involvement in the Witmores' case and Ray recalls that one of the officers talk about Tek being at the THES building. Ray gets in car and drives down there.

As Ray's concerns increase, he uses the siren to move through traffic quickly in his patrol car. After forty-five minutes, Ray finally makes it to the THES building. Ray sees the building's security people closing for the night, but he uses his badge to try to get inside. The security guards refuses to allow him to go any farther, and they tell him to leave the premises. Ray doesn't want to argue with them. He walks out of view of the security, but he remembers visiting this place a few times. Ray uses his memory to guide him around the back of the building, where he notices the shift change taking place between the afternoon guards and the overnight guards. Ray swiftly goes past them into the dock area and discovers a back door to the elevators. He sneaks in the door and finds work clothes from the maintenance crew. Ray goes into a vacant room and put on an old gray uniform with black oil stains.

Ray begins to sweat with nerves about being here, but his family's safety drives him to move forward. He walks into the dark, half-lit hallway and takes the elevator to another floor to search for his family. Ray suddenly recalls Tek taking him on a tour of the THES building months ago, but he remembers Tek not allowing him to go on a certain floor which he said was being isolated.

Ray slowly sticks his head out of the elevator for a second to watch for people. No one is around. So he moves from the empty floor to the restricted floor, but there isn't anyone there either. He begins to smell the aroma of cinnamon, nutmeg, and the light scent of a rose. Ray spots a bright light coming from one of the offices, and he approaches the door to find it unlocked. He opens the door very slightly to recognize the attractive woman, who is the same friend of Tek's, resting on a couch near the front door, but she isn't moving an inch on the couch.

He checks her pulse, but there nothing is out of the ordinary. Ray is mulling over his next options when a mist-like fog surrounds her whole body. He looks around with trepidation but the fog vanishes without a trace. When he looks back, he sees an empty couch. Ray becomes convinced this is all a part of an even larger mystery, but he keeps his focus on the location of his family. Without warning, a sobek comes into the room with a sword in his hand. The sobek tosses Ray to the floor very hard and points his sword at him. But the creature bursts into flames, and the sobek turns to cinder Ray recovers enough to see an elderly man standing over him, and he holds out his hand to help Ray off the ground.

Ray recognizes this man as Mr. Hardgrove, the teens' neighbor since he had questioned him about them. "You aren't just a regular neighbor, are you? How did you make those flames appear over the creature? What kind of creature was it anyway?" Ray asks.

"The creature was a sobek and they protect this building for their master," says Hardgrove. "You want to know my identity. That's a story for another time, but I was trying to get something from the dark creature called Seth. It was a lucky thing for you, or this sobek would have captured you like your wife and daughter."

"No! If my family is in the hands of some evil creature, then I have to save them," says a frantic Ray.

Ray isn't concerned with Hardgrove's thoughts, and he pushes his way past him.

Hardgrove seizes Ray just in time. Two of the sobeks walk into the room. The sobeks move past both of them without paying any attention, and Hardgrove tells Ray that he made them invisible to the sobeks and everyone else. Hardgrove gives him a quick synopsis of Seth and his involvement with the Witmores. Ray remembers reading about Egyptian mythology when he was a young teen. But he couldn't get himself to believe in any of it until now. It takes some time for Ray to accept this, but he loses focus when two more sobeks enter the room with his wife and daughter. The creatures are growling at them. Ray can't watch the scared and panicked looks on their faces, and he strikes Hardgrove in the face. But it isn't Hardgrove who is in pain, but Ray screaming in agony. Hardgrove's hand feels like concrete to Ray, and he uses his ability to reduce the pain in Ray's hand. It makes him feel a lot more relaxed and comfortable than before.

"What, is your face made of granite? Why won't you help them?" asks Ray.

"My power isn't strong enough to help them or to protect you from harm," says Hardgrove.

Ray can't deal with his inability to help his family. Just then, Tek enters the room with delight on his face. Ray realizes that Tek must be a follower of this Seth. Hardgrove senses Ray's rage upon seeing him; Ray tries to run at Tek. But Hardgrove places his hand on Ray's shoulder to increase his discomfort, and Hardgrove proves his point to him with only a finger.

Seth steps into the room, and he looks at the others with dominance. Mrs. Hightowers demands to know why Tek would help a monster, but Seth just laughs at their weakness. He doesn't consider the people of this century capable of stopping him. Seth fears the teens only because they hold the keys to his power.

"Tek chose to join forces to share in the great power to come, since my destiny is to conquer the world," says Seth. "Once I receive my items from the young Witmores, I'll rise to power as was meant to happen long ago."

"My friend will never help a horrible monster like you, so don't hold your ugly breath," shouts Eyeshadow.

"You both enjoy calling me a monster like it means something, but I've read about the history of the people of this world," says Seth. "I take the term 'monster' as a great honor, since the people of this world have done more crimes and horrible acts to each other than anyone from my time."

Hardgrove explains that Seth broke free from his prison almost a week ago. Hardgrove reveals that if Seth gets these items by the beginning of the seventh day, then he shall have the power to unleash the plagues of Egypt upon the modern world. In addition, Seth will become fully corporeal with the power to open the underworld on the eighth day and rule the world. Hardgrove concludes that the Ousias chose not to interfere with the human race and instead chose the Witmores to help mankind.

"This was my choice to assist them and you," explains Hardgrove. "The other Ousias diminish my powers for interfering here."

"I don't care about your rules and breaking them. My concerns are with my family," says Ray.

One of the sobeks gives Seth an original glass canopic jar, and he carefully opens it. The sobek backs away from them, and Seth releases the contents of the jar in front of them. A hideous musky odor comes out of the jar, and everyone covers their noses to avoid breathing in the smell. Eyeshadow and Mrs. Hightowers breathe in the odor and begin to shrink to the size of an insect.

Ray and Hardgrove watch this assault with horror. Seth orders Tek to put Mrs. Hightowers and her daughter in the jar, and Tek grabs them with both hands. Tek looks at Mrs Hightowers with desire in his heart. He holds her with his right hand and tries to kiss her, to the anger of Ray. A minimized Eyeshadow bites Tek's hand to protect her mother, and Tek squeezes Eyeshadow tightly with his left hand. As Eyeshadow screams with anguish, Seth orders him to place them in the jar. Tek obeys his order and he places them inside of the canopic jar. Seth reminds Tek not to disobey his orders again, and he tells him to keep an eye out for his partner.

"I want them to bear witness to my triumph of this world, and then you can do as you please with them," says Seth. "In the meantime, my future queen is about to get my items to me, so I'm going to meet her. What in the world is…?"

Seth stops to survey the room, since he had briefly seen images in front of him. But Seth couldn't see anything or anyone now, and Tek moves over to inquire about his leader's discomfort.

"I thought I saw someone in front of me for a second, but the image wasn't clear enough to be sure," says Seth. "But I don't see anything now, so it was just my imagination. I'm going to my room to wait for my future queen to accomplish her plan. There are only a few hours left to claim those items before the seventh day begins. If she is able to complete her goal, then I'm going to win."

Seth tells Tek to prepare the area for his return and promptly leaves Tek's presence. Ray stands dejectedly with Hardgrove. He is frustrated by his inability to help his family. But Hardgrove takes him out of Seth's room and walks to an empty office down the hallway.

"Why couldn't you have done something more to stop this evil creature, since you have the power to make us invisible?" Rays asks. "Besides, my duties as a cop won't let me just stand by and do nothing to stop Seth. Not to mention—what are you in the first place, since you're not all human?"

"That would take too long to clarify, but you can be sure of my desire to help mankind," says a serene Hardgrove. "In any event, I don't possess the power to stop Seth or confront him directly either. If you are willing to trust me here, there is a way for you to stop Seth."

"No. I can't now or ever put my trust in you," says Ray.

Hardgrove touches him on his left shoulder, and Ray turns into a statue. "Please forgive me, but I couldn't risk your life in a failed attempt. You can't move, but you can hear me. When the time is right, you will know what to do in regard to your family."

Hardgrove continues to talk to him about his importance not only to his family but to all mankind. He tells a silent Ray the whole story surrounding the Ousias, since he fears not being around to tell this story to anyone. He speaks to him for a while, and Hardgrove uses Ray's subconscious as a storage area to hide this information deep within him for safekeeping. He thinks of one last message to add to Ray's memory. "Mankind shall someday face a terrible time like no other, and the key to mankind's survival lies in keeping hope alive." Hardgrove thinks about this message being understood in the proper time. Until then, he moves Ray's lifeless, invisible body into an empty office and prepares to leave him.

He uses his power to keep Ray invisible for the time being, and Hardgrove searches every inch of this room with a fine-tooth comb to find for an item belonging to Seth. He gets a strong sensation coming from a closet in the corner. Hardgrove looks inside in search of this mystery item with no results. He wants to use his ability to find it, but he can't use too much of it, since Seth almost saw him and Ray earlier. So Hardgrove uses his senses to probe the darkness of the closet, much like a bat using radar to find its way around. But he doesn't find anything. Hardgrove doesn't give up the search, though, and finally he touches something underneath in the far end. He examines the item to his satisfaction, and Hardgrove magically disappears with it out of the THES building.

19

RIDDLE OF THE SPHINX

After moving around within the map for a while, the four teens fall hard to the ground. Everybody recuperate nicely from the fall, and they observe the appearance of sand in all directions. Kendra concludes this is a desert area, so she tries to determine the location. Meanwhile, Roland, Juan, and Drake notice the nighttime view of the sky and remember fleeing from Apophis in the middle of the day in Las Vegas. Kendra tells them to turn around. They turn to see themselves several feet from an incredible 241-foot-long structure that possesses the body of lion and the head of a human with a missing nose. Kendra realizes this is the city of Giza, and she recognizes this structure as one of the seven wonders of the world, the Great Sphinx.

Roland and Drake view the desert with awe, aware they have traveled halfway around the world to Egypt. None of them has ever been to Egypt, and this is truly an amazing sight for them to see with their own eyes.

"Wow," shouts Kendra. "Seth doesn't have much time left till the seventh day begins. There is no way he can reach us in time. Now we can throw those pyramid pieces into the abyss and help free Malcolm and Thoth from their comas."

Kendra had just finished her thoughts when the map's arrow appears to glow toward the Great Sphinx. No one notices that Juan is the only one without any feelings or reaction to being in Egypt. But Roland looks at his brother, silent in a daydream, and he worries about his lack of emotion. He begins to shake Juan's shoulder to snap him out his stupor. Juan comes out of it, and he informs them about viewing a vision of his mother and father. He says he saw them being held as prisoners of Seth's followers in the sphinx.

"Are you sure? No one knows about us being the chosen ones," asks Kendra. "So how could the followers of Seth know to kidnap your real parents? Even Thoth didn't know about us."

"No!" screams Juan. "How can you tell me that my vision is wrong, since all of my visions have come true so far?"

Roland and Drake side with Kendra. A small sandstorm blows next to Juan. It temporarily blinds the whole group, but then the storm subsides to reveal an attractive woman with ruby hair standing next to Juan. He recognizes her as his mother.

The boys are dazed by this woman's beauty, but Kendra isn't so affected. She smells a strong fragrance radiating from her. Kendra identifies the strong scent of jasmine, and she begins to realize the effect of this hypnotic scent on Roland, Drake, and especially Juan. Kendra tries to get the others to ignore the woman, but no one can resist the temptation. Roland and Drake are too immobilized to do anything, so Kendra decides to stop Juan from trusting this woman. Juan explains to Kendra that his mother gave me up for adoption to protect him from Seth's followers, but they found her anyway. He says that his mother was being held in the abyss, and his father as well. Kendra scratches her head, since Juan's father was separated from his mother before his birth. She tries to convince him to rethink his decision, but he refuses to turn his back on his parents.

"I won't let you do this, since I seem to be the only sane person left here," says Kendra. "I don't believe your lies to my brother. You aren't Juan's mother."

Kendra moves toward the woman, but Juan steps in to snatch the map from her.

She tries to grab the map back from Juan, but he pushes her to the ground. Kendra gets back up in an attempt to retrieve the map, and she runs into an invisible barrier between her and Juan's so-called mother. Kendra tries using her bracelet, but it isn't able to make a scratch in the shield.

Roland and Drake continue to watch like statues, and Kendra yells at the top of her lungs for Juan to stop. Juan doesn't hear her at all, and Juan and the woman walk rapidly toward the sphinx. Kendra turns to Roland and Drake, who are still in a spell, and she sees a light coming from the left side of the sphinx. Juan places the map in front of him like a key, and the door opens to allow them to enter inside. Roland and Drake come out of their daze like someone waking up from a dream, and Kendra moves toward them with distress in her heart.

"What's going on here, and where is Juan?" asks Roland.

"Yes, the only thing that I remember was seeing the actresses, Lisa Rise, from the movie, *The Inner World*," says Drake.

"I recall smelling jasmine and looking at the supermodel, Dee Moorehead," says Roland.

"Well, while the two of you were in a dream, this woman pretended to be Juan's mother," explains Kendra. "She convinced him to open a doorway into the Great Sphinx, and Juan led her into it. I tried to stop him, with no success. This must be part of Seth's plan to get his pyramid pieces back. Juan isn't willing to see through this deception, but there is another problem."

"What do you mean 'another problem'? Juan walked off with the stranger willingly?" asks Roland.

"When Juan pushed me away, I saw this woman's true appearance," says Kendra. "She had the face of a cow, and do you know what that means for Juan?"

"Are you trying to say that she's ugly?" Drake asks.

Kendra's face changes to stone with anger, but she can't waste more time proving her point. She says that they must go into the sphinx to stop Juan, so Drake and Roland put aside their confusion in order to assist Kendra. They approach the sphinx with amazement at its enormous size. They make their way to the left side of the sphinx, hoping to save Juan from making a big mistake.

As they walk steadily toward the sphinx, the ground begins to pulsate with powerful force. All of them fall to the ground, and they notice the sphinx coming alive with the rage of a wild beast. The face of the sphinx transforms literally into an angry man with the rage of a lion, and he stands up to shake the dirt off his back. The teens back away with thoughts of running for their lives, but the sphinx places his paws in front of them.

"Don't be afraid of me, since I mean you no harm right now." says a masculine voice.

"Why do you prevent us from entering your sacred area, since we only search for our brother, Juan?" asks Roland.

"We are the chosen ones of the Ousias, and we just want to save him from making a terrible mistake," adds Kendra.

"Your brother made his choice to allow someone to mislead him, so I don't see why I should allow you entrance to the abyss," roars the Great Sphinx.

"We have the right to enter your domain, and our bracelets prove our worthiness to cross the threshold into the abyss," says Kendra boldly, attempting to hide her fears.

Roland and Drake caution Kendra to choose her words with care. She knows the sphinx could rip them to pieces without breaking a sweat. The sphinx roars loud enough to shake several nearby cities in Egypt, but then it lowers its head at the teens, approving of Kendra's attitude and courage. The teens take a deep breath in relief. The beast removes his paws from them and makes an offer to the trio.

"You don't have the map anymore," says the sphinx. "But I'm going to make an exception for the three of you, since your boldness touches my heart. If you are willing to answer the riddle of the sphinx, then I will open the gateway to the abyss. But you must choose to accept this: there is no turning back. What is your choice?"

Kendra moves toward Roland and Drake, and they huddle together to discuss this.

THE OUSIAS

Neither Roland nor Drake approves of trusting the sphinx or trying to answer his riddle.

Kendra reminds them that they have no other way to enter the abyss and save Juan. They look at each other for a while, but finally Roland and Drake agree with her. Everyone chooses to accept the rules of this beast and try to answer its riddle. Kendra knows the riddle of the sphinx that is one of the most sought-after things in Egyptian or Greek mythology. Many people have found different texts with information on the subject, so Kendra believes she will know how to answer this riddle. The sphinx wants to know who is going to answer his riddle, since only one can give the correct answer. Kendra steps forward and volunteers to answer on behalf of everyone else.

"There are several recognized senses within a person, which you know of here," says the sphinx. "What is the most underrated sense that each person takes for granted here? You have a just a short time to answer me, or I'll consider this a no response to my riddle. The penalty for failing is to become my dinner, so make your choice wisely."

Neither Roland nor Drake supports this proposal of the sphinx, and Roland tries to use his bracelet. But his bracelet won't work for them and the beast laughs at their dilemma with merciless humor. The sphinx reminds them of their agreement to correctly answer the riddle or face the penalty, which only adds to Roland and Drake's fear. Kendra tells them to calm down, as they are making her nervous. As she thinks about the answer, the sphinx begins to lick his lips in anticipation of eating them.

"I think the answer is sight, since you need to see in order to get around," says Roland.

"No," says Drake. "I think the answer is hearing, Kendra, since you need to hear in order to know what's around you."

"Wait—there are people who make it through life without having either sight or hearing," says Kendra.

Then Roland and Drake try focusing on taste, touch, or the sense of smell as a solution. Kendra shakes her head to disagree with them, and the sphinx starts to roar at them for an answer. The sphinx mocks them. No one has ever come close to answering this particular riddle.

As they struggle to come with an answer, the sphinx says time is up for all of them. The sphinx delights in his first meal as a living creature in the last five thousand years, so the sphinx keeps his sight on them like a lion eyeing his prey. He won't deny himself the pleasure of watching their terror and their inability to solve his riddle. The sphinx releases his sharp fifty-foot claws to rip deep into the ground like a bulldozer. The teens develop a sickness in their stomach and wonder if the end is near.

"Your time is up, and my stomach is about to be full," says the hungry sphinx.

They beg Kendra to take any of their choices, but Kendra doesn't listen to them. She thinks for a second, and she turns to the sphinx with confidence. As the sphinx rises his claws to finish off the trio, Kendra speaks. "The answer to your riddle is common sense, since it is the most underrated of all the recognized senses."

The sphinx retracts his claws, and he returns to his in his original stationary position. A doorway opens to a swirling vortex on his left side, and the beast turns back into a statue. Roland and Drake turn to Kendra in confusion and want to understand why common sense was the right answer. Kendra reminds them about how the sphinx didn't say the answer had to be one of the five senses. But rather, the question was about the most underrated sense that everyone knows about.

"But maybe you two are the exception to this rule, since neither of you had the common sense to avoid being misled with false images of your fantasy women," says Kendra.

"Hey," says Drake. "She used some magic mind trick on us, and I would have seen through it eventually."

"Drake is right. She used her evil charms to fool us," says Roland.

"You can both just talk to the hand, since my ears aren't hearing either of you," suggests Kendra, walking to the entrance.

"This is why I find Kendra so amazing—she knows all the answers," says Drake. "She is just so totally hot and smart at the same time."

"I'm glad that we're friends now, but can you stop referring to my sister as hot?" asks Roland.

Kendra comes out of the doorway and ask what is keeping them. Roland and Drake won't answer her, claiming to be discussing some life issue. Kendra chuckles at the idea of them talking about big issues, so she goes back through the doorway. Roland tells Drake that he is fine with him and Kendra. But Roland reminds Drake that Malcolm will be another matter, when he comes out of his coma.

20

THE ABYSS

They cross through the Great Sphinx's doorway and into dark, creepy area. They find it hard to see in this dark place, but Kendra thinks about her bracelet. She uses it to emit a bright glow that allows them to see the inside of a mysterious place. Roland is able to take a step, but something pulls on his shirt to stop his movement. Roland looks to see that he's within seconds of stepping on a stalagmite, which is part of a row of cone-shaped stalagmites all around them. Drake and Kendra feel dripping water on their heads, and they look upward to see an entire column of stalactites. Roland offers a crazy observation: this cave's cone-shaped structures are reminiscent of the teeth in someone's mouth.

Kendra remembers this limestone cavern from a photo of Malcolm's last trip to Egypt. Roland wants to go looking for Juan, but Kendra cautions them to take one step at a time. She observes the sharp edges of the twisted cone-shaped stalactites moving a little above them, and she wants to avoid a possible cave-in. Everyone begins following her lead through the cave, and they walk slowly around the stalagmites. Kendra begins losing power with her bracelet, so Roland uses his bracelet to guide their way. They find themselves walking on soggy ground from the water dripping through the stalagmites.

"How far is this place anyway? This cave seems almost endless," says Roland.

"There are no rules here, since this is the abyss," says Kendra. "We need to keep on walking. I hope we don't find Juan too late to help him."

They move for what seems like hours and several miles until Drake sees two people in front of them. Kendra recognizes Juan and the woman masquerading as his mother. She refuses to approach Juan too fast, since Kendra senses a powerful mind game between this woman and her brother. Roland can't wait any longer and rushes in with no regard for the consequences. Kendra yells out for Roland to stop, but it doesn't make an impact on him.

Standing in an isolated corner of the cave, Juan doesn't see or hear any of them He has eyes only for this mysterious woman. He wants to know the story about his father.

But the woman can't answer him, and she uses some more of her perfume scent to further distract Juan. Both Roland and Drake get a sniff of it again, causing them to see their fantasy women again. Kendra calls to them to redirect their focus, and she talks out to Juan in an effort to talk to him down. The same invisible force field from earlier at the sphinx comes between her and Juan again. Kendra tries calling Juan's name, but the shield is totally soundproof. So Juan is unable to hear them, and the woman keeps him behind her so he can't see Kendra.

"I will explain everything, when your father is safe," says the mysterious woman.

She takes Juan for a walk, leading him farther into the cave. They approach the edge of a cliff. Both Juan and this mysterious woman look over the edge into swirling waves of fog, and she picks up a small rock to toss in the fog. They don't hear a sound, indicating a bottomless pit, but a voice shouts out from below. Juan looks upon a sturdy middle-aged man with long hair and fear in his eyes as he struggles to hang onto a piece of rock. Juan's mother says he is Juan's father. Juan is stunned to see him, and a small quiver rumbles through the cave. The ground suddenly collapses under the women's feet, and she is hanging onto the edge of the cliff for dear life as well. Juan reaches out with his hand to save her, but his bracelet prevents him from getting to her.

"Juan, please let me have your bracelet, so you can rescue your mother from falling," says his desperate father.

Juan is too full of fear and under the spell of this woman to see the truth; he takes off his bracelet to help his mother. As Juan hands it over to his father, he laughs with glee. Juan looks to see the woman not hanging on the edge any longer, and he realizes to his dismay this was all just an illusion. Juan sees the woman changing her appearance and discovers this person isn't his mother. He tries to regain his bracelet, but Juan's phony father transforms himself back into the evil Seth. He pulls Juan toward him and strikes him in the back with a needle, causing him to fall to the ground. Juan realizes that his vision about the needles came true.

Roland and Kendra begin to feel extremely warm, and they feel the heat the most near their bracelets. In fear for Juan, Roland and Kendra use their bracelets together to finally break the force field. Their bracelets create an opening through the field, and they run swiftly to locate Juan. As they run, they hear a loud scream of pain. Kendra and Roland distinguish the sound as Juan's voice, but they make it too late for Juan. Juan lies on the ground, holding his stomach in pain. Roland, Kendra, and Drake head for Juan, but they stop to see Seth standing over him. Seth also takes the opportunity to whisper in Juan's ear, which causes him to feel even worse.

"I shall say this one last time: I want my pyramid pieces and your bracelets," demands Seth. "He has twice as much poison in his system now, then what I put into Malcolm. Don't try any tricks this time, or I'm going to take your brother's life."

Kendra and Roland concern for Juan's safety, so they remove their bracelets. They throw them, along with Seth's pyramid pieces, to him. Seth takes all of the items and laughs at the teens' stupidity. Seth put his hands on Juan's shoulders, and he throws his body toward the others. They can see Juan isn't moving at all, and they listen for a heartbeat, finding none. They're forced to the horrible conclusion that he is no longer alive. Kendra and Roland try to attack Seth, but Drake grabs hold of their arms to stop them.

"You didn't need to kill him! We gave up our items," shouts Kendra.

Roland rushes toward Seth, but Seth magically lifts Roland from the ground, causing him to fall onto Drake. Kendra runs over to them. Both Roland and Drake struggle but they are able to stand on their feet.

"Several days ago at your home, I offered a quick death for the three of you, and you refused. This is your reward for your defiance," says Seth. "Besides, my future queen did the real work."

"Yes, Juan didn't have a chance to see through the lies of your queen, or should I say the lady Hathor," says Kendra. "I recalled reading that Hathor had the face of a cow."

"I'm sorry, my dear child," says Hathor. "But many of those stories wasn't completely true about me."

Hathor changes her form to prove her powers. She wears an Egyptian gold-and-silver headdress with two horns on either end. Seth is preparing to destroy the teens with their own bracelets when a cloaked figure appears in front of the teens. He takes off his cloak to show himself as their neighbor, Mr. Hardgrove, whose face also changes into Mr. A.R.'s for a second. It is a surprise to all the teens, with the exception of Kendra, as she was very suspicious of Hardgrove.

"I won't let you hurt them," says Hardgrove.

"No, Ra," says Seth. "I now have the power to conquer this world and to become the next pharaoh."

Hardgrove uses his powers to change back into a brownish-yellow falcon head, Ra, but Hathor aims a golden ring with Ra's face on it to drain his ability to turn into the great phoenix. Before Ra can react, a giant tail forces its way out of the ground to seize hold of him. The tail belongs to Apophis. It lifts Ra into the air. He tries to break free, but Apophis's tail is too strong to escape from. Ra uses his last ounce energy to release a small amount of flame at Seth's pyramid pieces. But Seth uses the teens' bracelets to reflect the flame right back at him and turns Ra into ash. The teens watch the fate of Ra with sadness, and they fear being the next ones to turn to ash. Seth casually mentions that Ra didn't know Hathor possessed the golden ring of Osiris. Osiris had used this ring to make his enemies weaker, but Seth had taken the ring in their last battle, and then he killed Osiris with the ring in Osiris's throne room. But he had risen again, thanks to the strange, unexpected magical force that mysteriously gave most mythological figures a second chance at life. However, Seth promises, there won't be another chance for Osiris or the chosen ones, since they shall all join Ra in everlasting death.

Seth brings out a small glass jar and opens it to release several blue scarabs with yellow stripes on their backs. The scarabs circle the teens like locusts in a field of wheat, and they begin to consume the teens, to the approval of Seth. A bright light shines on the bracelets and the pyramid pieces in his hand, which increases his level of excitement. The destiny of Seth is nearly at hand, since it is officially the seventh day. Seth turns to his future queen, Hathor, and he prepares the next phase in his plan to conquer the world.

He combines all three bracelets, and disappears from the cave. As Seth leaves the area, the scarabs fall dead to the ground. The teens recover to find themselves without a scratch, but they can't enjoy the moment. They look at the body of Juan, and it brings tears flowing out of them like water from a fountain. A small still voice speaks out to them, telling them not to lose hope. Everyone looks around to see where this voice is coming from. Kendra tracks the voice to a heap of ash that was once Hardgrove. But the ash spins around like a small tornado, and it changes back into their friend.

Their happiness changes back into sorrow when they look at Juan's body. Hardgrove advances toward the body and touches Juan's right shoulder. Within mere seconds, Juan leaps to his feet, exhibiting no injuries from Seth's attack. Juan's remarkable recovery brings nothing short of surprise and absolute excitement to the others. All of them run over to release a flood of hugs and head-rubbing. Juan receives every bit of it in stride.

21

THE GREAT PLAGUES

Back in Chicago, on a mild clear morning, Seth stands triumphant outside the THES building. Hathor and Tek position themselves right next to him, and Seth holds the three bracelets in his hand. A sobek gives him the three pyramid pieces, and Seth uses the magic of the bracelets on the pieces. Shortly, the pieces begin to unite, and they join with the THES building. Soon after, the THES becomes an even bigger pyramid than before, and then Seth directs the bracelets at the Chicago River.

The water starts to flow out of the river, and it creates a barrier around the pyramid. Nearby people notice the approaching flood of water. They're driven away from the pyramid. The city police and other city officials can't get beyond the wave of water that surrounds the pyramid like a moat protecting a castle. But they won't have enough time and manpower to investigate this mystery. For it is the dawn of the seventh day, and Seth uses the power of the bracelets to fulfill his prophesy to rule over mankind.

"My Lord, the people of this world will never give up willingly, since they would rather fight than surrender," says a concerned Tek.

THE GREAT PLAGUES

"I know the strength of your people, but I also know their weakness as well," says Seth. "These bracelets have the power to force them to obey, and I'm going to take full advantage of it. For now, I shall unleash all manner of plagues to demonstrate my supremacy over to the world."

As Seth holds the bracelets above his head, waves of energy appear like yarn out of each bracelet. The energy wave splits swiftly in every direction from Seth's pyramid, bringing terrible disaster throughout the world. Over the next few hours, some people begin to fall mysteriously to the ground. Before long, this disaster strikes differently in other continents. People begin to panic and demand their leaders find a solution to the waves of unexplained devastation. This leads to a total breakdown as people struggle to leave the crowded cities. Many others take this opportunity to break into stores, banks, and businesses in their desire for food, money, and other items, further increasing the level of terror. Regrettably, there aren't enough officers and other law authorities to stop or even control the tide of violence worldwide.

Meanwhile in Europe, the people find themselves with festering boils upon their bodies. But while people are battling this epidemic in every corner of Europe, the people of both Asia and the Middle East discover their streets and homes are covered with unbearable swarms of flies and frogs. The power and horror of the energy wave spread like a powerful plague, traveling to parts of Africa and South America. Before long, this force provokes large swarms of locusts to consume every bit of grain, plants, and other vegetation on the two continents. With every corner facing a different terror, the people of Australia face their own trouble when deadly hailstorms strike and devastate the entire continent.

As the entire world faces terror and unforeseen horror, more people fall uncontrollably into unexplained comas. The doctors can't find any solution to stop these plagues. With the world in chaos, Seth orders Apophis to release its power at the sun. Seth uses the magic of the bracelets' conjunction with his powers and magically drains Apophis's power. Apophis follows Seth's command, and a dark cloud goes from his body toward the sun. A powerful solar eclipse forms in the sky, and the sun turns black to bring more fear upon the world.

People are told to stay home, and the world comes to a standstill. The plagues continue into the night. No one can tell night from day. Scientists can't make any sense of this, since no solar eclipse is expected for this time of the year. Also, the moon is still in its regular orbit, so it isn't causing the eclipse to occur. It only increases the ever-growing mystery.

"My plan is working now. It is coming to the final phase of my destiny," says Seth. "Tomorrow, I'll become fully corporeal. Then I shall gain control of the great armies of the underworld, and I will become pharaoh of a new world very soon."

After Apophis gave up its power, the creature shrank to ten feet long. Seth calls for his sobeks, who run to respond to his command, and they carry Apophis to Seth's room for rest. Seth tells Hathor to prepare for the ceremony tomorrow, when Seth will take this world by force. He walks away, leaving Hathor with Tek, and she tells him to guard the pyramid against threats. Tek and the rest of Seth's followers carry Seth's protective tattoo on their left and right arms, making them immune from the plagues.

Hathor touches her head as if she is having a headache. She doesn't understand the reason, until she looks at Osiris's ring. It shows the image of Ra, inducing panic. She doesn't want Seth to know of this change in events, so Hathor goes to Apophis. Hathor uses the ring to regenerate Apophis's powers, and she orders him to eliminate Ra once and for all. Apophis slowly regains all of its size and strength, and Hathor turns the ring upon herself and Apophis. They both vanish like smoke from the room without Seth's knowledge. Meanwhile, Seth employs the bracelets' power for a peek into the underworld. He views with delight a large army of men, sobeks, and other creatures.

In the caves of the abyss, Hardgrove consoles the teens over losing their bracelets to Seth. Juan, who stands silent in the corner away from the others, feels the worst. They try to deal with Hardgrove in his true form as a falcon-headed person.

Ra senses the teens' questions and knows their concerns. "Hathor isn't the only person who can create an illusion, so I used my powers to make an illusion of those scarabs eating you all," says Ra. "Seth redirected my power back at me, but I altered it in the direction of those attacking scarab beetles. Seth and Hathor didn't notice the illusion, so Seth believes no one survived his attack."

Everyone marvels at Ra's trickery. He knows time is running out for the entire world. Ra asks Juan to come join them for a much-needed discussion. Ra asks the teens if they're OK with this falcon face, or should he just change his facial appearance back to human. But the teens agree that Ra can stay as he is, and they try to figure out what to do next.

"I know how badly you're all feeling about this situation," says Ra. "But we have to stop Seth."

Juan speaks out. "No, it is my problem that I brought to the world with my stupidity. I didn't see through Hathor's lies until it was too late. Also, Seth told me that Thoth had passed away at the hospital. He had used the last of his power to protect Malcolm. It led to Thoth's demise. So what is left for me to believe in here?"

They feel sad hearing this from Juan, but Ra tells them they must maintain their focus on the immediate problem. Agreeing with Ra, Roland and Kendra try to make Juan feel better, reminding that they had also given their bracelets to Seth willingly. Juan refuses to listen to either of them, and Drake offers his advice with no success. Ra makes a strong statement to Juan, and they listen with open ears.

Ra begins with the story of how Thoth tries to stop Hathor, who had betrayed Horus because Seth tempted her with promises of riches. Ra talked about how Hathor had changed her appearance into Thoth's wife, Ma'at. Ra finishes with the hard truth about Thoth losing his wife because of Hathor's deceit, for Ma'at's name means truth and justice.

Ra mentions with sorrow that their love wasn't meant for a long marriage. It started with Ma'at who wished to share in her husband's desire to protect others, like Horus. Against his better judgment, Thoth successfully mentored Ma'at to protect Hathor against her enemies, but Hathor was the real enemy. She betrayed Horus to Seth and used her powers of deception to fool Horus. But Horus was too smart to fall for her tricks, and he attacked Seth directly in a great battle to get revenge on Seth for killing his father, Osiris. Even with Horus's victory, the news wasn't all good, since Hathor tricked Ma'at in a trap that Thoth couldn't see through to save her life. Ra tells them that some beings like Ma'at didn't get a second chance at life, adding to Thoth's pain of losing his beloved.

Roland and Drake ask Ra for a description of this trap, since they didn't fall into the same one. Ra couldn't get Thoth to tell him. He was ashamed of failing his wife; they were the most in-love couple in the palace, next to the pharaoh. He thought that their love would stand the test of time, until Hathor used her deception to end their marriage. She was imprisoned for her crimes for eternity, until Seth recently set her free to help with his plans of subjugation. Thoth became an Ousia who wished nothing to do with mentoring anyone again, but the Ousias refused to honor his request. This led him to blame them for forcing his role as mentor, and it put a division in his relationship with the other Ousias, especially his best friend, Osiris.

Ra tells Juan how this caused Thoth to lose faith in his cause of helping others. Ra tells Juan to stop hating himself. Kendra listens with intensity to Ra and recalls learning about the history of Ra. She realizes Ma'at wasn't just the wife of Thoth: she was also the daughter of Ra as well. Kendra senses his desire not discuss this fact with the others, though, so Kendra keeps these thoughts to herself, since she figures Ra wants to concentrate more on stopping Seth.

"If the wisest man on earth can be tricked with a lie, then there is no shame in anyone else being misled," says Ra. "The real shame is to give up the fight against evil and allow evil to overcome good. Thoth gave up the fight against evil when his wife died in his arms. Seth's arrival caused Thoth to rekindle his fighting spirit against evil, so he took Seth's pyramid pieces to delay his plan. But once Thoth learned of your being the chosen ones the prospect of facing Seth was too much for him. So he chose to get you out of the city, since he cares very much for all of you. Please don't let Seth win."

"Ra is right. We can't let Seth and Hathor get away with this," Juan finally agrees.

As everything seems bad, the teens let a little humor slip in to relax them. They start to tap each other on the head and shoulder. Drake asks Ra about the Ousias. Why couldn't the Ousias stop Seth in the first place, since they were so powerful? Ra knows time was running out here, but he also knows the value of knowing the truth. Ra magically creates an illusion about the past to show the teens their war. It took place several millennia ago, when the dark and evil figures of other mythologies disagreed about working with mankind, leading to war.

This Great War began as the good and bad figures of Egyptian, Greek, Norse, and other mythologies fought to the death, but this war took place on another plane of existence. The war continued seemingly without end for months, until the good mythological figures were victorious over their evil rivals. The bad figures were imprisoned for the crimes against mankind, but then a new battle took place. Many of the good Ousias tried to help a city as an example of their desire to aid mankind, but instead they brought chaos and destruction to the people of this city, which people refer to the city of Atlantis. Kendra doesn't recall any story about how Ousias had caused the fall of this city, and Ra senses her thoughts on this matter. He talks about how the other Ousias had erased their involvement with Atlantis and had rewritten the history of this great city. Ra declares this event brought about debates and arguments about their plans to aid mankind, and how it was about to spark another war among the Ousias.

Pangu is the most influence of the Ousias, and he used the yin and yang philosophy as a way to help bring balance and order for everyone. Many Ousias questioned this idea at first, but eventually they went with this yin and yang's plan. This gave balance to both the good and evil figures from each mythology, ending all of the fighting, and this led the good Ousias to form the Society to help maintain peace. Ra says Thoth had come up with the name "Ousias," since it refer to the entity or essence of a living being. After the tragedy of Atlantis, the Ousias decided not to interfere in the affairs of mankind again, but they agreed to allow three human controls of three magical bracelets to fight the evil Ousias if needed.

"I understand why Roland, Kendra, and Juan are the chosen ones, but how do I fit in?" asks Drake.

"One may not understand his or her purpose in life, but there is a purpose for all of us," says Ra. "You will see your purpose isn't just as a spectator, but as someone who assists those in need. I can't say any more, but please trust my words on this."

Drake feels a weird sense of peace within himself from listening to Ra. The teens are ready to follow Ra's instructions to the letter. But they notice him showing signs of getting weaker, and he tells them about losing his power due to his assisting them against Seth. Everyone is concerned for him, but Ra reminds them about the yin and yang rule of maintaining order. This has kept the Ousias, both good and bad, from using their powers irresponsibly. The teens understand why the Ousias placed a limitation on their powers.

Ra tells them there is only one way to help save the earth now. He tells them they must travel into Duat, so they can find Osiris, who can help them. Roland inquires about the meaning of Duat and Ra tells Roland that Duat is another word for the Egyptian underworld. None of them wants to leave him, but Ra knows his time is almost up. The teens want Ra to go with them.

"I'm sorry," says Ra. "This is a journey that the chosen ones and Drake must travel alone."

"We don't have our bracelets anymore, and it makes this journey impossible to survive," says Kendra.

"Listen, your world is getting closer to belonging to Seth, and you can't let him win," says Ra. "Trust me—you all have great strength within each of you, and this includes you as well, Drake. Duat is a dangerous place, and there are a couple of things to that can assist you on this journey."

Ra pulls out a five-foot silver-and black-spear. Ra gives the spear to Roland for protection and tells him to use it only in a time of trouble. They agree with heavy hearts to go to the underworld, and Roland agrees to keep the spear near him. Ra walks over to Kendra and murmurs something to her, something he didn't want to share with the others. As they prepare to go into the underworld, Ra reminds Kendra to remember his true name as an access code to travel through Duat. They ask if they will ever see him again, but Ra doesn't answer their question. Ra uses the last of his magic to open a portal under their feet, and they turn into vapors. The teens go slowly down through the portal like steam. Ra couldn't tell them about this being his last day on Earth, for he had used his last ounce of power to protect them. Ra expresses his confidence in the teens and fades away into nothingness.

22

JOURNEY THROUGH DUAT

Following their long journey through the portal, the teens find themselves sitting on an ancient boat. But this isn't just any boat. Kendra looks around to remind her about such boats. She observes the forty-two-foot-long, crescent-shaped papyrus ship. It contains ten papyrus oars on the left and right sides of the boat. The teens look over the side of the ship and find it flying through the air. The teens further witness something unbelievable: they see several heavyset black bulls with reins attached to them. These bulls are pulling the boat through the air like sled dogs carrying a sled through the snow.

"How are those bulls able to fly?" asks Drake. "And who is guiding these bulls, anyway?"

No one can answer Drake's question, and soon the ship stops moving as the bulls sit down. The teens notice a powerful, menacing muscular man with the face of a falcon. He's wearing a kilt-like piece of linen tied around his waist. He draws near them with a sharp sickle blade in his hand.

The teens move away from this creature and try to reason with him. The stranger notices a spear next to Roland's right leg, and he moves at the teens to kill them. Roland tries to use the spear to defend the others, but the man knocks the spear to the ground. He takes aim with his sickle to strike the teens, but Kendra remembers Ra's message to her.

Kendra speaks with authority. "We come in the name of Khepri in the morning and Ra at noon and Atum in the evening."

He stops in midattack and places his sickle on the ground. He glances at the teens, but there is no malice in his eyes, not like before, when he thought the teens were servants of Seth—he had noticed Roland holding Seth's spear. The man knows Ra wouldn't trust his true names to just anyone. The stranger asks the teens for forgiveness and offers to take them the rest of the way to Duat.

They introduce themselves as the chosen ones of the Ousias and state their desire to seek Osiris's help in stopping Seth. He reaches out to shake their hands and introduces himself as the fearsome warrior, Montu. His handshake causes great pain to Roland, Drake, and Juan, since his grip is too strong to handle for long. They are worried for Kendra as Montu reaches over to shake her hand. But he is as gentle as a lamb.

"Ouch," yelps Roland, rubbing his hand. "Your grip is as strong as pliers. How long do we have to travel through the underworld to find Osiris?"

As Montu is destined to travel throughout Duat, he offers to guide the teens through the underworld. Drake admits to being very uncomfortable about this place, since he was always terrified of the stories of the Greek underworld. This place doesn't make him feel any better until Juan tells them to gaze over the side of the boat. Montu says that this solar barge, which he refers to as one of two boats, belonged to Ra who once used it to travel through the sky.

Everyone looks over the right side of the boat, and they see images of people floating below like clouds in the sky. Kendra asks if this is what people go through in Duat, but Montu refuses to utter a single word. Montu looks uneasy about talking to them, since the secrets of Duat aren't something to share with the living. Montu tells them the journey isn't too long, but the dangers are many to behold.

Montu orders the bulls to make a left turn, and the bulls follow his order to the letter. The boat moves, and they start to feel hot, like being inside of an oven. They begin to smell an overwhelming odor of sulfur, and they lookout on the left side of the boat to a mighty lake of fire. Montu tells them to remain inside for their safety, but something horrible has got other ideas for them. Many bandaged hands reach out to them from below the boat, and they see dozens of mummies covered in torn wrappings. The faces of embalmed, decaying corpses attack them. Montu orders the teens to move away from the sides of the boat, but not before Juan sees mummies riding on the backs of large vultures.

Foul, stinking mummies hurl their rotting and decaying bodies from several huge black-and-gold vultures with a thirty-foot wingspans to climb onboard the boat with their decomposing hands. Montu reaches for the oars and knocks many of the mummies off the boat. The teens don't want to just stand by without helping him, so they strike the mummies with the other oars. More vultures approach from above the boat, and they redirect their assault toward the incoming mummies. They successfully knock the mummies from the boat, but more of these decaying monsters continue to attack them.

"I never thought I'd be fighting a mummy as a part of the journey, but I guess this must be one of the traps here," says Roland.

"I'll never look at another mummy movie in the same way again when we get out of this mess," says Drake.

Montu tells the teens that the mummies were once followers of Seth who betrayed Osiris and Horus. They are bound to Seth to serve as the living dead for all time. Montu calls out to the bulls in an ancient Egyptian language. Kendra listens to intently. They battle both the vultures and mummies to a standstill, until one of the vultures strikes the bulls with its sharp talons. The solar barge turns upside down, but they manage to hang on to some oars. However, Montu falls off the boat, as he fights with a mummy.

Even as Montu heads for the lake of fire, Kendra reacts to save his life. She speaks the exact words that Montu had when he ordered the bulls to change direction. The bulls obey her commands, and she orders them to rescue Montu. The bulls move the boat with increased speed,

JOURNEY THROUGH DUAT

and Montu drops back into the boat before landing in the lake of fire. They cover their noses to keep from breathing the deadly sulfur from the lake, and everybody pulls Montu back onto the boat safely. Montu offers gratitude to them, especially to Kendra, for rescuing him.

As the boat travels rapidly ahead, the mummies discontinue their pursuit of them to return to their home near the lake of fire. Everybody is relieved to see the last of them, and they look forward to smooth sailing for a change. However, the danger isn't over, as they find themselves traveling near an isolated desert. But this desert is full of thirty-foot-tall marble figures of sobeks holding stony sword blades in their hands. Roland and Kendra desire to go in the other direction, but Montu tells them this is the only way to get to the gateway to find Osiris. Upon approaching the statues, one of them moves its sword to attack. The heavyset bulls move to avoid the first strike. The rest of the sobek statues swings their stone swords at them, but the bulls use their swiftness to evade the attacks with ease.

As the statues become a distant memory, everyone begins to relax about living another day. They have traveled about halfway through Duat, which Montu mentions to calm their nerves. But as they get closer to leaving Duat, the sands blow from the desert like a storm, bringing out the revenge-seeking Apophis. Apophis instantaneously consumes two of the bulls off the boat, and it snatches Kendra and Juan with its tongue. Apophis uses its mighty tail to take hold of the boat, and Drake, Roland, and Montu aren't strong enough to break Apophis's grip.

Drake uses the oars to strike Apophis, but the attack doesn't faze Apophis, who uses his head to toss Drake to the other side of the boat. Roland looks behind him at the old wooden spear that Ra had given to him for protection. But this spear is too small to hurt something as large as Apophis—that is, until the spear grows another five feet. Apophis tosses both Juan and Kendra high up into the air, so it can swallow them whole.

Roland releases the spear at Apophis, throwing it like a javelin. The spear increases in size again before piercing its neck, and the mighty snake cries out in pain. Apophis roars with rage, attempting to strike back at Roland, but the razor-sharp spearhead, which is embedded in

Apophis's neck, grows large enough to cut the head off the great snake. Apophis's head and the rest of its body plummet like a boulder to the ground. Montu, Roland, and Drake use their bodies to catch Kendra and Juan before they hit the ground. They shake off their fear and thank for saving their lives.

"Hopefully, there aren't any more dangers before we can see Osiris," says Drake.

Montu's solar barge flies for several more miles until it comes upon to two golden gates and a grassy area. The boat lands firmly on the ground. Montu points to the gate on the right side, which leads to the Field of Reeds. It is a type of paradise where the righteous can enjoy a life of happiness for all time. After everyone consider this place, Montu walks over to the door on the left. He tells them that this gate leads to Osiris. But Montu warns them of possible dangers to those who enter this gate. Montu tells the teens that they could choose the Field of Reeds, allowing them to enjoy paradise.

"But then, what happens to the world under the rule of Seth?" asks Roland.

"OK," says Juan. "Paradise or unknown dangers. These are very tough choices, but I won't allow Seth to dominate the Earth. My decision is to go left."

"I vote for the left gate," says Roland.

"As much as paradise would be my dream place, I'll take my chances and open the left door," says Drake. "What is your decision, Kendra?"

"I don't want to go against the majority, since it's our fault that Seth is on the threshold of ruling mankind," says Kendra. "Then the majority rules—we choose the left gate."

Juan doesn't agree with Kendra about giving Seth the power, since he feels the most responsible for their situation. They settle on going through the left gate to find Osiris. Montu gives Kendra a piece of paper from *The Book of the Dead*. Montu tells them how Ra had kept the original book in his possession for safekeeping, but Ra had given Montu this page long ago with the hopes of the chosen ones coming here. Ra had told him that the true chosen ones would know his true full name or

JOURNEY THROUGH DUAT

face certain death. Montu gives Kendra the page, which includes information on getting through any challenges within the gate.

Kendra takes the page from Montu, and they thank him for his help. Montu promises to repay the favor someday for them saving his life. They stroll through the gate and head swiftly down the tunnel, hoping to avoid any more dangers. But they begin to smell an atrocious smell in the tunnel—a combination of manure, rotten eggs, and methane gas. Everyone holds his or her nose, since it is very difficult to breathe in those awful smells. They walk for a little while until the smells slowly decrease enough for them to breathe again. Roland observes a particularly dark area within the tunnel and hesitates to go any farther. Kendra looks at the page from *The Book of the Dead*, and she reads its reference to dangerous animals living in the tunnel.

"Maybe we should think about taking another direction, since I don't want to see what kind of dangerous animals are living here," suggests Roland.

"No, I brought this mess upon us, so we need to get through this creepy place," says Juan.

As they continue into the dark, mysterious tunnel, they hear a crackling sound under their feet with every step. They catch another unpleasant whiff of a rancid, decaying, musty stench that smells like decomposing meat. This makes them want to leave faster, but they begin to feel something unknown moving on their bodies. They can't see in the dark, though, until a dazzling light shines brightly enough to illuminate the entire room and the page of *The Book of the Dead* in Kendra's hand, showing them a scary sight.

Kendra screams and drops the page on the floor. Their hearts stop at the sight of yellow and light-brown scorpions, each about six centimeters long, crawling all over their bodies. The scorpions enjoy tasting the flesh of those intruding in their home. They want to swat the bugs away, but Kendra recognizes these scorpions are poisonous creatures that are capable of bringing instant death. She insists that they remain still without moving a muscle, and they follow her instructions. A clicking sound echoes throughout the tunnel, increasing their levels of panic, and they turn to see a twelve-foot yellow scorpion approaching them from behind.

"Wait—I need to look at that page again. Montu mentioned this page could help us out," says Kendra.

Kendra slowly bends down to pick up the page from the ground and takes the page gently to avoid upsetting Mother Scorpion or her babies with any hasty movements. Kendra quickly reads the page in a speed-reading manner before the fear of the scorpions overtakes her. As the young scorpions continue to crawl their way upon the teen's body, it only serves to increase their discomfort. Drake, Juan and Roland express the desire to swat the scorpions off them and make a run for it. But Mother Scorpion gets upset with them and begins to click her claws faster. The smaller scorpions move their poisonous tails to sting the teens, but Kendra tells her brothers and Drake to remain calm. They follow her suggestion to remain quiet and immobile, and the giant scorpion clicks her claws slower this time. Within moments, the smaller scorpions move off the teens, and their mother leads them to the opening of the tunnel where the teens had entered.

"OK, please explain to me why Mother Scorpion decided to spare our lives," asks Roland.

"This page has a reference to Mother Scorpion. That she'll attack those entering her home to feed her children, but not any who hold this particular page from *The Book of the Dead*," answers Kendra. "But they must not seek to harm her children, or they will die a painful death."

Everybody agrees to leave Mother Scorpion alone forever, and they walk for some more miles. They are happy to come upon the end of this tunnel and prepare to find Osiris. To the right of them, one of the wall collapses to release powerful airstreams from it. In an instant, the teens are pulled through it like a vacuum picking up dirt.

23

FEATHER OF MA'AT

After what seems like an eternity, the teens finally come to a stop in a gigantic room. Everybody can smell the exotic aroma of blue lotus in the room, and it is truly a delight to their senses. They observe the massive room with astonishment, since the room makes them feel like mice inside of a house. They see seven mammoth limestone pillars to the left and right sides of the room. Kendra, a lover of playing board games, is the first to recognize the oversize black-and-white marble floor under their feet as a giant version of a chessboard.

Across the room, they see a rectangular lavender box with seven empty chairs. They see hieroglyphics of pharaohs dating back to many thousands of years ago. Images are hanging on the walls of the room like a memorial. Kendra sees other hieroglyphics of people in line, as they wait for Pharaoh Osiris to judge over them. She realizes this is Osiris's courtroom, and the lavender box in front of them is an enormous jury box.

As they try to leave this place, magical chains materialize out of the ground to bind them to the floor. Without warning, a twenty-foot-tall ominous-looking person, who wearing a dark gray tunic around his waist and several gold bands on both his arms and legs, appears in the room like magic. But he looks downward at the teens with great fury in his beast-like eyes, and they react to him with uncontrollable dismay. He has the face of a jackal, and he carries a ten-foot-long sword in his left hand, which he angrily waves at the teens. Kendra knows him as Anubis, the protector of the dead, and she fears for their lives as she pleads for their lives. Anubis demands the instant death of the teens, since they have committed the greatest crime against the Ousias.

"Why is Anubis treating us like the enemy?" asks Roland.

"Because we lost the bracelets to Seth, so we are now in the judgment seat of Osiris. He will determine our fate of going to paradise or being tortured for eternity," says Kendra.

The teens become very nervous about Anubis's attitude. The strong purring sound of a cat doesn't help to calm their nerves. They turn their heads clockwise to see a nineteen-foot female human named Sekhmet with the head of a lioness. She wears a black headdress and a gold-and-silver linen tunic and has a long golden furry tail. Sekhmet once sought to punish mankind with her armies of lionesses for their disrespect of Ra, but Ra convinced her to forgo this plan to work side by side with Osiris as an Ousia. Both Sekhmet and Anubis express strong anger at the teens, since their armies are about to be forced to serve Seth. Long ago, they had placed their armies in Duat to guard over Seth's army and prevent him from using it against mankind. The Ousias had created the bracelets with Anubis and Sekhmet's magic. When the teens gave their bracelets to Seth, they gave Seth control of Anubis and Sekhmet's armies.

Amazingly, a thirty-foot-long silver scale appears in front of them, and a huge white feather lies next to the scale. At the same time, the empty jury-type box fills with other Egyptian figures, and they want the teens punished for their action. Roland and Kendra want to prove their innocence. Juan doesn't share in their view of being innocent of everything. Kendra recognizes some of the jury members with distress. They're dressed in fancy royal tunics arrayed with expensive diamonds and sapphires. They look furious.

"What are our chances of making through this alive? It looks like they want a verdict without hearing our explanation," says Drake.

Kendra cries out for them to release Drake, since he isn't a chosen one. Anubis gives him a chance to walk away with his life in one piece. Roland, Juan, and Kendra tell him to accept Anubis's offer and leave them, but he wants to stand with his friends to the end. Sekhmet roars out her frustration, but she agrees to let Drake stay and share in the punishment.

As the other Ousias in Osiris's court shout out for their blood, Anubis calls for the servants of Osiris to appear. Two eighteen-foot-tall, brawny soldiers appear dressed in a long white linen with swords in their hands, and they open a trapdoor under the scale. An earsplitting growl comes out of the pit, and a thunderous blast of fire shoots out of the pit like a lightning bolt. But it becomes secondary to the sight of a twenty-five-foot-tall creature with the head of a crocodile, the body of a male leopard, and the backside of a hippopotamus hungrily staring at the teens.

Roland asks Kendra with worry, "What kind of creature is that anyway?"

"It is called Ammut, the eater of the hearts," says Kendra. "She eats the lives of those whom the scale declares unworthy of paradise. Our weight will be judged on the scale against the feather of Ma'at. So, if a person's evil deeds weigh more than the feather, then Ammut shall eat the heart of the unworthy."

They yell for Anubis to feed them to Ammut, but a loud, strong voice speaks out to silence the crowd. Everyone sees straight ahead to see a sturdily built man dressed in white linen. He wears a long black straight beard and a white crown upon his head with red feathers on opposite ends. Kendra knows him: it is Osiris, the great pharaoh who rules Duat and shows no emotion on his throne.

"I'm here to decide the fate of these chosen ones, but there isn't much to judge on here," begins Osiris. "We chose the three of you to receive our bracelets, and it was your task to keep them out of Seth's hand. You gave up your powers to Seth of your own freewill, and he can now conquer mankind with the armies of Duat. There are only a few hours left prior to the next day, when Seth will regain his corporeal form to control the world. Thanks to the three of you, Seth is now able to use the armies of Anubis and Sekhmet to dominate the world."

Osiris tells the teens that three-fourths of the world's population is infested with these plagues, and the remaining one-fourth is unable to keep up with the demands of the people in need. This brings no joy to the teens, and they know it will only gets worse when Seth becomes corporeal. Osiris tells the teens that Seth will use his powerful dark magic and his army in combination with the warriors of Anubis and Sekhmet to overrun mankind.

Many of those seated in the seven-seat jury box request Osiris to chastise the chosen ones. But Kendra bravely speaks out about a fair trial, so they can explain their side to Osiris. Anubis and the others raise their voices to refute their claim to a fair trial, but Osiris motions for silence again. Osiris asks someone to defend these teens as their legal representative, but the room turns as quiet as a library. Suddenly, a man leaps into the room from above, and it is their teacher, Thoth. The teens are excited to see him.

A giant Thoth, with the face of an ibis, speaks. "I could feel your pain of losing the bracelets to Seth, so I pretended to die in order to stand with you all here. Listen, these teens are worthy to receive a second chance to stop Seth. He used Hathor as a wolf in sheep's clothing to mislead them. I believe in their ability to stop Seth before he becomes fully corporeal."

Osiris and the crowd scream out for justice, not mercy. Osiris reminds Thoth of his own faults, and how he had given the chosen ones his map, opening the door to their current situation. Osiris brings up the fact that each Ousia is responsible to follow the Society's own rules against interfering. They cannot interfere directly. As Osiris points at the scale, he offers Drake one last opportunity to leave or face judgment with the others. Drake moves over to his friends to stand with them. Roland, Juan, and Kendra urge him to go, but nothing changes his mind.

Thoth fears their death at the hand of the devourer, Ammut. Juan, unable to resolve his own failure, can't take Drake's willingness to die. He wiggles loose from his chains, runs under Anubis like a rabbit, and moves straight for the scale. One of the warriors places him onto the left side of the scale for judgment. The other teens can't just stand by and watch Juan face Ammut alone, so they burst free from their chains as well, and the warriors put them on the scale with Juan. Juan tries to get them to go back, but they rebuff his offer to bear this alone.

"I was the one who allowed Hathor to deceive me, so I'll take responsibility for my actions," shouts Juan.

"We gave our bracelets to Seth, so we shall face the judgments of Ma'at together," says Roland.

"I'm part of team to the end," says Drake.

They valiantly look downward to see the beast, who delights in her chance to devour them, and the teens hold each other's hands to stand together. This may be their last moment, and they don't desire to give the beast the satisfaction of seeing their terror. Osiris orders Anubis to place the feather of Ma'at onto the right side of the scale, and the teens watch the warrior advance with resolutely. Everyone becomes eerily silent, and Anubis gently places the feather of Ma'at onto the scale. The scale tilts up and down for several moments before it balances.

Osiris and the other Ousias shout out loud with enthusiasm. "We rejoice on this day, for the chosen ones are all true of voice and justified in their actions to all of us."

They celebrate the teens' act of courage, and then each of them disappears from the courtroom. Thoth and the teens are the only ones left in the room. They run over to Thoth in order to get answers. Thoth reduces his size, returning to a normal man.

"Why did they allow us to go free? Osiris and the others clearly wished to sacrifice us to Ammut as a punishment," says Juan.

"It was never their desire to punish any of you, but they couldn't ignore their own laws and rules," says Thoth. "Juan desired to face Ammut alone. But the rest of you couldn't let him do this, so you all went onto the scale to accept the judgment of Ma'at. This act of selflessness helped to balance the feather of Ma'at, and it provided Osiris proof of your worthiness as the chosen ones. Plus, when Drake refused to abandon his friends, it was further proof of his courage and loyalty to everyone else."

Drake finally feels like part of the group and sighs with relief on surviving his ordeal. Thoth can't keep this conversation going on for long, since there is only a short time left to save the world. Everybody offers sympathy to Thoth for Ma'at, since they know the truth now. Juan understands how Hathor was able to deceive him so easily. Thoth admits that he was wrong for not mentoring them from the beginning, but he offers a way for them to stop Seth. "There is only a little time left before midnight in Chicago," says Thoth. "If Seth is still in control of your bracelets, then the world is lost in his darkness forever."

Thoth gazes meaningfully at Juan, but no one understands why. Thoth tells them about his connection to something that he once hid in a Las Vegas hotel. Thoth asks Juan to reach inside of his pocket and give him the coin with the picture of the Eye of Horus on it. Juan hands the coin to Thoth the coin, who informs them that the coin holds the powers of the Eye of Horus.

No one could believe their ears. Kendra thought it was a fake earlier in Vegas. Thoth uses his powers to show them Seth's pyramid in Chicago, and they see their bracelets in an invisible shield on the top.

People, who aren't immune to the plague like the followers of Seth, are suffering and the percentage of the world's unaffected population starts to shrink from one-fourth to almost zero with each passing moment.

"How are we going to get our bracelets back?" asks Roland. "Seth isn't going to just allow us to take them without a fight to the death."

At that exact moment, the teens begin to experience brain freeze or ice cream headache inside of their heads. Thoth checks on the teens, and they tell Thoth that they know how to stop Seth. Thoth concludes that Osiris gave the teens the information to saving the world. Kendra is the first one to speak about two levers in Duat. She tells them the levers control the invisible shield and maintaining the connection between the underworld and Earth. Roland interrupts Kendra to mention that someone must pull down these levers at the same time to remove the shield over the top of the pyramid. Juan speaks next about a door in this room, saying that it will open up into Duat so they can find the levers.

"The levers are in an upward position within Duat, and the invisible shield will disappear from the pyramid," says Drake. "You must choose someone to move the levers in the downward direction, and then the bracelets can be removed safely from the pyramid. Toss the bracelets in the air, and they will immediately return to their rightful owners. Seth will lose control over his pyramid, spelling his end. But this must occur before midnight tonight, or all is lost for everyone. You should also know there are traps within Duat that protect the levers from Seth's enemies."

"I guess—you don't need my help," says Thoth. "Its just as well, since there is nothing else left for me to add."

"You talk like you're not going with us to face Seth," says Kendra.

"Yeah, we can't face this without your help," says Juan.

"I won't be able to help anymore, since the other Ousias won't let me help out this time," says Thoth. "But they—and—I have confidence in your ability to stop Seth and save the world. There is great inner strength and hidden talents in each of you. One more thing—the Eye of Horus's powers will only last a little while, and the bracelets need to be released from Seth's control before the power dies for good."

"Thoth, what was the trap that Hathor used against you?" asks Juan.

Kendra thinks that Thoth might be uncomfortable with the question. But Thoth doesn't mind, since he knows Hathor used a very dangerous trap. Thoth was going to tell them when a powerful wind whirls around him, snatching him away from the teens.

"OK," says Drake. "What just happen here?"

"Osiris and the other Ousias didn't want Thoth to interfere," says Kendra.

"I guess we are completely on our own. Where do we go from here?" asks Juan.

He looks at the others, expressing doubt at stopping Seth. Roland refuses to let Juan and the others doubt themselves. "We can't allow any doubt to creep into us like a virus. We must stand together, since we don't have any other choice."

Roland places his hand forward and motions for everybody to do the same. They all place their hands on top of Roland's hand. The four of them agree to prevent Seth from enslaving the world. They release their hands, and each one of them promises to do his or her part.

"I'm going to confront Seth and end his bid to rule the world," says a bold Roland. "I think Kendra and Juan should get to the levers, but you need to evade those traps."

Kendra and Juan rebuff their brother need to confront Seth, but he refuses to waver from decision. Roland expresses his desire to follow his brother's brave example of facing Ammut. After hearing the courage and determination in Roland's voice, they reluctantly decide to support their brother's choice. As Drake listens to them, he offers to complete his role as well. "If we are going to do this as a team, then I shall do my part to remove those bracelets from the pyramid?"

Whereas they prepare for their separate journeys, Roland notices an inscription on the coin that wasn't there a moment ago. The inscription was in hieroglyphics, so Roland gives it to Kendra to interpret the message. Kendra looks for a moment and tells him to claim this power to use against his mortal enemy, Seth. Roland takes the coin from Kendra and claims the power.

Instantly, Roland is empowered with the Eye of Horus, and he sees Chicago in complete darkness from the solar eclipse. Roland hears the sound of ticking clocks in his head and he senses Seth's moment of triumph at hand. Kendra, Juan, and Drake hear this development from Roland, and they decide to go on their separate ways immediately. They wish each other good luck.

Drake pulls Kendra closer to him and kisses her on the lips, entreating her to return safely. They share one last kiss, and he promises to return in one piece to finish this discussion. Kendra reminds him about keeping his word and tells Drake not to do something stupid, like die. Drake reaches over to hold her, since this might be their last moment together. Roland and Juan begin to feel sick, and they wonder if it's from the pressure of saving the world or watching their sister with Drake.

Roland drags Drake away from Kendra, and he uses his new powers to create a swirling, multicolor vortex. Roland and Drake travel into the vortex to get to Seth's pyramid. They are astonished to see the different patterns of color and light, like a kaleidoscope. Kendra and Juan watch them disappear with some concern but then prepare for their part of the mission. They are looking for the doorway to Duat when they hear something rising from below the ground. They look to the west end of the room to see a reddish-pink granite slab, standing almost seven feet tall. Juan wonders if this is the entrance, and Kendra examines Egyptian hieroglyphics writing on the top of the door. Kendra interprets the message: "This false door opens to the underworld, Duat, and your challenges wait within. Enter at your risk."

"I refuse to enter some false door. We should wait for the true door to appear," says Juan.

"The words 'false door' simply refer to a passageway between the worlds of the living and dead," answers Kendra. "We have no choice here. This is the only way to those levers."

Juan isn't too comfortable with this false door, but he wants nothing more than to set things right. Within seconds of their decision to enter, the granite slab opens up to reveal a partially lit, creepy, and foreboding entrance to Duat. They walk together through the door, which slams itself shut behind them to indicate the start of their journey.

24

THE EYE OF HORUS

On a dark windy Friday night in Chicago, mostly people are succumbing to the numerous plagues and comas around the world. The military and the medical community can't solve these worldwide disasters, and people hide to avoid risk of becoming the next victims. Many of Seth's followers, who are immune to the plagues of Seth, traveled to Chicago from all corners of the globe. Several days prior to the plagues, many of Seth's followers took planes, boats, buses, and other transportation, waiting to witness Seth becoming pharaoh of the world.

As Roland and Drake travel through the vortex, they find themselves inside of Seth's pyramid. They attract no attention and sneak into an office without being noticed. They observe the Chicago River surrounding his pyramid outside of the window. Roland and Drake watch Seth greeting his followers. He's wearing a red crown on his head with a distinguishing high crest at the back and a long rigid line angling upward to the front. He's dressed in a golden linen cloth around his waist and gold sandals on his feet. Seth wants his followers to appreciate his enriched power and glory firsthand. Seth walks to a dark podium, and he hears the crowd roar: "There is no power greater than Seth on Earth, so who is able to stand against him?"

Seth holds out his silver scepter to the crowd for their silence. "I'm in the midst of my transformation to pharaoh in the next one and a half hours."

The crowd begins an energetic roar at Seth, and he starts to become fully corporeal as midnight hour draws near. Roland and Drake notice Seth becoming more corporeal at every second, and it prompts Roland to act immediately. But two sobek guards hear their voices through the door, and they burst into the room with sharp crescent swords. Roland uses his new power to fling them in the air and toss the sobeks extremely hard against the wall. The sobeks land comatose on the ground, and Roland takes this opportunity to make his move on Seth.

Roland and Drake look outside of the room for more sobeks, but there are no sobeks in the hallways. They take the elevators to the top floor. They see their bracelets at the very top. A powerful force field surrounds a twelve-foot-long gray pole with several steel bars on the side. They watch the bolts of energy from deep in the ground and understand how their bracelets connect the human world and Duat. The teens observe with horror the armies of Anubis and Sekhmet and other underworld creatures, including decomposing mummies, waiting to attack. Drake and Roland stand on the edge of the pyramid and hear the crowd chanting Seth's name.

"I'm going to attack Seth. I need you at the top of this pyramid," says Roland.

"Kendra and Juan are heading for the levers so they can turn off the force field."

Drake listens with difficulty to Roland's reckless plan. "This plan is too dangerous. Seth will kill you in a heartbeat. Maybe we should wait for Kendra and Juan to turn off the shield first."

"No, there isn't time to debate this. Please trust me to keep Seth and his followers distracted," says a confident Roland. "Besides, it is nearly the eighth day, and Seth is going to be all powerful. Wait for Kendra and Juan to shut down the shield, and then you can get to our bracelets."

Drake agrees to trust Roland, even though his fears stand out like a sore thumb. Drake offers to walk with Roland to the elevator, but Roland has ideas of his own. Roland doesn't want to delay in the face of Seth's winning this night, so he makes another vortex. Roland jumps into the vortex before Drake can prevent him.

As Seth addresses the masses, an unbelievably powerful vortex appears on stage like magic to quiet the crowd. They see Roland walk through the vortex to stand boldly without fear before him. Seth is surprised to see the teen, since he believed they all died in the abyss. In fear of coming too close and failing now, Seth places his scepter down and tells Roland he made a big mistake on coming here. But Roland doesn't show any hint of backing down, and Seth's face changes from a human to the face of a jackal.

Seth launches a firebolt at Roland, and the fire instantly consumes Roland. The fire disappears to reveal Roland without a scratch on his body, and Seth realizes Roland is empowered with the Eye of Horus. Seth promises this won't stop him, so he makes some of the water around the pyramid flow upward in an attempt to drown him. The water completely covers Roland, and the crowd cheers jubilantly. But the water turns to steam, and Roland thanks Seth for the nice steam bath.

A defiant Seth bellows, "You dare to mock me, so I promise this place will be your tomb!"

"I'm not afraid of your powers, so please give me your best shot," says a fearless Roland.

Roland doesn't give Seth a chance again, moving the water at Seth. Seth counters Roland's magic to take control of the flowing water to redirect it at him. But Roland reacts quickly as he observes the podium. Roland smirks at Seth and decides to demonstrate the dangers of mixing water and electricity.

Roland uses his magic to move the electrical wires from the microphone, and the wires touches the water to give off an electrical charge. Seth falls in pain to the ground. Many of Seth's followers rush over to help him, but Seth orders them to stay back. Seth quickly recovers from his injuries, but he can't let his followers see him struggling to defeating a child. So he uses his power to create a violet bubble that covers both of them like a blanket. No one can see into the bubble.

Seth doesn't want to fall short again, since victory is within his grasp. He changes his scepter into a long sharp-edged sword with an engraving on the hilt. But Roland refuses to walk away from this challenge and he picks up a piece of the microphone. He uses the power of Horus to change it into a red-and-gold sword with the face of Horus on the hilt.

"My destiny is at hand, and I'll deliver your dead body to the underworld for my creatures to feast upon!" yells a furious Seth with sword in hand.

Seth runs at Roland to kill him, but Roland engages Seth with the strength of a warrior. Seth swings his sword at Roland's chest, but Roland quickly blocks it. Roland decides to counterattack with a quick thrust that strikes Seth slightly on his right arm. Seth feels the impact of Roland's attack, which hurts. Seth is almost fully corporeal but he isn't powerful enough to resist Roland's attack. Seth regains his strength and moves with the quickness of a cheetah, launching a massive strike at Roland's chest.

Roland spins around like a jackrabbit to avoid Seth and counters to leap at Seth, kicking him seven times in his chest to knock him on his rear end. Roland begins to feel weaker as the power of Horus starts to fade away. Roland thinks about Kendra and Juan's task of removing the force field. But time is running out for them, and Seth regains his strength for another assault.

Tek is one of the many followers watching the bubble, and he takes his binoculars to scan for trouble. He looks upward and gets a glimpse of another teen on the roof. Tek runs into the pyramid, making a quick stop in Seth's office for something important.

25

HIDDEN TALENTS

As Roland and Drake prepare to complete their part of the plan, Kendra and Juan travel through a dark, damp passage within Duat. They notice a tiny bit of light shining in the passage. It is coming from some fireflies to light their way. These fireflies reside in several holes within the walls, and they remain motionless like lamps lighting their way. Kendra and Juan are happy for any light at this point, but they find themselves tired from walking through the soggy ground. They notice some dark green weeds growing from the ground next to the wall. They have a musky skunk-like odor, and they have to hold their noses to avoid breathing it in.

Eventually, they discover another chamber with a message in hieroglyphics on the doorway. The teens can't smell the odor any more, to their delight. It appears dry and sandy. Juan looks at the message with her and decides to take a chance. He takes a step into the room, but Kendra stops him from entering. She reads the translated message to Juan: "To travelers seeking to find the levers and survive the traps, your hidden talents are the key."

But Juan wishes to redeem himself, so he takes one step forward, against his sister's orders for him to stop. Juan moves three more steps straight ahead with nothing happening to him, until he starts to sink into the ground as if in quicksand. Kendra tells him to remain stationary.

"I'm sorry," says Juan. "I'm worried about Roland and Drake, and I mess up."

"I understand your fears, but this isn't the time for regrets," says Kendra. "But there might be a way out."

Juan isn't moving an inch, but he is gradually sinking. He tells Kendra to forget about him: she can save the world without him. Kendra ignores his request and stands back to better survey the room. Kendra mimics her brother's movements, walking one step forward. But as she move three steps to the left, she sees the ground become solid around her. Then Kendra takes three steps to the right side, and the ground turns solid like the left side. Without warning, Juan flies out of the ground like lava flowing out of an active volcano. Kendra runs to look at him, but Juan stands on his feet with only a slight bump on his knee.

"How were you able to figure this trap out?" asks Juan.

"I had a theory about this trap, so I put it to the test," says Kendra. "The trap works on those people who try to move straight ahead in this room. I saw footprints on the left and right sides of the room, and the footprints were similar on both sides. So I took a chance that the trap works on people moving straight ahead, but it doesn't affect those moving on the left and right sides of the room. However, people must travel on one side first and then the opposite side to escape this room unharmed."

Juan and Kendra progress to another room, and Juan decides to let Kendra make all the decisions to avoid another life-threatening situation. They enter a room consumed by blue and red crystals on the ceiling and walls, giving it a multicolored lilac appearance. The floor tiles are made of pure white diamonds. Some of the tiles are numbered from one to nine.

"What kind of trap would put numbers on some of the tiles, but not all of the tiles?" asks Juan.

Kendra scrutinizes this nine-by-nine structure and sees it's a three-dimensional man version of a Sudoku game. Kendra tells him about this game from Japan and how it became an overnight sensation in the United States. Kendra looks around at the numbers in different spots on each tile in each row, but she doesn't know how to get this particular game started. Juan doesn't want to rush in without thinking again, but then Kendra asks Juan to move forward.

Juan walks to the first row on the top left side and sees the numbers: two, six, three, and seven. He lands on a tile with no number on it, but Kendra moves downward to the right side of another row to see numbers nine, one, and four, which she's standing on. Kendra tries to figure out the solution or the rules to this game. She insists that Juan not move away from the tile; however, Juan, who is trying to figure out the number of the blank tile under his feet, accidentally called out the number three. Kendra worries about another trap. At first there isn't a sound. Then the entire room begins to sway for several moments. It finally comes to a halt, and they look at each other, thousands of feet in the air on top of the game.

Juan gets panicky over another mistake of his doing, but Kendra tells him to calm down. Kendra thinks about Juan's calling of the number three, and how it caused the game to float higher and higher in the sky like a balloon. Kendra determines this is another trap and orders that Juan not to call any other numbers without her permission.

"Please let me pick the all the numbers from now on," says Kendra.

Kendra was able to solve the hardest level of a Sudoku game in a San Diego tournament in three minutes last year, but this is more nerve-racking for two reasons. One is they are standing several thousand feet in the air with nothing except the tiles for support, and two, they can hear the sound of tiles crumbling slowly under their feet. So Kendra doesn't have too much time to waste in solving this game, or they will fall to the ground like rocks. She uses her skills to call every number correctly within seconds, and she tells Juan which numbers to choose. They are 98 percent finished with the game, but Kendra can't figure out the last two rows. There are only a few squares left to solve. Figuring out two numbers would win the game. She rubs her head for an answer, and the tiles begin to crumble even more.

Kendra is trying frantically to finish solving the game when Juan falls through the tile. She screams out his name in fear for his safety, but she soon relaxes to see Juan on top of Montu's solar barge. Montu, who wishes to repay them for saving his life, has been waiting for such a chance. Montu tells Juan about not able to assist him further. He places Juan gently on another tile, apologizing for not being able to do more to help. He leaves them quickly, so the other Ousias won't get angry with him for interfering. As he flies away, Montu yells to the teens, "We're even now."

As the floor collapses, Juan tells Kendra calmly, "We can't stay here forever. Just make your best guess. I've got more confidence in your worst guess than I do in my best fact."

Kendra dislikes having to guess at something; she enjoys knowing the answer. But her brother's confidence gives her the courage to call the numbers correctly, making those two rows stop moving. Kendra discovers that they are back on the ground again. Both Kendra and Juan relax, and Juan laughs at her for taking years off his life.

They don't have long to celebrate, because Kendra falls through the ground. Juan yells out for her to return, but there is only silence. A light shines into another room, and Juan walks cautiously into an empty room, looking for traps. He feels a cool breeze in this room, and Juan sees an average-looking dry sand prairie. He doesn't notice anything unusual at first, but then he sees something to his right that horrifies him. Juan sees two man-size tubes with holes for breathing, and each tube contains the exact likeness of Kendra.

Juan isn't sure on what to do, when a voice speaks out: "Here are two images of Kendra, and you must pick your sister. One of them is your sister, and the other one is Hathor in disguise. You have ten minutes to pick one. If you are unable to come to a decision, then Hathor will get to choose. And the loser will go into the pit of hungry scorpions."

Both persons claim to be Kendra, speaking out to Juan in her voice, and he finds it difficult to tell the difference. Each Kendra talks about events that only the real Kendra would know about. Juan still can't tell the difference, and time is running out. Juan thinks about how Hathor had deceived him into believing she was his mother, and he doesn't want to fail his sister this time. Things get worse for Kendra when a dense fog forms around each tube to cover them. Juan understands this was the trap that Thoth lost his wife.

"I can't make the call. I could send my sister to certain death, like Thoth's wife, Ma'at," says a terrified Juan.

The fog gradually lifts to reveal both version of Kendra. There is only a minute left for him to choose. Juan gets a whiff of jasmine from the Kendra on the left, and she speaks with Hathor's voice. The other Kendra, on his right, asks him to trust in his common sense and his worst guess for the solution. Juan gazes at the tube on the right, believing he knows the truth, and just then Juan gets a vision without the headache.

"My sister is the one on the left," says Juan.

Juan picks the Kendra standing inside of the left tube, the one with the voice of Hathor. The tube disappears to reveal his real sister, Kendra, and the Kendra in the right tube changes back into Hathor. She cries out in pain that a mere child has seen through her deception, and she falls helplessly into a pit of scorpions, who consume her entire body. Juan hears the words about making the "wise" decision.

"How did you figure out who was the real Kendra, since I spoke with the voice of Hathor and smelled just like her as well?" asks Kendra. "I'm never going to complain about your lack—"

"You were about to say your lack of intelligence again. So did I finally finish your thoughts correctly?" says Juan.

"Yes, but we don't have our bracelets to aid us so how did you get a vision without the bracelet?" Kendra asks.

Juan tells her about seeing them having this conversation in a vision a minute ago, and Kendra admits to him about getting a strong feeling on the correct number to pick in the Sudoku game. She remarks about that this feeling is similar to when she wears the bracelet, and Juan mentions that Thoth and Ra talked about using their "hidden talents." So he trusted in his hidden talent over his lack of outer talent to choose his real sister. They both come to the conclusion that Thoth and Ra's theory about their hidden inner strengths and talents is true, and they take a deep breath of relief over their survival. As Kendra struggles to credit Juan with his inescapable logic, the wall behind them opens up to reveal two silvery levers, and they run over to pull them down to remove the shield over their bracelets.

26

ON THE EIGHTH DAY

While the world remains in chaos, Seth's armies of mummies and monsters encircle every part of Duat prior to midnight. This includes the armies of both Anubis and Sekhmet, since Seth controls the bracelets of the chosen ones. Seth must wait to become fully corporeal to spread his dominance over humanity. But he and Roland remain inside of Seth's bubble, fighting to the finish. Drake observes them from the top of the THES pyramid, and he knows the force field prevents him from completing his mission.

But the force field disappears from around the pole, and Drake knows that Kendra and Juan have completed their task. Drake uses his skill at rock-climbing to aid him, and he gets to the top of the pole within minutes. Drake is getting ready to remove the bracelets off the pole when he hears a voice from the ground. Tek orders Drake to come down, but he doesn't pay any attention to him. Tek shifts his right hand from behind his back and presents him with a small glass jar containing a tiny Eyeshadow and her mother inside, whom Drake recognizes from his vantage point. Tek holds the glass jar over the side of the roof to establish his seriousness.

"No, you can't do it—it would kill them," says Drake.

"You know my terms. Either come down or watch them fall to their death," demands Tek.

Drake looks at the bracelets, thinking about ignoring Tek, but he can't let anything happen to Eyeshadow and her mom. He climbs down off the pole and asks Tek for the glass jar. Tek brings it close to Drake's hand, but then he abruptly throws the jar off the roof. Drake reaches over to catch the jar, and he manages to grab the jar with one hand. But he falls off the building in the process, and he is barely able to grab ahold of the rooftop.

Tek ridicules Drake for helping two insignificant people and ignoring the chance to save the world from Seth. Drake tries climbing back onto the building with his left hand, but Drake isn't capable of maintaining his grip with the jar with his right hand. Tek walks over to him and places his foot on Drake's hand. Drake can't disregard the pain, and it gets tougher with every second. Tek bends over to tell him that he could simply drop them and save his life. But he refuses to give in, so Tek decides to further torture Drake. He begins to lightly press his foot on Drake's left hand, increasing the pressure with every precious minute.

As Drake fights for his life on the roof, Roland is battling in the bubble. They continue their sword fight until Seth feels the disappearance of his force field. He uses his power to create an energy bolt and sends Roland flying away from him. Seth takes this occasion to release another energy bolt, but he aims it toward the ground like a lightning bolt striking the earth. The bolt travels several feet deep within the surface until it strikes the levers, which Kendra and Juan are holding in a strong grip.

The powerful bolts of energy completely immobilize Kendra and Juan, and their best effort isn't good enough to break free. The force of Seth's bolts returns the levers to their original position. This leaves the teens frozen like statues with the clock continuing to tick on the fate of mankind. Roland feels the midnight hour upon him, so he and Seth run toward one another at top speed. But Roland can't hide his lack of strength from Seth. Seth increases his movement with his sword and is able to injure Roland on the arm. As he falls to the ground with blood dripping from his arm, Roland turns the shiny side of his sword at Seth to show him his reflection.

Seth sees his reflection in Roland's sword. "Sorry, but I'm almost corporeal now and my former weakness doesn't bother me anymore. I should just kill you now, but I want to savor this moment."

Seth gets pleasure from watching Roland helpless on the ground with no strength left to fight with. Seth kicks Roland's sword away from him in triumph. He then releases string-like energy from his hands to remove the bubble, and soon his followers see Seth's foot on Roland's chest with his sword at Roland's neck. With midnight looming, Seth thrusts his sword in the air and tells everyone his destiny is at hand. The crowd screams and yell at the top of their lungs at Seth being their pharaoh forever. "The power of Horus failed this foolish teen, and this is the fate of those who are foolish enough to stand against me," taunts Seth. "Do you hear that, Roland? My people want to see your body ripped to pieces as proof of my strength as Pharaoh Seth, and it would be a crime to disappoint them. But look at it this way—your death is only the beginning. The Ousias will die for a second time, and this time Osiris won't have a second chance at life."

But as Seth celebrates his triumph over Roland, a mysterious man, standing near a window in an office within the pyramid, witnesses the celebration of Seth's followers. This person looks upward to view Drake's situation, and the stranger quickly moves away. Seth creates a giant indigo bubble to remove every drop of water from around the pyramid. He bursts this oversize bubble over the Chicago River, and finally Seth splits the ground encircling the pyramid to reveal the underworld, Duat.

His followers observe flames shooting out of Duat as hundreds of mummies crawl to the surface. The crowd doesn't know these mummies were once people who followed Seth: He had betrayed these followers. They blindly cheer with excitement.

Drake views the terror of Duat, fighting to hold onto the ledge with his hand. From inside the jar, Eyeshadow and her mother watch Drake trying to keep them from falling to the ground, and they know Drake can't hold them for long. Eyeshadow and her mother hold each other in preparation for their death. Drake starts to lose his grip on the edge of the pyramid, and Tek decides to end this struggle. He lifts his foot, preparing to end this. But someone pulls Tek away from Drake and punches him in the face.

Tek falls to the ground, and he looks up to see his partner, Ray. "How did you get into this building?" says a shocked Tek.

"Ra brought me in here and hid me," says Ray. "I was able to see and hear everything, but Ra made me invisible from everyone here. That is, until Ra's magic released me just a little while ago. Now I'm going to make you pay for hurting my family."

Tek and Ray fought against each other like prizefighters, each one striking mercilessly. Drake puts the jar on the edge of the pyramid and pulls himself back up. From their vantage point, Eyeshadow and her mother laugh with excitement over being rescued, and they both cheer for Ray to repay Tek for endangering them. Drake catches his second wind and hears the crowd shouting. There is only a minute left until midnight. Drake runs back to the pole again, but the force field is back in place.

Seth aims his sword at Roland's neck, but Roland uses his last ounce of strength to release Horus's power. Seth prepares to deflect the power with his sword, but Roland releases his magical power at the ground instead of Seth. Seth, believing Roland was too weak to aim his attack, smiles with evil delight over Roland's decision, but the energy of Roland's magic travels deep within the earth. It reaches the immobilized Kendra and Juan, and it frees them from Seth's evil hold. Kendra and Juan pull down on the levers. Drake sees the force field fall, but he struggles to move the bracelets apart with only mere seconds left. The crowd begins counting down the last second to midnight like people at a New Year Eve's party.

Seth's holds his sword over Roland, "My day as pharaoh is about to begin, and your time is over!"

The crowd counts down the seconds. "Ten, nine, eight..." Seth prepares to deliver the death blow at Roland's neck, but Roland doesn't show any fear. Just as the eighth day is about to begin, Drake finally breaks the bracelets free from the pole with a second to spare, and the bracelets soar through the air back to their owners. Seth notices immediately that his body feels weak, returning to his incorporeal state. He realizes to his horror about the bracelets.

"No!" shouts Seth. "This was my moment of triumph over the Ousias, and a pathetic teen prevents my rise to power! You won't live to enjoy it!"

He thrusts his sword at Roland, but Roland's bracelet lands onto Roland's injure arm in time to magically toss Seth across the stage. Soon after, Roland notices that his arm is completely healed. Seth's followers watch Seth on the ground in defeat and lose all hope in their leader to fulfill his destiny. Meanwhile, on the roof of the pyramid, Tek flips Ray over his shoulder near the edge of the roof. Tek brings out a sickle-like seven-inch sword from his back and moves swiftly at Ray. Drake spots Tek from his view on the pole, and he cleverly leaps from the pole. Drake lands on Tek to knock the sword out of his hand.

"How could someone could turn his back on being a cop and choose to serve an evil creature like Seth?" asked Ray.

Tek recovers, getting to his feet. Turning, he focuses his wrath upon Ray and Drake. But a minor trembling causes Tek to lose his balance, and he falls headfirst into Duat from the roof. Drake recovers the jar, handing it over to Ray. In his enthusiasm, he jostles the jar too hard, which makes his wife and daughter feels they're in a mixer. Ray hugs Drake for saving their lives and explains how Ra had turned him into a statue for his own protection.

"Ra allowed me to see my family, but he wouldn't let me help them," says Ray. "It was truly the most terrifying and horrifying experience to live through."

"How did you know to come here, since you were a statue?" asks Drake.

"When Ra turned me into a statute, he told me his real name," says Ray. "Ra also told me that I would be able to help my family at the right time. That's the last thing that I remembered until I heard a crowd of people cheering for Seth below me, and then I heard some more noise from above as well. I looked upward to spot someone—who turned out to be you—trying to hang onto the edge of the roof, and then I caught a glimpse of Tek trying to make you fall. But I have a question for you—is there any way for my wife and daughter to return to their normal size again?"

Drake couldn't think of anything at first, but then he thought about the Witmores' bracelets. But before Drake can tell Ray this, the pyramid begins to come apart. Drake and Ray head for the stairs to get to the main floor, Ray keeping a strong grip on the jar.

While they escape the collapsing pyramid, below, Seth crumbles completely to pieces like a sandcastle. Roland tries to use his power to help others in need, but the speed of this powerful earthquake (which measures 7.2 on the Richter scale) moves too fast for him to react. It is also occurring in Duat, and Kendra and Juan hold on to each other for support. Above them, the pyramid falls totally apart like a house of cards.

Soon after, a mighty dust storm blows surges of dust around the globe, and every continent finds itself in the midst of this imposing force of nature. The swirling dust storm makes it difficult for the teens to see anything, but the storm lasts only for a brief time. In a blink of an eye, the dust storm disappears from the earth, and the heroes who fought against Seth find themselves together again. Roland, Kendra, Juan, and Drake are able to regain their vision. They look around to find themselves standing outside of the highly polished Cloud Gate, a stainless steel bean-like structure erected at Millennium Park, on a bright sunny afternoon day, but they are too happy to be being alive to notice their surroundings right off.

"Awesome!" says Roland. "We kicked the pants off Seth, and everyone helped to save the world."

"I don't remember much of anything after Officer Ray and I fell off the pyramid," said an amazed Drake. "I hope Ray is OK, since Tek kept Eyeshadow and her mother inside of a jar."

Kendra's face turns red to hear this about her best friend. She demands an answer from Drake, who explains how Seth had shrunk them and how Tek was crazy enough to throw them off the roof. Drake tells her to relax, since he and Ray saved them from Tek. She takes a deep breath in relief, and the news brings a sunrise to her face. Both Roland and Juan share in Kendra's pleasure, but they wonder about what happening in the world. Kendra reaches into her pocket, and amazingly finds her iPhone. Roland and Drake also discover their iPhones in their pockets as well. Juan is equally amazed, since those iPhones were destroyed to keep the authorities from finding the teens. Kendra doesn't have an answer to it but looks more surprised, seeing the date is September 4, 2011, a Sunday. She informs everyone, and they conclude that the other Ousias caused this change in time to occur, as well as the reappearance of their iPhones.

"I'm grateful about not spending anymore time in Duat," says Kendra. "But I can't believe our fortune in surviving this crazy ordeal. We face certain death many times during this crisis."

"Is it just me or is there a reason for this creepy scene around us?" asks Juan.

Everybody stops their celebration to observe what Juan is trying to tell them. They discover people frozen in their tracks like statues around the whole park, and it brings an eerie feeling. For the next couple of minutes, they watch unmoving people on their bikes across the park and other people looking at themselves in front of the Cloud Gate. The teens enjoy to view oneself in the stainless steel like a mirror, but the weirdly frozen people take the joy out of appreciating this wonder.

They see a figure of a man inside of the Cloud Gate, and he moves gently toward the teens. They look around to find the person who is casting this image. None of them can see any individual outside of the structure who can account for the image there, but still, the person walks within range of them. The teens fear this is one last attempt by Seth or some other evil person about to attack them. Juan recognizes the man in the Cloud Gate. He tells them to calm down, and they see Thoth walking toward them in a brown three-piece suit. They can't hold back their excitement. They hug and high-five him.

"I thought that I would be happy to see all of you," says Thoth cheerfully. "until, I almost got hugged to pieces. I'm deeply proud of everyone here. I apologize for freezing the people of Millennium Park, but I didn't want anyone to see my grand entrance through the Cloud Gate."

"By the way, is Ra or Mr. Hardgrove really gone?" asks Roland.

"Yes, I don't sense his presence anymore—he gave his last bit of life force protecting the three of you against Seth at the abyss," says Thoth.

Everyone shows their sadness, losing Ra. But Thoth reminds the teens that Ra made the choice to assist the chosen ones against Seth. He tells the teens Ra had foreseen his end to me. Ra never told Thoth the details, but Ra told Thoth that his death will help chosen ones to save the world from a great evil. It was hard for them to hear but they come to accept it.

Juan expresses regret for Thoth, having heard the details of Ma'at's end. "Oh, I shouldn't have brought up the subject," says Juan.

Thoth gives him an understanding smile. Thoth expresses sadness that he didn't trust in his own hidden talents. Thoth recalls his own failure to see through Hathor's deception and save his wife, Ma'at, but he is proud of Juan, trusting in his hidden talents to save Kendra.

"You overcame insurmountable odds to stop Seth. Thoth tells them that the power of the bracelets was within each of you. For the record, Ra visited me at the hospital, and he admitted being proud of the chosen ones, including Drake," says Thoth.

"Thoth, your and Ra's message on trusting our hidden talents and inner strength saved our lives many times without our bracelets," says Kendra.

Thoth explains that the bracelets didn't just give a special ability to each one, but they increased the skills and talents of each person. Drake looks on, thinking about not having a bracelet of his own, but Thoth tells him that he has power of his own without possessing a bracelet. Thoth tells Drake that the teens' bracelets reacted with power to increase Drake's ability to rescue Ray when he leaped from the top of the pyramid. Thoth mentions that this is very rare, since the bracelets' power normally doesn't work for someone without one. But Drake's friendship with the Witmores formed a special connection, and it empowered him to courageously face unimaginable dangers. Roland and Juan pat Drake on the shoulder to congratulate and welcome him as a member of the chosen ones.

Kendra doesn't feel like celebrating like her brothers, though, since she remains upset at the Ousias. "How come they couldn't use this power to stop Seth themselves without involving us in the first place, since they can alter time at will?" she asks.

"I understand your feelings, Kendra, but there are rules," says Thoth. "They couldn't risk upsetting their grand design and destroying the order of things. We refer to this as the rules of order against the rules of chaos that many evil Ousias would like to bring to this world. It helps to allow mankind to keep free will without the risk of chaos, and the Ousias don't want humanity to know about them being real. There are the rules with which all Ousias, both good and evil, agree to live. In the end, Seth destroyed himself trying to conquer the world."

Kendra thinks about it with some approval and agrees to accept Thoth's justification. Roland and Juan begin to think about Thoth's words on good and evil Ousias living with these rules, and Roland is the first to discuss his concerns with Thoth.

"Wait—is there a chance that more of these evil Ousias might be running loose on Earth?" asks Roland.

"I haven't heard of any other Ousias escaping from their prison, so I'm going to assume the worst is over for now," says Thoth. "I almost forgot—Malcolm is OK."

The news brings cheer to the teens, but the loudest cheer comes from Juan, feeling vindicated for his earlier mistake about Malcolm. Kendra is happy for Malcolm's recovery, but she stares at Thoth, seeking to discuss a more pressing issue with him.

"That is some very good news to hear, since I want to live a normal teenager's life," says Kendra. "A life without large snakes, scorpions, and flying creatures, or finding myself scared to death in Duat. I would like to get back to talking to and texting my friends. There is one good thing about turning back the clock; my best friend will be back to normal size. I'm going to enjoy my life like any normal teenage girl."

Thoth shares in her relief, but he secretly wonders on if any other evil Ousias had escaped from their prison like Seth. Thoth wants them to hide their bracelets, and they follow his suggestion to see an interesting twist. The bracelets transform back into tattoos, and Roland, Juan, and Kendra's tattoos contain small images of Roland tossing a spear at Apophis's head. They also include Kendra and Juan playing the Sudoku game. Drake finds a tattoo on his arm that shows him grabbing hold of the canopic jar before it went off the roof. Thoth turns to Kendra and offers to remove her tattoo. But Kendra agrees to keep her tattoo like her brothers, but she doesn't want anyone to get the idea that she's rethinking her decision to help the Ousias.

"I have to return to Utopia, but I have one last thing to say," says Thoth. "With the apparent death of Ra, I'm the next person responsible to keep *The Book of the Dead*. I would like to have the missing page from this book. There is another book with historic significance, and it is *The Legacy of the Ousias*."

As Kendra returns the page to Thoth, Thoth wants to say more about the book, but the Ousias wouldn't allow any non-Ousias to read this book. Nevertheless, Thoth, like Ra, loves to go against the Ousias, so he mentions to them about sending this book to his old address for safekeeping. Thoth doesn't know if he will teach at their school again, but he does hope that Osiris will give him another chance to see them all someday. Roland and Juan want to see Thoth as well. Thoth offers his good-bye to the teens, and he disappears from their sight like the wind.

They wonder about this mysterious book, but none of them know Thoth's address. As they begin to miss their friend, mentor, and teacher who helped them to save the world, people start to move around the Cloud Gate like nothing ever happened to them. It is a typical Sunday in Chicago, and Drake recalls aloud memories of running away from fortune hunters on top of bronze lions. The teens notice Ray Hightowers near the chess and checkerboard tables several feet from Cloud Gate.

They observe Ray and his new partner approaching the Cloud Gate. Ray calls out to the teens, since he knows them as friends of his daughter. Ray wants to say something more to the teens, but he gets a weird feeling that stops him from asking. Ray experiences a creepy déjà vu about being on the roof of a pyramid in Chicago, but he doesn't remember any such structure in this city. Ray disregards this crazy feeling and leaves to return to the police station with his partner.

Everyone reflects on their experience with Seth until they see Malcolm carrying a large blue sport bag. Roland, Kendra, and Juan run over to embrace him with gladness, and he wonders what brought on such affection. Malcolm doesn't know that a few days ago he was fighting for his life in the hospital.

Juan doesn't let this stop him from hugging Malcolm. "I'm so glad to see you, Dad."

Malcolm stops in midthought upon hearing those words from Juan. Malcolm figures that time has got a way of changing a person, so he doesn't question it in the least. He is too thankful for Juan calling him "Dad," and hopes this is sign for better things to come. Juan hugs his Malcolm, and Malcolm decides to just go with it rather than question it.

"Dad, how did you find us here?" asks Kendra.

"A teacher from Higher Learning, Mr. Thoth, called me at home a little while ago and told me about your visiting the Cloud Gate today," says Malcolm. "I told him his name is unique, and it's the same name as a great figure from Egyptian mythology. Thoth told me that he is being reassigned. He is a substitute teacher and the company hired him to work at Higher Learning for the semester, but they changed their mind at the last minute. I inquired about the name of this company. Thoth would only tell me that the company is called, the Society."

Everyone begins laughing nonstop at Malcolm, who wonders what was so funny. Malcolm says he came out because it was too good a day to waste at home, and he offers a little surprise to Roland and Juan, bringing out two items wrapped in brown paper out of the bags. He says he planned on giving the gift to them for their birthdays next month, but something came over him to give it to them now. Malcolm can't explain his change of attitude: it almost feels like he has received another chance at life. Roland and Juan want to know what is inside of the packages. Roland grabs hold of the mysterious item, feeling two wheels inside. Juan and Roland doesn't understand why Malcolm needs to hide such an obvious item, considering the wheels are a dead giveaway to the teens. Malcolm says that he added something special to their gift. Malcolm gives the OK for his son to tear off the paper, but Juan stops to feel his head. Malcolm runs over to check on him, but Juan says it was just a minor headache.

Drake takes this opportunity to ask Malcolm for his permission to go on a date with Kendra. Malcolm is a little surprised to hear this. He sees the hint of strong feelings upon Kendra's face, and he decides to talk to both of them over lunch. Malcolm offers to take them to a restaurant, and he agrees to listen with an open mind. It isn't easy for him—or for any father—to hear about his daughter growing up. However, Malcolm promises to keep his own opinions to himself until he listens to both of them. Roland and Juan contemplate Drake's chance of getting through lunch in one piece, and Malcolm tells Roland and Juan not to come home too late.

Roland and Juan agree to come home at a reasonable hour. They thank Malcolm for the gifts, and he promises something unique inside. Drake gives a high-five to both Roland and Juan, and he walks with Kendra and Malcolm, ready for an interesting lunch. Roland waits for them to walk out of range, and he gives Juan a suspicious look about his mild headache.

"Juan, you may fool Dad and Kendra most of time, but you can't fool your big brother none of the time," says Roland. "What did you see just a moment ago? And don't spare the detail?"

"It was one of the weirdest visions so far," says Juan. "We were standing in New York City, looking at the Statue of Liberty, when a dark shadow fell over the statue like an eclipse. I could feel the severe heat of the sun, and people start to scream nonstop at the sight of something horrible coming out of the shadows. But the vision came to a stop with no hint of its meaning, and I don't even know when or if this vision may occur. Do you think we should tell Kendra about it?"

"Your visions haven't been wrong so far, and I don't think this one is any different," says Roland. "But there is no way to know for sure; nevertheless, I'm going to keep an open mind to this vision foretells something in the future. I don't want to freak out our sister, though, so we won't mention any of this to her. In the meantime, I want to see what Malcolm meant by a surprise."

Juan tries to remember seeing another vision, but he couldn't see anything except a white wall. Juan is standing like a statue, and Roland shakes Juan to get him going. Roland asks if he is having another vision.

THE OUSIAS

Juan responds to Roland's question with a weird statement. "You must keep hope alive in the dark times," says a confused Juan. Juan didn't have anything else to add to this, so they decide not to reflect on it. Roland wants to go to an isolated place behind Grand Park where no one is hanging around. Roland tears off the wrapping paper, finding two rainbow-patterned skateboards and skateboarding equipment. But as Roland and Juan enjoy their skateboards, they notice images of Horus with the face of a falcon, battling jackal-faced Seth. Both teens are surprised to see the images, and they recall Malcolm talking about adding his own touch to their gift. They become curious about Malcolm's choice of picking these Egyptian designs until they see a note taped to one of the skateboards. It is a message from Thoth, "I told Malcolm that Roland and Juan were huge fans of Horus defeating Seth in battle. Malcolm found a store that places unique images on items like skateboards. One more thing—the others Ousias have removed some of the limitations on the bracelets. But they still maintain the rule that the chosen ones can't use their bracelets to hurt an innocent, or chaos will be unleashed on the world. I shall miss all of you. Farewell."

As they enjoy their skateboards in privacy just outside of Grant Park, Roland decides to test his new skateboard. He uses his bracelet to move across the ground very fast. Roland and Juan discuss their new freedom with their bracelets, since Thoth had mentioned there are no more limitation on the bracelets. Both boys realize that they just have to keep from accidentally or purposely hurting an innocent person. Juan jumps with cheerfulness and can't wait to try it for himself. After many practices runs, they move off to a park in the city, a place where skateboarders like to go to for fun and to display their skills.

"I wonder what's in the future for us. What if there are other evil Ousias threatening to mankind?" asks Juan. "I hope that we will get to see Thoth again someday."

"Me too, but to answer your question about the future," responds Roland. "I don't know what is coming tomorrow here, but I know nobody is going to hurt my world. Especially since we are here to stop them in their tracks. I want to test the limits of these bracelets. We should go to the Wilson State Park. It is an excellent area for skateboarding there."

"I wonder if you want to test the bracelets' powers or test your skills to the girl who you saw over the summer," said a prying Juan.

"You are going to stop listening to other people's conversations on their iPhone," says Roland. "So why don't we make it more interesting here? We could race to see who can get to the Wilson State Park first, and the loser must wash every dish after dinner for the next two weeks."

Juan chuckles at his brother's idea, since he knows his skateboarding skills outweigh Roland's. They travel on their skateboards to Wilson State Park, each one hoping to outperform the other. Juan zooms out of the area like a jet plane first, but Roland doesn't give up the chase. They move miles and miles within seconds. People they pass can feel a heavy breeze, but they don't notice anything out of the ordinary, and they make it to Wilson State Park in no time. Roland is the first one at the park, and he tells Juan to prepare to wash some dishes. Juan doesn't care, so he slaps his brother on his back to congratulate him for his victory.

Roland and Juan spend the next few hours enjoying their fancy high-flying stuns in the air with their skateboards. They accidentally tap into their bracelets' power and find themselves leaping and twisting in the air higher than any other skateboarder. They both land safely on the ground without a scratch. People including a friend of Roland clap and cheer their performances as the teens take a bow together.

Roland goes over to talk to his good friend, Marilyn, a skinny young girl with long blond hair and blue eyes who knows Roland from her regular skateboarding sessions at Wilson State Park, and she brings her curly-haired younger sister, Lacey and equally blue eyes. Both girls have on their black-and-silver protective gear. Roland introduces them to Juan. Marilyn says she feels nervous about being here, since she isn't as good as the other skateboarders. But Roland tells her to ignore it, and he offers to assist with her skateboarding. They don't get a chance to utter another word as a flash of light streaks through the sunny midafternoon sky. Marilyn says she thinks it is a comet and is suddenly embarrassed she might be wrong.

"Don't be embarrassed. Seeing a comet in the daylight isn't so rare," says Roland.

Marilyn wonders at Roland's knowledge, but Juan can't just keep his mouth shut once again. "I'm also impressed with his brain power, since he wasn't quite so smart with his last—"

Juan is about to mention Roland's ex-girlfriend to Marilyn when he observes Roland's left eyebrow twitching. This lets Juan know to walk away from him before Roland does something bad to him, like stuffing him in his closet with nothing to breathe except for his smelly socks and shorts again. Juan decides, for his own good, to go show Lacey some fancy tricks.

Lacey and Juan laugh together as they take turns flipping in the air. Marilyn tells Roland she read about a legendary comet with two tails called comet Destiny. Roland says that if a people see the comet, then they are about to begin a journey to fulfill their destiny. But Marilyn doesn't believe in the myth, and Roland knows she would never accept his story as fact. She changes the subject and talks about his skateboard with the Egyptian figures on it, saying she is a big fan of Egyptian mythology.

Roland talks about Seth resurfacing in Chicago, and Marilyn laughs at such a crazy idea. But Marilyn wants to hear the story anyway, so they sit on the park bench, and Roland begins to tell her about an invisible realm named Utopia. Lacey and Juan sneak back to Roland and Marilyn, since no self-respecting little brother or sister would pass up a chance to overhear their conversation. Lacey asks Juan to imagine such a story being true. Juan partially grins at her comment, since he doesn't want to admit any of his experience to Lacey. Juan proposes to show Lacey some more skateboards tricks of his own, and they run off to enjoy the rest of the day together.

Meanwhile, at an Italian restaurant near Millennium Park, Malcolm, Kendra, and Drake enjoy their meal. Malcolm still isn't comfortable with Drake and Kendra sitting together, but he's learning to trust his daughter. However, when Kendra goes off to the restroom, Malcolm takes the opportunity to remind Drake to treat his daughter with respect, or face the consequences. Drake fears what "facing the consequences" means, but Malcolm says that he was just being funny. Malcolm shakes Drake's hand to show he has no hard feelings, and Kendra returns to the table. Observing the look on Drake's face when he sees his daughter, he accidentally squeezes his hand like someone does to a stress ball. Malcolm gives a creepy laugh about not knowing his own strength. Drake laughs about the whole thing to Kendra's enjoyment. They eventually walk back to Malcolm's car, and he drives Drake home first.

Drake whisper to Kendra, "Is your father ever going to trust me, or am I just thinking wishfully here?"

"Yes, when it's snowing in summer, and there is a heat wave in January," jokes Kendra. "Please don't lose confidence in Malcolm; he's come a long way from his past mistake earlier this year."

"I'll be waiting for that," says Drake. "I won't forget about the kiss at the Willis Tower. It was a kiss for the ages."

"Yeah," says Kendra. "I can't forget it, either. But don't ever throw me off another building again."

The sun is setting, and Marilyn and Lacey have to go home. Roland whispers to Marilyn about going to a movie without their siblings, and she whispers yes to Roland. Juan, who has great hearing, wants to go with them. Roland brings up a certain smelly closet to change Juan's mind, who wisely keeps his mouth shut. After the girls walk away, Juan asks Roland about the comet Destiny with respect to their future. Roland tells Juan he doesn't know the answers to his question, but he advises Juan to not tell any of this Kendra. Juan agrees with Roland to remain silent, since Kendra would just want to ignore it anyway.

"I'm happy about your change in attitude toward Malcolm, since it was long overdue," replied Roland.

"Sometimes it takes a while for a little common sense to sink in my head, and this common sense talk reminds me of the Great Sphinx at Giza," says Juan.

"Please don't bring up the sphinx again. I'm still seeing it licking its lips," Roland says.

Roland and Juan laugh together as they ride their skateboards toward home. Kendra checks her iPhone for text messages, and she finds messages from Eyeshadow and Glitter about going to a dance. Malcolm talks about learning to trust his daughter more, and Malcolm gives Kendra and Drake permission to go to the school dance together. Kendra screams out in her excitement, and Malcolm covers his ears. Kendra hits the speaker button her iPhone, and her friends shout out their approval to the news. At the same time, Kendra grabs ahold of Drake to show her friends. Malcolm looks uncomfortable with Kendra hugging Drake, but he doesn't say a word about it. Malcolm reaches Drake's home, and he says his good-byes to both Kendra and Malcolm.

As they continue toward home, Malcolm mentions that he received an interesting text message from his ex-researcher, who had found a job at the White House a year ago. He tells her about the message, which talked about his daughter's school trip to the White House being canceled last year, and he demands to know where she and her friends gone to. Malcolm figures this wasn't just a solo stunt, and he stares at her for an answer. Kendra doesn't know what to say to him. She is as white as a sheep. She admits to going to a concert instead of the White House. She thought that Malcolm was going to hit the roof.

"I should be upset here, but I'm not mad with you," says Malcolm.

"I'm speechless," says Kendra.

Malcolm admits his own fault as well. "I didn't trust you enough when I should have in the past. I had an interesting discussion with Thoth, when I received this message. Thoth told me that you are normally a responsible person. I shouldn't be too hard toward someone who wanted to be treated like Roland. He reminded me that I was a kid too. Thoth talked about how you are the type of person who would risk her life to save the world from evil. I found that very weird for him to say. However, I think that we should sit down and talk this over as a mature father and daughter."

"I won't be punished," says Kendra. "I—mean—I feel bad for going to a concert with my friends."

"Kendra," says Malcolm. "Please stop embarrassing yourself any further. In fact, I'm glad that you feel so bad. Since I'm going to need a research assistant with excellent computer skills and guess who just volunteer to help me this summer."

"I'm all too willing to help out," says Kendra.

Before returning back home, Roland and Juan walk into a nearby store to look at some great skateboard shirts. They browse around the store for a long time. The store owner notices their Egyptian-designed skateboards. Roland wants some custom-made shirts of the different mythological figures, so he asks the store owner to create them from his ideas. As the store owner agrees to design their unique shirts, Juan says he wants one with phoenix flying over a large serpent. Roland says he'd love one with Horus fighting Seth. The store owner tells the teens to come back in three days, and he guarantees that the order will be ready. As the teens leave, the store owner scratches his head at their request. The store owner concludes that both teens have a very activated imagination.

Both teens swerve wildly to avoid hitting people on the sidewalk. They also maneuver around people crossing the street. While they move through the city at great speed, Juan thinks about Malcolm's career as an archeologist. He couldn't allow himself to appreciate anything about Malcolm for a long time, but Juan has finally come to view Malcolm as his father at long last.

After traveling for a little while, they make it home. They open the door to see Kendra and Malcolm smiling together. Roland thinks that he is in the wrong house. Malcolm offers to order out for dinner, and Juan wants Malcolm to show his artifacts and scrolls. A happy Malcolm agrees, and he wants to show them one scroll in particular. Malcolm says, "It makes reference to beings called, the Ousias. I have never heard of any such beings, and the scroll also mentions chosen ones that are destined to save the world." Kendra and Roland didn't have a comment. However, Juan offers his own thought, "Here we go again."

Made in the USA
Charleston, SC
29 August 2014